THE HOUSE WITHOUT A KEY

MARIN MONTGOMERY

WILTED LILLY L.L.C.

ALL RIGHTS RESERVED

COVER DESIGN: LOUISA MAGGIO

EDITING: THE PASSIONATE PROOFREADER

All rights reserved. No part of this publication may be reproduced, distributed, or transmitted in any form or by any means, including photocopying, recording, or other electronic or mechanical methods, without the prior written permission of the publisher, except in the case of brief quotations embodied in critical reviews and certain other noncommercial uses permitted by copyright law. For permission requests, write to the publisher, addressed "Attention: Permission Coordinator" at the address below.

This is a work of fiction. Names, characters, places, and incidents either are the product of the author's imagination, or if an actual place, are used fictitiously and any resemblance to actual persons living or dead, or business establishments, events or locales is entirely coincidental. The publisher does not have any control and does not assume responsibility for author or third-party websites or their content.

This e-book is licensed for your personal enjoyment only. Thank you for respecting the author's work.

❦ Created with Vellum

DESCRIPTION

Madeline Pruitt and Allegra Atwater are strangers, nothing more in common than their ages and the city they live in. Or so they think. Both grew up on opposite ends of town, one struggling to survive, the other heir to one of the wealthiest families in the state.

Madeline's father, Brian, is an alcoholic with a quick temper and a rough hand. Not one to be tied down, he spends his time drinking and dating a married woman, his seventeen-year-old daughter, Maddy, an afterthought. When Maddy goes missing, Brian's the last to know, but the first to be interrogated.

Allegra's parents, on the other hand, control her every move. Her mother, Valerie, tries to be the voice of reason between Allegra and her overbearing father, Darren. But even she is under Darren's thumb when it comes to enforcing his rules.

Except there is a deadly game going on behind the facade of wealth and privilege. When Brian becomes tangled up with the Atwater family, a complicated web of deceit unravels itself as those involved try to unlock deadly secrets.

For Sarah Avila.

Thank you for being my rock.
You worry about not being 'further' ahead in your career. I see an amazing woman who balances family, work, school, and friends. I'm continually amazed by your work ethic, how hard you love the people in your life, and the care you always take of those around you.
I look forward to the journey you have ahead of you now that you've completed your degree. I can't wait to see what you accomplish.

PROLOGUE

The dumpster at the rest stop's overflowing with garbage, the large metal bin unable to accommodate any more junk. A nasty stench permeates the air, and I wonder if roadkill's roasting in this metal oven. The summer months are hot and humid, the Texas sun blistering everything beneath it. It's the beginning of September, and it still hasn't cooled any.

Gagging, I turn to shield myself from the waste, but whether it's the sun making its first appearance of the day as it rises from the east, or the reflection off my sunglasses, a flash of color makes me face the pile again to consider the culprit.

It's green, except it's not a typical shade of green.

Darker. With yellow mixed in. Olive.

I don't know why I'm drawn to it specifically. There are mounds of trash piled up, the usual fast-food wrappers, cigarette butts, and diapers.

The now-empty jumbo coffee cup in my hand I've reused over and over again starts to shake, and it's not from the caffeine I've inhaled over that distance. As I reach forward to toss it, the green, I mean *olive* piece of fabric, catches my eye again.

I slide my sunglasses up before I step closer to inspect it.

At first, I think it's an ornament of some sort. Lots of people have angels or crosses that dangle from the mirror in their vehicles as a sort of talisman. Myself, I have 'truck nuts', a replica of dangling balls that hang as a joke off my bumper, much to the disgust of women I date and the laughter of my friends.

I realize it's a makeshift bracelet of some sort, since really, it's nothing more than a piece of fabric acting as a trinket. I finger the material. It's shiny, kind of like the stuff dancers and figure skaters wear. Taffeta. Or maybe chiffon?

Perplexed, the fabric seems to darken as it goes from olive to a putrid color, becoming greenish-black. When I pull on the material, I realize the bracelet is wound around a wrist, and that wrist belongs to a hand.

No, it can't be.

It's gotta be a collar on the neck of a dead cat that ran in the road and got hit.

Except I'm staring at a hand that appears as if it's sticking out of a grave. Jumping back in horror as if someone branded me with a hot iron, I gasp for air. This can't be happening. It must be some kind of sick joke.

But the hand is small...and human. I count five fingers before my mind goes into overdrive.

An overabundance of flies swarm the open air around the skin, aiming for an empty spot to settle on. Their intent is to feed on her. I'm going to be sick from the stench, or maybe it's the fear of my discovery.

I stare at the olive fabric gathered around a wrist that's sticking up out of the garbage at a rest stop in Texas. After pawing through the trash on top to discover whose arm it's attached to, I make out the torso of a woman.

It's a body, my mind screams as I hurtle backward, unleashing a violent storm of liquid coffee onto the concrete next to the dumpster. This, I do know.

At least I think she's a woman, or she could be a teenage girl.

The smell of the garbage mixed with the putrid odor of the corpse is enough to make me drop my nose into my shirt. She's naked except for a tattered jean skirt with frayed edges. I tell myself the red stains are from ketchup. Surely someone left packets in a paper bag that spilled.

From the many episodes of Law & Order and CSI I've watched, they instruct you to not move or touch a dead body in case you disturb precious evidence. I can hear an actor playing a detective say, "Every crime has a trail of fibers and hair follicles and skin we don't realize we're shedding,"

But let's face it, I never thought I'd be in this situation, staring at a dead body in a dumpster at a rest stop in Texas.

It seems inhumane to just leave her in the trash. As if *she* didn't have feelings or a purpose. As if *she* is merely garbage to be dumped and taken to a landfill and tossed. I ignore the fact that maggots and rodents are taking a stab.

I grimace at my choice of words.

Insects and flies have taken a liking to *her*.

Maybe she suffocated in here, or perhaps she was dead on arrival at the dumpster. But I'm staring at a dead *her* in a metal bin at a rest stop twenty-seven miles from Laredo, Texas.

I wheeze, trying to catch my breath. I decide I can't leave her to rot any more than she already is.

After I lay the body on the ground, heavy and stiff and purplish, I take a step back, as if to offer *her* some space.

Shaking my head in disbelief, I try to distance myself from the situation. I stare vacantly at the big white star painted near the rest stop sign, signaling I'm in the Lone Star state.

I say a silent prayer and mumble my condolences out of respect for the deceased. When I end with "Amen," the only sound is the highway traffic whizzing by, a deafening roar where the rubber meets the pavement.

Not only am I in shock, I'm brutally tired. For the last fifteen hours, I've been on the road. I had planned to sleep in the cab of my semi after throwing out my garbage and taking a leak.

But not now.

Now the police will come. The cops will ask a million questions. Will they think I'm somehow involved? That I'm a cold-hearted killer?

I won't be able to sleep, I won't be able to eat. I'll see *her* every time I shut my eyes, and who knows what that does to a person.

I'm not a bad man. At times, lost. I've done some questionable things. Had affairs. Stolen money. Slept with prostitutes.

Wait... my hands tremble. Now that I think of it, there was a woman in my cab last night.

No. There's no way. I've been driving for the last fifteen hours, right?

I let out a grunt, as if the sound can guide my attention back to last night. I did stop and pick up a hitchhiker at a truck stop a few hours back. She was blonde like this girl, but this girl's been dead a long time, hasn't she?

I feel nauseous just from the recall. It reminds me of a bad experience that twists your stomach from memory, like drinking enough rum and Coke to hug a toilet all night.

Speaking of alcohol, the woman and I drank until the

road blurred into something other than the glare of oncoming traffic. And we did more than get drunk.

Her name slips my memory, if she even gave me one.

She had a baggie of drugs, and we snorted and got high and lost our inhibitions, if we had any to begin with.

We must've stopped here at some point during the night, because in the back of the sleeper cabin, we snorted and screwed and slept. Then we repeated all three.

In fact, I sling my hands on the hips of my Wranglers, my high came crashing down when I caught her trying to steal money from me, out of the stash I keep for emergencies in an old, rusted metal box.

It ended in a vicious fight. Not a screaming match, but worse.

I choked her.

Closing my eyes, I attempt to remember how luminous her blonde hair was as I dragged her out of the cab by it. *Maybe I should forget*, I think nervously. It's nothing but a haze with puzzle pieces that don't seem to fit into the big picture.

Could I have done something like this? Am I really capable of murder?

Yesterday, I'd say no, except for the pit in my stomach that's enlarging as if a massive tumor has overtaken my intestines.

I think again about the cops. They will contact my employer since they own the rig. Now my company will be suspicious and start watching me closely, picking apart my route and my hours on the open road. And who's to say the police won't try and connect me to other disappearances around the country. What if they think I'm a serial killer? There was some guy who committed murder up and down I-80 back in the eighties in California.

Or maybe it was the nineties?

Disgusted, I shake my head. Who fucking cares when it was?

What if I'm fired over this? I can't lose another job. This route suits my wandering eye and nomadic tendencies.

Hesitantly, I check to see if I've been spotted by any other folks. I peer at the couple of brick buildings with square windows filled with shitters and vending machines outside of Laredo, Texas. It's pretty empty this morning.

Now that the body is out in the open, lying on the ground, I can't leave it.

I walk briskly to my truck and grab a blanket in the back of the cab. Sure enough, an empty plastic bag rests innocently on the floor, along with a couple empty condom wrappers.

I ignore the evidence and tuck the old, worn cover over her body, making sure her eyelids are closed.

Glancing to make sure I'm alone before I move the body into plain sight, I heave her over my shoulder and place her in the empty trailer, the blanket wrapped tight around her frame.

After I'm finished, I'm tempted to wipe my hands on my jeans since I feel unclean. I can't decide if it's the washable kind of dirty. But then I feel guilty, since I doubt this poor *her* asked to be dumped in a trash bin and left to decay.

But it was *definitely* not by me. I'm saving her from the birds.

"I'm going to go wash my hands," I say out loud.

When I enter the dark restroom, I'm grateful for the dim lighting and the separation from the sun and my trailer and *her*. The filmy mirror above the sink gives away my emotions as I glimpse my haggard appearance. I stare at my

The House Without A Key

dilated pupils while I wash my hands. The tremors subside as I press them together under the lukewarm water. You're supposed to count to ten or recite the alphabet to get them entirely clean, except I can't seem to stop lathering them under the soap dispenser. The faucet's one of those annoying types that suddenly turn off and on, leaving you with soapy residue on your hands. I keep washing and re-washing them, scrubbing as if I can remove the touch of her warm and mottled skin.

The door slams and shakily, I lift my head to consider another male in the mirror as he heads into a stall.

Could he be the killer?

I mouth to the mirror, "They wouldn't hang around after dumping a body."

But what about you?

The sound of the man pissing reminds me I still have to go, so I move to a stall, barely able to stand upright. Leaning forward, I rest my hand against the cracked concrete wall for support.

When I emerge, I continue the repetition of washing my hands like I have OCD until another man walks in dressed in a uniform.

A Texas Highway patrolman.

I nod at him in the mirror, my heart racing as I jerk my hands from the running water. Careful to not draw attention by running to my semi, I walk with purpose, my head held high.

The lack of sleep has my eyes weighted with sand, not to mention the images of *her* flash in rapid succession like I'm watching an old home video.

I can no longer manage the drive home without stopping for a shower and a real bed. As I stand underneath the scalding water at a seedy motel, I let it wash over me as if it can cleanse me of any mistakes I've made, absolving me of them.

Then I cry.

I break down, the running water mixing with the tears.

As I dry myself off, I feel like I should call someone, a substantial need to unburden myself. I scroll through my contact list and decide on Marge, my ex-wife. We've been divorced for almost ten years. A lifetime, it feels like. I was never good at being married. A shit husband, worse father. So, I left, and now we've never been better. Once you take the piece of paper away and the vows and quit sharing the same roof, it's incredible how much better your relationship can become when you're not under someone's thumb.

When I call, Marge's television is on in the background. She mutes it when I begin to speak, and telling my ex I found a body doesn't help. She shrieks, and instead of feeling relieved, it brings up more questions she peppers me with, none of which I can answer.

I was throwing out a coffee cup at a rest stop outside of Laredo, Texas, I tell her. I omit the part about the young woman in the back of my cab. I don't want the inevitable jealousy that will sneak into her voice, ten years gone or not.

Of course, I'm not capable of murder.

The woman stole from you, I remind myself. I could claim self-defense but the tiny voice in the back of my head reminds me she weighed barely a buck ten and I'm double that.

Marge is gabbing, the topic now changed to an infomercial or something equally unimportant. I make up an excuse about work calling and disconnect.

I try and sleep, but it's useless.

She flashes across my mind, followed by the what-ifs of

how someone could reach their breaking point and kill another human being. *But what if I did this?*

With no choice but to swallow a couple of sleeping pills, I toss and turn through a few hours of sleep.

Then I climb into the cab of my semi and drive home, another few hundred miles to Oklahoma, and bury the body where I know it won't be found. Six feet deep in a makeshift grave in my backyard.

Over the next couple of days, my senses are heightened, expecting the blare of sirens to upset the peace and quiet. I picture someone pounding on my door, demanding to know where *she* went. Parts of our night together come back at the damnedest times, like when I'm mowing my lawn or watching television. I pass on the true-crime channels and focus on game shows or reruns of Happy Days.

I now remember her telling me she was on the run, but from what or who, I don't know.

But it wasn't from me.

Deep down, maybe *she* knew she'd never make it far, dead or alive.

PART I

PRESENT DAY

1

MADELINE

"Brian, stop," I yell. "You're hurting my arm." As if in a trance, he loosens his grip as he watches me wince in pain. I take the opportunity to shrug out of his clutch and slither away from him. I lean back against the beige walls, trying to catch my breath, feeling as if I've run a marathon instead of just had the usual fight with him.

I hate these fucking beige walls and this shoebox of an apartment that closes me in and suffocates me daily. But nothing smothers me more than Brian's endless frustration with me. Maybe my hate is misdirected at the red and sweaty face of the man-child staring back at me as we stare each other down. Perhaps it should be at my absentee mother.

Brian and I both struggle to catch our breath and put our tempers in check.

And no matter what, I can't hate him. And I certainly can't leave him. At least not until my boyfriend, Dane, and I have a solid plan locked down.

He steps back for a moment, giving me space, which is not his strong suit. Pursing his lips into a thin line, he struggles to remain calm. "How many times are you going to run away?

"Depends," I snap. "How many times are you going get drunk and push me around?"

"Why do you always have to be so dramatic?"

I say nothing. Instead, I point to the evidence of my latest scar, this one on my right shoulder. A shoving match ensued, and I lost against our hand-me-down coffee table. When I fell on top of the scarred oak, it buckled underneath me, and I ended up with my own permanent reminder. Brian ignores my gesture and steps forward.

Unsure of his next action, I cross my arms over my chest as if this will protect me against his wrath. Closing the gap between us, he leans down to pinch my chin with his fingers. "When are you going to stop talking back?"

I don't think before I respond, a severe problem in this household. "When you stop being a drunken asshole." I pop off at the mouth when I wish I could just shut it, swallow the words, and bottle up my anger, but just like him, I can't.

He responds with his fist. I go at him with vicious words.

"What did you say?" He squeezes my chin tighter, his brown eyes glaring into my blue ones.

"You heard me."

"Repeat it." He moves his fingers to press against my lips. "Say it one more time, Madeline."

"When are you going to admit you're an alcoholic?"

"When are you going to stay out of my damn business?" He drops his hand from my face, covering his own with his hands. "Why do you keep sassing me?"

"I don't 'sass' you."

"You know I'm sick."

"Being drunk isn't a sickness, Brian."

"It's a disease."

"It's no more a disease than your inability to be a parent." I feel it before I even realize it, the sharp strike across my cheek. Flinching, I try and move out of his grasp. He boxes me in against the wall, his hands on either side of my frame.

"Watch it," he warns. "You're already in hot water."

Tears start to wet my cheeks, but I refuse to let him see me full-on cry. "I'm going to bed," I snap, attempting to sneak underneath his long arms so I can remove myself from the situation.

"You can't keep escaping to Dane's," Brian says tersely. "I mean it. I don't want you around that boy."

"Why not?" I argue. "I should feel wanted by *somebody*."

"That's not the way to feel wanted. That's the way you end up pregnant in high school and ruin your life. You don't want to be a parent right now, trust me." With a loud sigh, "I should know." An annoyed hand runs through his thick dark hair, the only shared feature between us besides our aquiline jaws.

"I hate you," tumbles out of my mouth.

"Then next time you run away, don't come back, okay?" He taps my leg with the toe of his boot.

"I won't."

"Good."

"Agreed."

"You'll be eighteen soon, right?" He strokes his chin. "I'll make sure to have a cake made with a 'congratulations, get the fuck out' sentiment."

"Classy," I murmured, keeping my eyes glued to my knees. I order myself not to cry in front of him.

I fail at this as the tears pick up speed, rolling down my cheeks. Thankfully my hair partially covers my face.

"And speaking of accomplishments," he smirks, "you've earned yourself a grounding, so congrats."

"Joke's on you since there's nothing to ground me from." I almost giggle. He can't take away my phone because I don't even have one. Or my car, I don't have one of those, either. Pathetic, I know.

"Really? Tell that to your boyfriend."

"This fucking place is a prison," I jeer.

"You're not seeing Dane for a week."

"Whatever."

"I mean it, Maddy. If I have to lock you in your room, I will." Again, I try to scuttle away, scooching over before I try and stand. It doesn't work. He's faster and in an instant, he grabs my wrist, yanking me towards the couch. He practically pushes me onto the worn leather. "Have a seat."

I land with a thump and a scowl. "Why am I being grounded for running away when you never want me around?"

He sinks down on the opposite end of the couch. "Maddy," he sighs. "Come on."

I glare at him. "You're a shitty dad, and trying to act like a good one because you found a new insta-family isn't *my* problem." He's kept his girlfriend and me at arm's length, but I know she has a kid because I hear them talk on the phone in hushed voices.

"I'd prefer we concentrate on your senior year of high school." His jaw is set. "You're going to start doing better. You're only a few weeks in."

"I don't even have a laptop," I point out.

"Then spend time in the computer lab before or after class. This is your last chance to improve."

"Why do my grades matter now?"

"Because you need to figure out what you want to do with your life."

I seethe. "What I want to do with *my* life is none of *your* business."

"Madeline." The steely tone in his voice portrays his anger. "You're excused. Whatever you decide, you better hope the cops don't get involved because that'll be the end of this living arrangement. And as much as you think you hate me, being a foster isn't any better."

"Next time, don't look for me." With a sneer, I jump up. "Hopefully I'll be gone before I meet your fucking girlfriend."

I know I better run for my room or risk him throttling me. He's hot on my heels as I slam the door in his face. The lock on my door was removed after I snuck out of my window a few weeks ago. He threatened to take it off of the hinges the next time. This *is* the next time. All I can do is lean against it, my back pressed hard into the wood.

Panting, I catch my breath as he does the same on the opposite side. He utters a curse word and then his footsteps retreat, back to the kitchen, back to the fridge, back to his favorite companion. Alcohol.

When he's drunk, he gets belligerent. That leads to destruction, which leads to him blacking out with no recollection of what he said or did. Wearily, I slide down my door and curl into the fetal position. I have to be ready in case he comes back to take a swing.

This is where I will fall asleep, using my hands underneath my head as a pillow. Tomorrow I'll wake up with circles underneath my eyes and a red mark on my cheek from his palm.

But tomorrow is another day.

And when I shut my eyes, I remind myself how bad it used to be with my mother, who was just as selfish. The problem, Brian emphasizes, is *me*. How easy his life would be if I weren't around.

He'll soon get his wish when I leave for good. I've been saving money, and he doesn't know this, but I started my own business. It's not exactly legal, but I've got a stash saved up. It's cliché to hide it underneath my mattress, so I shove it in the pockets and lining of a jacket that I never wear. I outgrew it years ago but leave it hanging in my bare closet. It was the last thing I was wearing when my mother hugged me for the last time and disappeared into the snow.

I blame him for that, and he blames me for being born. I guess we're even.

The start of a throbbing headache pounds as he plays death metal at full volume and resting my head on my hands, I close my eyes.

2

MADELINE

"Eyes closed," Dane instructs, pushing me gently into the recliner. He smells like a combination of gasoline and sweat, both left over from his day job as a mechanic and his dedication to the gym. Apparently, it was enough of a surprise that he decided to forgo his afternoon shower.

I arrived home from school to find him impatiently waiting for me at my door, his feet tapping the concrete and his hands waving all over as he told me he had a surprise. He led me down the stairs to the building next to ours, where he lives in a first-floor apartment with his twenty-one-year-old roommate, Robbie Atlas. We are too poor to afford a cell phone for me, it would only get shut off anyway, so it's lucky he lives in the same apartment complex, which is how I met him.

I coined the phrase, 'Proximity is everything when you live in poverty.' I'm dying to trademark it, or at least screen-print it onto t-shirts. Not surprising, when I told Brian, he didn't find it the least bit funny.

"Are they closed?" I feel his calloused hands grab for

mine. He moves my much-smaller hands in front of my eyes. "Keep these here, okay?"

I nod, my face twisted in a smile.

His heavy boots stomp across the floor, which is unusual for him since he leaves them by the door, first thing when he gets home. He must be really excited. The heavy footfalls move in the opposite direction of the secondhand recliner, where I'm seated.

He checks again. "Still closed?"

"Yes." I giggle to myself. "Hurry up already! I can't stand the suspense."

"Then remind me never to surprise you again." His laughter radiates across the room, and I can picture the big goofy grin on his face.

"Hurry!" I yell.

His footsteps echo closer before something thin and lightweight flutters into my lap and on my bare thigh.

"Now?" I ask.

"Now," he affirms.

I remove my hands from my face, staring down at the white envelope.

"Babe, don't rip it in half," he warns. I'm glad he gave me a heads-up. I usually like to tear open gifts regardless if they're wrapped in pretty paper or tied with a bow. The same goes for an envelope in my outstretched hand.

I slowly open the unsealed flap. Inside is a yellow sheet of paper. Scanning the message, it says *IOU* in bold letters at the top. Underneath, a sentence is scrawled in his boyish handwriting.

Concert tickets are on their way for the most beautiful girl in the world.

Love, Dane

"Um...babe?" I don't want to ruin his good spirits, but

tickets have been sold out for the Taylor Swift concert for months. I'm certainly not going to mention that I'm also grounded from spending time with him.

He tilts his head. "Oh no, what is it? You can't go?"

"No, it's not that. It's just...tickets are gone. It's sold out." My voice wavers as I try not to let the disappointment shine through. I don't add that the concert's next weekend and it's T Swift, so why would there be any tickets available?

"Then you're lucky you picked the right guy." He flexes his bicep. "I found a pair for sale on one of those ticket finder websites."

I didn't realize I was holding my breath until I gasp. "Oh my God, thank you!" I jump up and into his arms, clawing him with my fingers as I wrap my legs around his waist and clasp him around the neck. "I can't wait, babe."

Nuzzling me, he whispers, "Me neither." Kissing me, he murmurs in my ear, "You deserve a special night out. We'll go out to dinner, go to the concert." Then with a wink, he adds, "Maybe you can even stay here." We both know that's a big fat no. We skirt over the issue that my thirty-six-year-old father's biggest problem with Dane Burns is that he's nineteen and I'm seventeen.

As if this isn't the biggest hypocrisy in the world, Brian doesn't trust that Dane and Robbie aren't out to corrupt my underage self with drugs and alcohol. If you met Robbie, you would find this concern outrageous. The two of them get along but looks and personality-wise, they're polar opposites. Where Dane is tall, over six feet, with dark hair and a permanent five o'clock shadow that never disappears, Robbie is short with sandy blond hair and intense green eyes. He's rail-thin, wears glasses, and is studying to become a mechanical engineer. He'll graduate soon and get a job.

They met when Dane's ex-girlfriend moved out and he

needed a roommate. They connected on a housing finder website, and the rest is history. I wouldn't call them friends, more like acquaintances. They live together, so they're close to one another's confidences and secrets, privy to what happens behind closed doors, but have little in common. The two agree on video games and pizza toppings. What more could you want? Dane thinks Robbie has a crush on me, but I think he's just socially awkward and I'm a female.

The door opens, and Robbie walks in. "Hey," he greets us. "You both look super happy. What's the word?" We tell him about the concert, and he gives us both a high five.

"When are you going to get the tickets?" I ask Dane after Robbie heads into his bedroom.

"I have to grab them tomorrow."

Worried I'm still going to miss the show, I scrunch my nose. "And they're legit tickets?"

"Yeah, girl says she has them in hand. Hard copies."

"This is going to be the best night ever." I kiss him hard as we let the world fall away, let my problems, his problems, melt into a ball of nothing. Even though I'm grounded, I'll think of a legitimate excuse. Brian did tell me to study.

So, I will...he doesn't need to know I'm studying a crowd full of super fans known as 'Swifties.'

All I can think about is the thrill of the concert, Dane's mouth on mine, and the blank slate of life we're about to begin. I can't wait until we ditch this town and move in together, far away from Brian and the constant reminder that I'm the reason behind his disappointment.

When Brian's upset, he always says 'like mother, like daughter.'

She was smart to leave him, and soon it'll be my turn.

3

MADELINE

A knock on the door startles me as I unload the dishwasher and tidy up the hurricane Brian left during his poker game with his buddies the night before. He's passed out in his room, so I rush to answer it. I don't want him to wake up, grumpy and hungover.

Surprised to see Dane, I give him a hesitant smile, checking over my shoulder to make sure the sleeping lion is still in his den.

Dane seems depressed, his attitude the opposite of yesterday. Eyes downcast, he greets me with a nod.

"Hey, you," I whisper.

"Hi." He leans in to give me a kiss. "Would you mind giving me a ride to pick up the tickets?"

"Oh no, is Magda having issues?" 'Magda' is Dane's sixteen-year-old car. She's a piece of shit, a real metal trap, but he loves her for life. And I can't deny that loyalty is an attractive trait. She needs a new engine, and though he's a mechanic, some miracles can't be imagined, such as a new 'heart' under her hood. Dane can replace it himself, so it cuts out the cost of labor, but it's still not cheap.

"No, a flat tire." His brown eyes flash in annoyance. "Robbie had to give me a ride home from work." He points to the duffel bag in his hand.

I don't have a car, but Brian does. Brian doesn't have a license, and I do.

Hesitating, I look again over my shoulder. The hard part isn't stealing his truck, it's finding his keys. I'm not going in his bedroom, where I'll likely slip in a pile of piss or vomit.

"Okay, we just need to search." I wrinkle my nose. "I hope they aren't on him."

Lucky for us, I find them underneath the scarred table where they played poker last night. It's no surprise they're on the floor next to a beer can and an overturned ashtray.

Dangling them in front of me, I press them into his hand. "You wanna drive?"

"Sure." He shrugs. "But let's at least drive down the street before I do."

It makes sense he's careful about who spots him driving Brian's truck. In our complex, Brian has acquired friends that watch his possessions like a hawk and me even closer. Our fifty-something neighbor lady, Katrina, has a mad crush on him and has made it her mission to give Brian a play-by-play of every hour of the day he's not at home.

Unfortunately for me, because there's assigned parking, she always knows when his battered pick-up is here, frequently finding a reason to knock on our door, sometimes with a casserole, sometimes with a light for his cigarette, sometimes with gossip.

I dart my eyes around as we slide into the truck, aware of the flutter of her curtains. Nosy bitch, I think to myself.

Slamming my hand on the steering wheel, I mutter angrily. "I bet she knocks on my door as soon as we pull out of here."

Dane directs a smile and a wave through the dirty windshield at her.

"I'm more worried about the smell in here." His fingers pinch his nostrils. "If I'm around sweaty men and rotten egg smells in a shop all day, and I notice, it must be bad."

"It's awful," I agree. "He's such a slob."

I drive through the broken gates that never seem to close or open when you need them to. When I reach a side street down the block, I turn right and park the pick-up.

"Your turn." I crawl over his lap to reach the passenger side. "Where are we meeting for the tickets?"

"Just up the street at the convenience store. I thought it would be, well, convenient." He squeezes my knee. "I'm so excited about this."

"Me too." I press a hand to his neck as I rub his shoulders. "You're the best."

"No, you are, babe. You deserve what's coming to you." He taps my nose with his finger. "All good things, baby, all good things."

The drive to the gas station is a short one, so I busy myself with tidying up the truck and putting the fast-food wrappers, empty Styrofoam coffee cups, and the cigarette butts in an empty plastic sack I find at the bottom of a pile of clothes and tools. We pull into a space around the side of the gas station. A gray Toyota Camry idles next to us and in the driver's seat is a girl with jet-black hair. She flips it over her shoulder and stares at us, squinting.

Motioning for Dane to roll down his window, her passenger one lowers as she leans over to holler. "Are you here for the tickets?" She finishes with a drumroll on her steering wheel.

"Yeah, we are. I'm Dane."

"Dammit," she says with a smile, "I was hoping you

wouldn't show." I watch as she grabs her purse and comes around the driver's side of the pick-up.

"Hi, I'm Sapphire." She's tall enough to lean through the open truck window, staring at us intently.

"Why didn't you want us to show?" Dane's curious.

She giggles, and her purple eyeliner lights up her green eyes. "My boyfriend hates pop music, but I really want to go."

"You can't take a friend?"

I elbow him hard in the ribs. "Stop trying to sell our tickets back before we even have them."

She stares past Dane at me. "And you're one lucky gal."

"Also known as Madeline." I offer.

"Nice to meet you." She reaches past Dane to shake my hand. "I love your nail polish."

I look down at my hands, the electric blue color starting to chip. "Thanks."

"Will you hand me my wallet in the duffel?" Dane motions towards the black bag resting at my feet. "I brought three hundred cash. All twenties. I hope that works."

Sapphire reaches into her purse and pulls out an envelope. I watch as her face drains of color. "Oh shit. Oh, shit balls."

"What's wrong?" Dane and I ask at the same time.

"I decided to sell my tickets for another band, Kings of Leon, and I accidentally grabbed the wrong set of tickets."

Dane whistles, "You have those, too?"

"Yep." Sapphire grins. "You live around here?"

"Yeah," I say.

"Cool." She digs around in her purse, pulling out her cell phone. "Let me call my boyfriend and double-check he's got the T Swift tickets with him. Are you guys in a big rush?" she whispers as the phone rings.

"Just to get the tickets." Dane shrugs.

I hear a male voice answer, and Sapphire steps away from the truck. We wait until she reappears next to Dane's side. Shoving the phone back in her purse, she says to us. "My boyfriend works at a bar, the Roosevelt. He can't leave work since he's about to start his shift, but we could go get them. Would you guys wanna follow me?"

Dane starts to nod, but I point out the obvious to him. "Dane, Brian will kill me. That's at least a twenty-minute drive from here."

"I'll put gas in his truck," Dane offers.

"He'll still check the mileage." To Sapphire, I say, "It's okay, we can wait until tomorrow to get the tickets. It's not a big deal."

"I'm so sorry." Sapphire looks crestfallen. She wrings her hands around the chain of her purse. "This is all my fault."

"Are you available tomorrow?" Dane asks.

"That's the thing." She runs a hand through her hair. "I'm going out of town for a week."

"Could we meet your boyfriend and get them from him?" Dane suggests.

"He works until 2 am and then sleeps. I can't believe I'm such an idiot." She taps a long fingernail against her cheek. "If gas is a problem, I can give you gas money or discount the tickets by twenty bucks, no problem."

As we consider her offer, she screeches. "Better yet, why don't you guys just hop in with me? I'll call my boyfriend back and tell him to come outside with them."

Again, hesitation on my part. "Uh, I don't think..."

Dane nudges me. "Babe, I'm here."

"But she's a stranger," I hiss under my breath.

"I'm a stranger, huh?" Sapphire hears me and cuts in. "Yeah, I can't help that part."

Brightly, she adds, "but I'll tell Sean to feed us when we get there. Platter of wings on

me." She bows down to us. "Again, my apologies."

"Really, it's no biggie," I say. To Dane, I murmur, "I guess we can drive."

"I have to come back here anyway." She nods her head down the street. "I live over on Marsh and Bellows."

"About five minutes from here?" Dane asks.

"Yep. Don't worry about inconveniencing me. I inconvenienced you guys big time."

Dane and I look at each other. Or, I should say, I try to meet his eyes while he tries to avoid mine, as if he's looking past me toward the gas station pumps.

"Will his truck be okay parked here?" I eye Dane with concern.

"I'll move it down the street." Dane peers over his shoulder. "That way they won't tow it in case they have a time limit here."

"I can't be gone that long," I groan.

"I know." He brushes a strand of hair off my face. "You look pretty when you're flustered."

"Aww, thanks." I smack him gently on the knee.

"Just follow us around the corner," Dane tells Sapphire. "I don't wanna park in this tow-away zone."

"Got it." Sapphire smacks her gum before she retreats to her car. I worry we're going to lose her because she is hell-bent on finding something in the backseat of her car. She's not even paying attention as we reverse, her neck never raises back up to watch us drive off.

"I think she's still hoping she can find the tickets," I muse.

"Kind of a dingbat, huh?"

"That or she's scattered." I shrug. "Who knows?" It's not

until I watch her turn the opposite way of us when we exit the gas station that I change my opinion. "Never mind, a total dipshit."

Dane attempts to get her attention by honking. We take another turn down a side street that's full of dilapidated houses that look like their owners abandoned them or they had a zombie apocalypse. I never said I live in the rich part of town.

"Think she'll find us?" I wonder out loud.

Dane gets out of the pick-up and stands near the rusted brown Chevrolet, facing the street. A gray blur turns towards us, and I watch as Sapphire finally makes her way down the road, slowing to a crawl.

She rolls down her window as she approaches us. "Ugh. I thought you meant the other way." Her face flushes crimson. "I'm having a backward day all around, if you couldn't tell."

"No biggie." Dane smiles at her. "We all have 'em. Let me lock the truck, and we'll get in your ride." I offer him the front seat, but he crawls into the back after opening the passenger door for me. "I'll let you ladies chit-chat."

"Or I can sit in the back with you and pretend we're in an Uber or Lyft," I joke.

Sapphire giggles. "That would be funny."

Dane buckles his seat belt. "You sure you're cool taking two strangers with you?"

"Yeah," she glances in the rear mirror. "I'm okay. You two seem like nice, chill people I would hang out with."

She rolls her eyes. "Sean, my boyfriend, says I'm too trusting of people, but whatever."

"Because you pick up strangers a lot?" I stare at her side profile and notice she's wearing a lot of makeup besides the purple eyeliner.

"No, I just think people are good, you know? One bad person can ruin humanity for everyone. I'm lucky I haven't encountered that, you know?"

I keep my mouth shut since I don't agree. You can be minding your own business and wham, run into the wrong person having a bad day, and suddenly their problem becomes yours.

Dane thankfully fills in the silence. "I get what you mean. I'm a mechanic, and I always want to help people if they're broken down on the side of the road or stranded."

"You are also a guy," I point out.

"What do you mean?" He leans forward, hands on his knees. "Like, I can fix shit?"

"Just that I wouldn't feel safe stopping to help someone."

"Oh true," Sapphire licks her lips. "What if it were another girl or a woman with kids?"

"Maybe." I tilt my head, considering her question. "But probably not, because I couldn't really be useful."

"You mean, because you can't actually fix their car?" Dane tugs on a piece of my hair gently.

"Yeah," I say.

"You could call them a tow truck," Dane argues. "Or let them borrow your phone."

"But everyone has a cell." Sapphire throws her glossy hair over her shoulder. "That wouldn't apply in today's world, you know? I get what you're saying, though."

She turns to look me straight in the eye with her purple-lined, almond-shaped ones. "I wouldn't stop either for random strangers."

"What about us?" Dane teases.

"You are officially no longer strangers." She gives a curt nod. "Plus, I messed up, not you." She taps her steering wheel with her extraordinarily long but fake fingernails. "Are you both in school?"

"I am," I say.

"I'm not," Dane replies.

"I just started my senior year," I offer.

"And I'll be a freshman," Dane mutters, "finally."

Sapphire looks confused. "Oh, you're the sugar mama, I get it. You're dating a younger man." She makes a sound like a cougar, letting out a loud cackle as if this is the funniest thing she's ever heard.

"No," I motion backward, "he means college."

Her face turns ashen behind her caked-on makeup.

"What about you?" I ask politely.

"Oh, I'm nineteen. I kind of like, dropped out of high school." She raises a hand up as if placing it on a bible. "Mark my words, I thought you guys were a lot older."

"What, why?" I ask.

"Because you look like you're at least eighteen."

"No, I mean, why'd you quit school?"

"It wasn't for me." A wistful look crosses Sapphire's face before it passes just as suddenly.

I'm curious as to what she's up to now. "What do you do with your time, then?"

She seems taken aback, as if I asked her to reveal her deepest, darkest secret. I watch her side profile as she tightens her lips into a thin line, as if I offended her.

Quickly, I add. "I just mean what do you do now, for work or whatever?"

"Gotcha. I'm way better off now. Got a better thing going." She seems flustered. "I make money, and I hustle."

In the rear mirror, Dane mouths, "Drugs."

I wonder if that's what she does for money. Suddenly, I

feel very uncomfortable sitting next to this stranger. Even with Dane in the car, I get a bad vibe.

"Do you like school?" she asks, her smile pasted back on.

"Not really," I confide. "I just don't see the point, and my grades suck."

"Yeah, what *is* the point?" She chomps down on her gum. "It's not like I'm going to use chemistry or figure out complex math equations. You can still have a nice life without going to school."

But the look in her eyes tells me she doesn't even believe that. "Take this, school." She cackles again as she flips the bird.

Dane and I exchange another glance in the side mirror.

This girl seems lost.

I look at the clock on her dash.

We should be at the Roosevelt in just a few minutes. Maybe we can make an excuse and grab an Uber home, so we don't have to ride back with her. I can tell Dane's thinking the same thing, and I'm grateful I have a guy that's so dialed into how I think and feel.

Giving him a small smile in the mirror, I settle back against the headrest as Sapphire turns up the radio. It's a good sign – Kings of Leon are wailing through the speakers as if beckoning us to go along and exchange the tickets.

Laughing as Sapphire sticks her tongue out at us, I begin to feel at ease.

4

MADELINE

A sign announcing the Roosevelt hangs in cursive, and a billboard boasting about their 'famous chicken wings' towers above it. This isn't in the best part of town, but it's not the worst, either. It's brick, slightly rundown, yet in such a way it could be considered 'hip.'

Sapphire pulls into a spot as she shuts down the engine. "The tickets are inside. Let me go in and grab them. You guys want a drink or some wings?"

"Nah, it's okay," Dane says. "We don't wanna impose on your time. If it's easier, I can go in with you to get the tickets."

"Nope, I'll grab them, you guys wait here." She grabs her purse and shoves her door open. "I'll see if Sean's got a batch of wings we can take to go. They seriously make the best, spiciest, tastiest ones here." I watch in the mirror as she disappears through the back door marked 'Employees Only.'

Turning in my seat, I grab Dane's knee. "Is this weird to you?"

"Jumping in with a complete idiot to get the concert tickets she forgot?" He rubs my shoulder in agreement. "Totally."

"If it had been a guy in her place, would we have got in with him?"

"Doubtful." He grins. "But I can kick anyone's ass, especially when it comes to you."

"I know, babe." I scratch the dark shadow lining his jaw gently with my fingertips. It makes him look rugged yet dangerous.

I tease. "I'm surprised Sapphire wanted to take us with her. With those muscles, you look like you could *do* some shit."

"Good, then I'm useful." He moves my hand to his lips to kiss my fingers. "I'm so happy with you. I hope you know that."

I gaze in his eyes. "I do." My reflection mirrors how I feel, happy and giddy. "This concert is our first big outing."

"I know." He runs a hand over his face. "Look, I know you could have anyone, and I'm not much, but I care about you and even though I'm not good at saying..."

Entirely focused on Dane and his words, I miss Sapphire spitting out her gum as she exits the back door of the bar.

I don't notice the man that steps forward, clamping a hand on her mouth so she can't scream.

I don't see her raise her hands in the air to try and warn us.

Or watch as he half-drags her to the car we're in.

It isn't until the passenger's side door is yanked open that Dane and I, both wearing matching horrified expressions, watch as she's shoved into the seat beside Dane.

This can't be her boyfriend. What was his name? Sean?

What a dick. He can't be that upset about the concert tickets. It was an honest mistake that Sapphire mixed them up.

It takes a second for me to realize she doesn't know him, to understand that the metal object in his hand is a gun, and he's waving it at us. With a menacing glare on his face, the man tells us there's been a change of plans.

Dane springs to action and twists his body like a human shield, trying to shelter me in the front seat from the man with the gun while yanking Sapphire behind him. My boyfriend has muscles, but this middle-aged man looks like he's been injecting steroids in his veins since he came out of the womb. The gun's steady in his hand as if this is a typical afternoon. It's as if he's not afraid to murder anyone who interferes with his day.

"What do you want?" Dane tries to keep his voice level. "You want money?" He nudges Sapphire, who is cowering behind him in the back seat. "Where's the money I gave you for the tickets?"

"He took it," she whispers tearfully.

"What about my girlfriend's purse?" He motions his head towards me. "Babe, can you lean forward and grab it?"

I want to argue, but now's not the time. There's nothing valuable in my purse unless you have a craving for a 'buy one, get one free' iced coffee or a coupon for ten percent off your next eyebrow wax. The man doesn't seem like either would be of interest. Moneywise, there might be a wrinkled twenty-dollar bill.

"Sure," I squeak.

"Hand it over." The man reaches forward to take it from me. My hand shakes as I toss it at him. The gun is still centered in the middle, pointed viciously at all three of us. Not wasting a minute, he dumps it out on the seat. He unclasps my wallet and checks in the pockets for cash. He shakes his head at the lack of money. "Where's your phone?"

I'm a little slow. "Phone?"

"Yeah, you dumb bitch." He fixes me with a glare. "Where's your fucking cell?"

"I don't have one."

"Get out." He jabs the gun toward me. "Get out of the car, take your clothes off, and show me."

"She's not lying." Dane raises his voice. "She doesn't need to do that." As if pleading with me like I have a choice in the matter, he begs, "Please don't do that."

"She's telling the truth," Sapphire confirms in a shaky voice. "She doesn't have one."

I've decided to name the unhinged man 'Crazypants' because his low-slung jeans are at

risk of falling off his hips. He directs the gun and his anger towards Sapphire. "Why would I believe you?"

She lowers her eyelids as he cocks the gun at Dane. "Where's your phone and wallet?"

"It's in my bag. Not here," Dane explains, "in our truck." I'm floored that Dane doesn't have his cell on him. He *always* carries it with him. How are we supposed to get help?

The man looks at Sapphire, then back to Dane. "Out." He chews his lower lip in disgust. Sapphire and Dane exchange quick glances.

"Go ahead," Crazypants murmurs. "No, not the girl, dipshit." He rolls his eyes. "*You.* You get out of the car."

Dane holds his hands up in protest. "I can't do that, man."

Crazypants scratches his head like he's about to blow a gasket, his face beet red. "Why the fuck not?"

"Tell me what you want."

"*Her*," Crazypants motions the butt of the gun at Sapphire, then at me, "and *her*."

"Please, man, let's figure something else out." Dane pleads.

This annoys Crazypants, and he kicks the panel of the car with a thud. "Do me a favor. Don't tell me what to do. There's nothing to figure out. I'm taking these pretty asses with me and ain't nothing you can do about it."

"No fucking way," Dane's thunders. "Over my dead body."

"What?" A scowl twists the scar above Crazypants' upper lip into a crease. "Get out. It's not a question, or this will happen." He raises his leg to kick Sapphire in the side as she screams.

"Out." The man shrugs, "or I'll shoot her."

Trepidation builds in Dane's eyes, but I can tell his concern is for my safety. "Fine, I'll get out, but I'm taking my girlfriend."

"What's her name?" Crazypants asks.

Neither of us answer.

"What's your name?" Crazypants looks straight at me, and as much as I want to look past him, I force myself to stare into his cold green eyes.

Swallowing hard, I stay quiet.

"Fine, no one wants to play by my rules." He redirects his gun at Sapphire, and I hear a loud pop. At first, I think he shot her by the way she claws with her long fingernails at the cloth seat, her sobs reaching fever pitch.

I join in when I see the blood appear on her hands.

Realizing it's from the large gash on her knee where he kicked her with his steel-toe boot, I force myself to breathe, except a burning smell taints my nostrils. My eyes focus on the source - a patch of fabric upholstery, where a bullet hole entered the seat behind me.

I murmur, "Jenny."

"Huh?"

"Jenny's my name." I lie.

"Out," he screams again at Dane. "I'm not playing." Stomping his foot like a two-year-old having a tantrum, he aims the gun at him. "The next one is for real."

Turning to face me, Dane whispers, "I love you," before kissing me hard on the mouth. "Do what he says, and he'll let you go, okay?"

I will never forget the look on his face as he gradually climbs out, the gun trained on his back. It's one of sheer terror laced with disappointment, as if he knew at that moment how much he let me down. That he alone couldn't save me.

Crazypants yells, "Not so fast, hotshot."

Spinning around, Dane is met with a shot to his chest. This time there's no denying where the bullet hits. I watch in horror as the dark red liquid muddies his light-colored shirt.

"You said over your dead body." Crazypants shrugs.

Acting like a maniac who just watched the first guy she's ever loved get shot, I lunge forward to jerk the arm holding the gun.

Another deafening sound releases from the pistol.

I scream as it whizzes past Dane. I'm rewarded with a smack in the face from the butt of the gun as Crazypants leans past Sapphire to slam and lock the door Dane just slid out of.

My cheek goes numb with pain.

"Now that I have your attention." He points the gun at me. "You will stay up here with me. Buckle your seat belt."

"And you," gripping Sapphire's chin, "will stay in the

backseat. If you try any funny business, I'll put a bullet in both of you, it doesn't matter who did what."

Crazypants jumps into the front seat and throws the car in reverse before I can shove my own door open to escape. We peel out, the tires squealing in protest.

Dane is on the ground, his chest heaving, as he holds his hand over the wound. I watch in the mirror as he tries to stand, stumbling after us. Horrified, I watch as he falls over and crawls, his hands outstretched.

My last memory of Dane is his bloody fingers waving in the air.

The excruciating pain on his face.

Shock.

My earlier thought about bumping into the wrong person crosses my mind. We just wanted concert tickets, I think wildly.

5

BRIAN

I wake up to a pounding and mistaking it for my headache, I ignore it. Ever since I got home from a job I didn't want, but I needed, the tension has been building in the form of blurred eyesight and painful throbbing that reminds me of a hammer striking my temple.

Except this time, it doesn't go away. It grows louder and more annoying. "Maddy." I holler, "Get that, will ya?" No answer. Not even a cuss word aimed in my direction.

"Dammit, Maddy," I roll out of bed, tripping on the sheets I'm tangled up in. I realize I'm wearing nothing but a pair of boxers. Whatever, if someone's going to bother me this late at night, then they can deal with my beer gut.

Another unwanted knock.

I fling the door open, with no expectation of who stands in front of me. Instead of it being pitch black, it's dusk. Rubbing my eyes, it's the lady from next door, Katrina. Close to my mother's age if I had one, she's annoying but harmless. She takes a disturbing amount of interest in us. I should be grateful, since it's like having a guard dog without the incessant barking. Though she'd probably hump my leg if I asked.

"What the, what time is it?" I grumble. Every time I encounter her, she's wearing black leggings and an oversized sweatshirt, reeking of smoke. But I can't judge, I probably smell the same.

"It's only a little past six." Katrina keeps her eyes on my bare chest. "I don't want to alarm you, but that daughter of yours took your truck."

"*My* truck?" I pat my boxers as if the keys will appear in the pockets I don't have. Squinting down the staircase to my parking space, it's empty, an oil stain the only reminder my Chevy was parked there.

"What the..." my voice trails off. I run a hand through my hair in disgust. "She alone?"

"Nope. Dane Burns from Building B was with her." She bites her lip. "Maybe I shouldn't say nothing, but he had a duffel bag. Looked like they were going somewhere to spend the night."

"She driving?"

"Uh-huh." She puts her hands on her hips. "Teenagers, right?"

"I'm going to blister her ass," I bellow, "and his, too."

Katrina plays dumb. "Oh, are they not supposed to be using your pick-up?"

"She's grounded." I sigh. "Anyways, thanks, Kat. I appreciate you watching out for us. Everyone needs a neighbor like you." I reach forward to pat her shoulder at the same time she leans in for a hug. It's awkward as I accidentally brush my hand across her boob. "Uh, have a good night," I say.

She leers at me. "Let me know if there's anything I can

do... I'm more than happy to keep you company while you wait for her."

"Thanks, uh, that won't be necessary." I give her a wink. "She's a big girl." After I slam the door in her face, unintentional of course, I head into the kitchen.

Reaching into the battered fridge, covered in dents, likely from my drunken fist, I yank the only magnet off the surface, a bottle opener. I tug the lid off a cold one and chug it down. It tastes like heaven, coating my throat, as I finish it and start on another one.

Then I settle onto the couch and flip on the television to wait. Except I'm not sure what I'm waiting for. If they went to spend the night somewhere, then she won't be back until at least tomorrow.

And I just want my rusted Chevrolet back.

I crack my knuckles. I don't need this shit right now. I've got enough to worry about. I consider going to Dane's apartment, but what's the point? Robbie isn't going to give him up.

I spend the night on the couch, moving only to grab the chilled bottles from the fridge, finally stacking them in their leftover box I never bothered to recycle, preferring instead to let them pile up next to the sink. This way, I don't have to keep transporting them two at a time back to the living room.

Eventually, I pass out, after chain-smoking and ordering a large pepperoni pizza. Unsure how long I slept, I wake up to a female voice pounding on the door.

"Again," I mutter. No way. I ignore it this time.

Since I fell asleep sitting up, I can feel the shooting pain radiating down my spinal column, an old injury that flares up from an earlier car accident. Choosing instead to retreat to my bedroom, I stop in the bathroom to take a leak.

I search in the medicine cabinet for some pain pills. A crumpled can of two-day-old Coors Light beer is next to the sink. Shaking it, enough remains to swallow the capsules with. I tilt my head back and let the watery piss run down my throat.

I don't know how long I'm out. All I know is when I wake up, I hear an unrecognizable male voice that's too raspy to be my friend, Chip's. Tempted to avoid answering, I peek through the blinds. It's a man, gray hair, gray suit, dressed professionally. He's chewing gum yet still manages to look pissed.

My stomach lurches.

The man looks like he could work for Child Protective Services, yet his suit is tailored and screams 'expensive.' It's not an off the rack one he picked up on clearance.

Deciding I'm unimpressed and he's clearly not CPS, I stomp back toward my bedroom. It isn't until I hear him rap his knuckles on the door and yell, "Police, open up," that I vomit all over the ugly beige carpeting in the hallway.

6

MADELINE

Sapphire wails in the backseat, repeating, "I fucked up, I'm sorry."

"No shit you fucked up." Crazypants lobs his hand out at me. "What was that, Sapphire? You didn't call. You know better. You always call."

"I couldn't," she huffs, "and you could be a little more understanding. And what's with kicking me?"

"Good point." He gives her a slight smile in the mirror. "I shouldn't do that." At a stop sign, he turns to backhand her across the cheek. "I should've done this instead."

Her eyes fill with tears as he forewarns her. "Don't ever fucking talk to me like that again."

When I turn to glance back at her, she stares straight ahead, refusing to meet my eyes, arms crossed over her chest. I silently beg her to tell me she doesn't know this man, that she didn't set us up. That the thoughts running through my head are insane.

Instead, she chews her lip and stares glassy-eyed out the window, pretending not to notice. Crazypants does, though.

"Don't look at her." He smacks me on the shoulder. "Don't you dare look at her."

Is this Sean? Were they planning to rob us all along?

I have to say it out loud. "Is this your boyfriend?"

"Hardly," she mutters.

"Who are you?" I ask the man who shot my boyfriend, the gun now removed from sight.

His response isn't surprising. "Your worst fucking nightmare. Shut up."

When I open my mouth to speak, the gun reappears next to my cheek. "We like 'em pretty and alive, but if you'd prefer, you can be dead."

Who likes them pretty? I want to ask, but my gut tells me it will mean instant death.

And right now, I'm not at a point where I want to die. At least not yet.

I try again to meet Sapphire's eyes in the side mirror, but she's frozen in place, her sight glued to the front windshield.

"What's going to happen to Dane now?" she asks him. "He took a bullet for you."

"It was hardly for me." Crazypants snorts. "He'll get paid."

"Paid?" I narrow my eyes at him.

He growls, "Shut it."

"Listen to him," is all Sapphire mutters to me.

I watch the scenery whiz by, my mind frantic to figure out where we're going now that I realize it's the opposite direction of where we came from. When I watch the news or crime shows, they always tell you to pay attention to every detail, every sound, every noise. This way, you can retrace your steps. It sounds straightforward enough, like common sense, except it's impossible to focus when you were just kidnapped and taken from your just-shot boyfriend.

Not wanting to lose my shit, I can't help it, the tears fall as I stare out the smudged window and silently cry. I want to be strong. I have to be strong, I remind myself. Remember what Brian always tells you? Not to let anyone see you cry. Don't let anyone know they can cause you pain. And up until now, he was the only one who could.

My mouth is bone dry, like a piece of cotton is lodged in my throat. How long will it take for Brian to realize his car is missing? I wish now that Katrina marched up to our door and woke him, explaining she saw me and Dane take it.

My heart sinks. He'll think Dane and I ran away together.

I let my mind drift to Dane. The pain on his face. The gunshot. What do they mean about him getting paid? He arranged for us to get concert tickets, end of story. *Dane wouldn't hurt you, he loves you*, a small voice whispers in my head. Another voice, a louder one, reminds me that money can solve a lot of problems. He needs money. He's always broke.

No, never.

He'd never let someone hurt me, he loves me.

I scrunch my face up as my stomach turns sour. The nagging voice in my head screams at me. *He* was supposed to get the tickets on his own, without you. How convenient to have a flat tire on the day you are robbed at gunpoint. He encouraged you to get in the vehicle with a strange girl.

But he got shot, I remind myself. It's not like he faked the bullet wound.

No. Stop it. Stop these thoughts.

I pinch my leg, directing my attention to the road. Crazypants makes a U-turn, and we lurch onto the interstate, his eyes gaze at the speed limit sign, and he sets his cruise control. With one hand on the wheel, he reaches into his pocket with the other, pulling out an old school flip phone.

He hits one button only, the 'redial' one. "I got her," he murmurs to someone. "Said her name's Jenny, but I checked her ID to confirm it's Madeline." My mouth caves at what he's saying. If Crazypants knew his target ahead of time, this wasn't a coincidence in the slightest.

And who is this girl behind me?

What could they possibly want with me?

Crazypants continues, "I know we're late. Sapphire didn't communicate on time." A long pause follows as the voice on the other end speaks. I can't hear the muffled words, but Crazypants responds with, "No need, I already took care of it."

"Be there shortly." He disconnects and shoves the phone back in his pocket. I focus on the billboards that sneak by, memorizing the content on them. One advertises a 'painless, needleless' six-hundred-dollar vasectomy, another an air-conditioning service. Safford Community College announces it's the next exit.

I recognize that name. We're about thirty-five miles from my apartment. It passes in the rearview as we get farther and farther away from what I know. A few more miles pass, and without signaling, he maneuvers off Exit 167-A. I keep repeating the mile marker in my head, still hopeful at this point we'll be stopping soon.

Except he makes a right turn, then another, and as I try and connect the dots and keep the directions straight, he goes in a loop and merges back on the freeway in the direction we just came. At the next exit, we hang a left and keep going until he turns onto a gravel road that's barely visible from the highway.

A large warehouse looms up ahead. My eyes scan for

signage or recognizable road signs, but a speed limit warning doesn't seem useful. Reading my mind, Crazypants says, "Don't get too excited. We're not staying for very long." He slows to a crawl and drives down another gravel road that leads to a tan building.

We park in the back, the gray Toyota hidden from sight.

He pops the trunk button before removing the keys from the ignition. Jumping out, he sticks his head back in to address Sapphire. "Get her ready."

"Yes, sir." She nods and leans forward to gently touch my shoulder. "Stay here, I'll be right back."

"Ready for what?" I shriek, "What...what're you going to do?"

"You're safe now. I got you." She applies pressure to my arm with her long talons. "Heads up, if you don't follow my lead, they'll kill you."

I shudder, jerking my shoulder out of her grasp.

Without another word, she exits the vehicle.

Holding my breath, I wonder what I'm getting ready for. Is Crazypants going to rape me? Is she going to hold me down and help him? Sapphire alluded to more than one person. Am I going to be part of some gang initiation ritual?

Frantic, I unbuckle my seat belt, darting my eyes wildly around me. If I hit the door locks, that won't buy me time. Crazypants can just unlock them and drag me out.

In the mirror, I watch as Sapphire pulls a dark navy pillowcase-looking thing that has a cord attached out of the trunk.

She yelps as another man slinks up to her, surprising her from behind. He envelopes her in his arms. This one is covered head to toe in tattoos, even his shaved head has a massive one in the shape of an eagle riding on something. Maybe a motorcycle?

They say a couple words to each other before he settles on a rough kiss. I can't tell if she enjoys it or it's unwanted, especially since his next move is grabbing a fistful of her jet-black hair. With a squeal, he holds her in place while he sucks greedily on her lip. I watch in the rearview mirror, scared to move, though I realize I should run. This might be my only chance.

But where will I go?

Does it matter?

If I don't run now, I might not get another opportunity.

And there is no such thing as 'pretty dead.'

Preparing to tuck and roll underneath the vehicle, a hand latches on to my ear. I quiver as it slides to my neck.

"You ain't going anywhere," a voice informs me from behind.

Before I can scream, a wet rag's shoved down my throat, and I feel a pinch in my arm as a needle sinks into my vein. I'm lifted out of the vehicle and pushed against something hard, maybe a man's chest, as I'm being shifted in the air. My eyelids are unable to stay open, and they press shut right before I fade into darkness, my last conscious thought of Dane.

BRIAN

I hear another voice, this one lower and gruff, but nonetheless female. I peek through the blinds and sure enough, Katrina's perched next to the railing outside of the red brick building. She's sidled up to the man in the suit as the two of them exchange words.

Shit. I wonder what she's saying.

His authoritative voice hollers, "Police," as he pounds on the door again.

Slowly, I unchain the deadbolt before I peep out. "Yeah, I hear you," I gulp. After rubbing the grit out of my eyes, I realize the gray-suited man looks familiar. His imposing figure isn't towering, it's more like his demeanor.

"Time for a chat?" He removes his badge to give me a glimpse. "Detective Delaney. We spoke recently."

My mind drifts to the events of the last couple of days. The sinking feeling in the pit of my stomach expands. Recognition flickers. "We met..."

"Indeed, we did." He frowns. "Less than a week ago."

"Uh, yes, I remember," I squint at him. "Not the best of circumstances."

He opens his mouth to respond, and his gum falls out, the stickiness landing on my bare foot. I meet his gaze with a glare.

"Accident," he shrugs. "I had no idea you were the father of Madeline Pruitt. I guess even law enforcement can be surprised at times." I never loosen my grip on the wood as he stares at me with contempt. "And my reason for stopping by, I'm afraid you're not gonna like," Delaney says.

"Then, by all means, make yourself at home." I lean into the doorjamb for support.

"Mind letting me in?" He pushes past me. "I've got some questions, and you better have some answers."

I forgot about Katrina, who has stood silently behind him until now. Her wrinkles are more pronounced today, or maybe it's the glaring sunlight, or perhaps it's concern. She gives me a wink and follows Delaney in. Is this woman batty, I wonder? Why does she want to be here when the detective is?

"I'd like to talk to you about your seventeen-year-old daughter," he scrunches his nose at me. "Or is she still an afterthought per CPS?"

I ignore him for a moment as Katrina appears at my side. "Hi, Kat," I say, nodding at her.

"I'm here for support, dear." She reaches an arm around my bicep. "Hopefully I can help since I saw her leave in your pick-up."

"Wait, you called the cops on Maddy?" I blurt out. This is *Unfuckingbelievable*. She knows I can't afford another incident involving CPS or law enforcement. Narrowing her eyes at me, Katrina shakes her head.

Both of them pause in the small entry, their eyes scanning the living room. I cross my arms as I consider the apartment through their lens. The television sits on the floor since I don't have a stand. Ashtrays are scattered in every direction. The same can be said for the overabundance of beer bottles and cans, empty and unopened cartons of cigarettes, dirty magazines next to earmarked auto mechanic ones, and a greasy pizza box. The coffee table has a broken leg, so it sags, the weight on its three remaining ones.

Irritated, I ask, "Want me to light a candle and set the mood?"

Detective Delaney shakes his head impatiently. "Let's get down to business."

"Whatever." I point to the kitchen table. It's still standing on all four legs. "Have a seat."

"Where?" He mutters, "underneath your unopened mail or the mildew-smelling clothes that are hanging from the chair?"

"Your pick, detective." I don't bother emptying one for him. I do for Katrina, who looks absolutely tickled pink that I'm catering to her. She sits down with a sigh of relief.

Fuck. I'll pay for this later.

Heading to the fridge for a beer or a glass of orange juice, I peer at the bare shelves. "Shit." I run a hand through my disheveled hair. "Nothing here." I step away from the fridge. "I've gotta get groceries."

Nonchalant, Delaney doesn't bother to take a seat. Instead, he asks, "Mind if I look around?"

"Not until you tell me what you're doing here." I stick my head under the kitchen faucet for a drink of water.

"Where's Madeline?" His eyes drill into the back of my head.

"Maddy," I sputter, "is at school."

"Are you sure of that?"

"Positive." I wipe a hand across my mouth.

"What about your truck?"

"It was borrowed." I skirt around him and Katrina to the front window, peeling back the curtains. "Still not here."

"Wait, your vehicle is missing?" Detective Delaney whistles through his teeth.

Katrina jumps in, thrilled to be part of the conversation. "His daughter stole his truck a few days ago."

"Yesterday." I correct her. I'm surprised at her senile moment. Usually, she's on her game. "It was yesterday."

She shrugs, "It was four days ago, actually."

Delaney stares at me. "Have you gone to work this week, Mr. Pruitt?"

"Of course." But a bead of sweat furrows on my brow. "I never miss a day of work."

"Your co-worker Chip said you were gone for the last three days in a row at the shop. He hasn't heard a peep from you. Your daughter hasn't shown up for school all week. And conveniently, your truck is now missing."

"Wait," I feel my temper flare, "what're you implying, dude?"

"*Detective*," he corrects me. "Not dude."

"Whatever."

"Maybe you're suffering from guilt?" He makes a face like he sucked on a sour piece of
candy. "Nah, not *you*."

I want to tell him to...never mind.

Point-blank I ask, "Detective Delaney, why are you here? To arrest me for Maddy
skipping class?"

"No." He shakes his head. "Not yet. I've got a couple questions, though. Do you know Dane Burns?"

"*Dumbfuck* Dane?" I swipe a hand across my forehead. "Wait, did that asshole wreck my truck?"

He ignores my sentiments. "We've been trying to get in contact with you. Not to mention the hospital and Madeline's high school." He steps back like I'm a rabid dog about to attack. "There's been an accident."

"Dane wrecked the truck, and they got hurt?" I scratch an itch on the back of my neck. "Shit. And let me guess, he wants to sue me since Maddy was driving and I don't have insurance?"

I notice Katrina's hands grip the back of the chair tightly as she rises.

"Aren't you going to tell me what you know?" I snap.

"Why?" His voice is laced with sarcasm. "You don't care."

I curl my hands into fists. "You don't know shit about me," I spit out. "Don't you dare come into my place and act like you do."

His disgusted gaze trails over every inch of the front two rooms. "I don't need to spend time with you to know who you are. I could walk through this place and give you a step by step."

"By all means," I wave my hand in the air. "Let's hear it."

"You numb yourself with alcohol," he kicks an empty bottle, then moves on to the patched walls and dented fridge, "you fight with your fists." He walks forward down the tiny hall, stopping at the bedroom on the left, which is Maddy's room.

His eyes inspect the missing door handle. "You probably removed Madeline's lock after a bad argument because you tell yourself that's the only way to control her." Stepping inside her room, he reaches for the blinds to peek out of the dirty window. "And you blame her for your mistakes." With a glower, he turns on his heel. "Would you like me to continue on to your bedroom?"

Flustered, I say, "Be my guest." My face burns as I

consider the bottle of pain pills on my bathroom counter, not to mention the invasion of my personal space.

"What's your point, detective?" I sneer. "I support Maddy in all the ways she needs."

"Then why don't you know where she's at?"

"In the hospital, according to you. In fact, it's a *blessing* I didn't know about the accident because I would beat the shit out of that loser boyfriend."

Detective Delaney sighs and a flicker of emotion crosses his hazel eyes. A touch of

sadness tinged with despair. "Mr. Pruitt, Madeline is *missing*, not injured, and I find it rather suspect that you don't know where your daughter is. In hindsight, it seems you hinted at a confession then."

"What do you mean?" I narrow my eyes. "Is this some kind of sick joke? What's wrong with you, dude? You can't go around putting words in my mouth. You're an officer of the law, aren't you?"

"Madeline is gone." He grits his teeth. "Dane Burns is in the hospital in critical condition, not from a car accident as you *presumed*, but from a gunshot wound. It's unclear if he will make it through the night." Taking a deep breath, he adds, "Though clearly he's a fighter. They said that a few days ago when he was found, and he continues to amaze the doctors."

My mouth is open, wide open.

Spittle flies before I realize I need to close it and then reopen it before starting a sentence. "He was shot? Where's Maddy? Was she shot, too?"

"We don't know where she is. That's what we're trying to determine."

"Where's my truck?"

"I didn't know it was missing until now." He runs a hand down his tie as if to smooth it. "So who knows?"

"Where did you find Dane?" I run a hand through my hair, exasperated. "She could be in danger."

"It wasn't until the school reported Madeline truant after three days and you couldn't be located that we connected the dots and determined she might've been with him, unless..." his voice suddenly halts.

Frantically, my eyes dart around for my phone. It's buried underneath a pile of clothes in my bedroom. Dead. "Shit," I murmur. I plug it into the charger on my nightstand, knocking over a lamp in the process. I catch the flimsy lampshade as it topples to the ground.

"We need to talk," Delaney insists. "Now."

"About what?" I'm in shock, my eyes unable to focus as I stare at everything but see nothing. I stare at my cell, watching the red battery light appear as if reprimanding me for my indifference to having a positive charge.

"Madeline," he says softly, "Can we have a seat now and get down to business?"

Katrina steps forward and grabs me by the elbow, gently guiding me to the leather couch, where I sit on a duct-taped patch to prevent the stuffing from sticking out. She sits next to me and lighter in hand, leans down for a pack of cigarettes on the floor, removing one for each of us. Delaney brings a chair from the kitchen into the living room and takes a seat.

"Mind?" I let the cigarette dangle off my lips.

"It's your place."

Under my breath, I mutter. "Finally, we agree on something," Delaney asks me question after question, rapid-fire, as I try to answer what I know, which isn't much. Katrina speaks for me, telling the detective she saw Maddy drive my truck with Dane beside her in the passenger seat.

"And you have no idea where she went?"

"He had a duffel bag, so I assumed somewhere overnight, to be alone," Katrina says, stiffly. "She's head over heels for that boy and doesn't seem to care about her responsibilities."

"What do you mean by that?"

"Her head's in the clouds." Katrina's face burns, and she adds, ""She's flighty, and Brian shared with me that she barely passed her junior year."

Delaney turns to me. "And why didn't you bother to report her missing, Mr. Pruitt?"

"I didn't know she was missing." I'm grim. "She's run away before, just a couple weeks ago, in fact, so she could be running again."

"What does she run from?" Delaney shoots me a pointed look. "*Besides* you."

"Life. How unfair it is. She wants responsibility she can't handle."

"Meaning?"

"A serious boyfriend. Her own place." I take a long drag. "Yet she has no money and no job."

"And you think she just ran away?" Delaney pulls a notepad from the inside of his jacket and examines his notes. "That this is another one of those times? What about the gunshot wound Dane was brought in with?"

"Maybe not now..." My voice trails off. "She doesn't usually steal my truck. That's off-limits. Unless she had other intentions with it. She knows better," I add, tersely stubbing out my cigarette.

"Then why didn't you report it stolen?" Our eyes lock, and we both know why. I'm under investigation by CPS and would lose custody of Madeline. And not that I want the responsibility of raising her, but I do have a little bit of a conscience. It's not like I want her to end up in the system. I know how that goes, and it's not my first choice.

He changes his line of questioning, but I don't find his interrogation any easier. "Was your daughter involved in drugs? Did she use or sell them? Did her boyfriend?"

"Any illegal activities or underage ones?"

"Are you aware of anyone that would want to harm Madeline? Could she be bullying another student or vice-versa?"

"Does Madeline have any enemies? What about Dane Burns?"

"How is the relationship between Madeline and Dane? Were they in a committed relationship? Any other individuals they might've been involved with? What about exes? Any tension or revenge-type issues?

"What about Dane's roommate, Robbie Atlas? How well do you know him?"

"Do you have a girlfriend or partner? What's their relationship with Madeline?"

Nervously, I lick my lips. "Since Maddy's seventeen, I don't let her have a phone to avoid most of those problems you listed off." I don't mention it's because I can't afford it.

"The only guy I know about is Dane." I light the next one. "She doesn't drink or smoke, or do drugs. Maybe she's smoked pot, I think Dane and his roommate do, but I don't think she's a fan. Said it made her tired when she first experimented with it." I don't mention Maddy's first time smoking pot was with me.

"Class has only been in session for a few weeks. Not many friends that I know about. She mainly hangs with Dane, and he's outta school. She skips class a lot, and I don't know about any particular trouble with other students." I rest my head in my hands as my voice breaks. "I don't know where her mom is. I don't know why anyone would hurt her or want to. I just don't know."

"What about a girlfriend? You have one?"

"She's never met Maddy," I say. "She has her own kid to worry about."

"That'll be all for now." Delaney slaps his notepad shut. "We'll keep on investigating any leads or tips that are called in." He thrusts his business card in my hand. "My cell is right here." Punching it for emphasis, he says, "Call me if you think of anything that could help us locate Madeline."

"Just find her." I rub my bleary, bloodshot eyes. "I'll deal with her when she's home. Try to steer this ship in the right direction. Be a better father. A more present one."

"By all accounts, you're a shitty alcoholic father." Delaney hesitates at the door. "Just so you know, I don't think there's anything to find. I think you know exactly where Madeline is because you put her there. She's cramped your style for a long time. So now you tell me, Brian, what exactly do you want me to do for you?"

"Find her." I slam my fist on the coffee table.

"And one more thing. Anyone else who might have it out for you?" Delaney yanks at his tie, as if it's suffocating him. I'd do him the honor, I think. "You know, someone you might've pissed off at the garage? Maybe a car not fixed properly or any issues with customers?"

My heart pounds out of my chest.

I can think of a particular person from my past that might want to do us harm. Before I can say the name out loud, I swallow it. I'm not ready to give it life just yet. If it turns out to be accurate, then not only is Maddy in trouble, her old man is too.

"No," I keep my voice steady.

"Damn, that's too bad." He sounds anything but contrite. "You should clean this pigsty up."

"Asshole," I mutter under my breath.

"What's wrong? I'm trying to be a friend," Delaney pauses at the door. "Saving you the embarrassment when I come back with an arrest warrant. We wouldn't want the media to add *slob* to deadbeat dad, would we?"

Because I can push him out the door and slam it, he takes my cue and exits.

PART II

THE WEEK BEFORE

8

BRIAN

"Isn't it slumming to come down here?" I ask the tall, leggy woman who just exited her fairly new Jeep Grand Cherokee at my piddly mechanics shop. "Don't tell me you had to trade the G-Wagen in for that?"

"Funny," she retorts, even though her mouth never twists into a smile. "It's Allegra's new Jeep."

"Thought she wasn't allowed to have one?"

"We just won't tell her father." She shrugs. "I'm giving it to her as a surprise."

"Where are you going to keep it?"

"I was hoping here." She gives me a tense smile. "I'd pay you to store it."

I raise a brow. "What happens if he finds out?"

"Allegra and I will be dead meat."

"You ain't lying." I stub my boot in the dirt. "And no need for payment. I'll store it behind the shop. There's a makeshift covered garage."

"You need money, right?"

"Val," I say with a warning tone.

"Can you do a tune-up on it? I bought it from someone

online and I want to make sure it's safe for her to drive." I can tell she's nervous by the way she wrings her hands. I want to give her shoulder a small squeeze, but I don't dare.

Instead I offer, "You know, you're a really good mom."

"Thanks." She blows a chunk of chestnut-colored hair off her face. "I need you..."

Chip, the only other mechanic, is staring at us with intense scrutiny so I interrupt, motioning her to meet me at the hood of the Jeep. "Follow my lead." I move the chew forward in my mouth, clipboard in hand, as I pretend to write down issues with the vehicle. A quick study, Valerie comments loudly on a rattle it's making so Chip overhears. He's a good man, ornery as hell, not good at talk but great at work, and damn nosy. I watch him watch her stride to my side, his eyes drinking in the sight of her.

When Chip notices my glare, his head instantly moves back down to the oil pan of another car he's working on.

"Oil change," she whispers. "And I want..."

"Valerie Atwater." I growl. "Not here."

"Okay, can you meet me on your lunch hour?"

"No. As much as I'd like to, I don't have time to take a break."

"Of course you do." She hastens to add, "I need your help with something. It pays well."

"Is this a get-quick-rich scheme?"

"I didn't get rich quick, so why would I pester you with that?" She tries not to roll her eyes as Chip replaces his stare, trying to place where he knows her from.

That, and she's a well-heeled woman, stunning today even dressed down in a beige trench coat and dark jeans.

"I need help," she pleads. "But you gotta keep a handle on the drink."

"You wanna start in on that now, too?" I grumble,

disgustedly spitting my chew in a plastic bottle. Chip notices my flash of anger and eyes us suspiciously, a rag paused midair.

She stuffs her hands in the pockets of her trench. "It involves driving."

"Okay." I shrug. "If you say so."

"I only say so if you can be sober."

"I can," I mutter, "and only if it brings us one step closer..." I don't have to finish my sentence, her eyes indignant with understanding.

Without another word, she starts to head into the office of the shop.

"Wait," I yell after her. "Mrs. Atwater," I clasp the clipboard to my chest. "If you can sign this slip, we can complete the job."

She turns on her heel and takes the pen and clipboard from me. With a flourish, she pens a fake name and pays cash.

Chip must've figured it out because he shakes his head and mouths, "What's an Atwater doing here?"

I shrug, unable to tell him that no matter where you go, you can't seem to get out from under the Atwater spell or curse, depending on which Atwater you're tangled up with.

9

BRIAN

My hands punch the steering wheel in emphasis as I belt out a Guns N' Roses tune. They just don't make grunge rock like they used to, I reflect. Looking for a parking spot at the mall is proving rather difficult today. I spot a silver sedan with a man standing near the tail pipe.

Slowing, I wait for him to throw his packages in and go.

He's not moving very fast, which makes me impatient. I have limited time and his slowness is cutting into it.

About to honk, I realize that he can't go anywhere, as his front left tire is deflated.

No wonder he's taking his sweet time.

I'm about to gun my engine and pass as he pops his trunk and fumbles for his spare. Except he's too good-looking, too dressed up, too *prim* to be able to handle this blue-collar job by himself.

Usually, I'd drive right by his type, but there's a familiarity about him. Maybe it's just his type - the quintessential rich, suave type who think the world owes him something.

Tilting my head, I catch a glimpse of the license plate. He's local.

I snort at the personalized plate. It's a silver Jaguar that identifies itself with MOMENTM. In my book, people who bother to set themselves apart with some bullshit tag are ridiculous. That might be because I'm not necessarily a calm driver, and I'd rather flip someone off and shake my fist at them, which makes having a customized plate unnecessary. I don't want them to be able to identify my vehicle.

Clearly, the man is a fish out of water when it comes to cars. He might be able to afford a luxury automobile, but that's where his relationship with them ends.

Disgusted, he kicks the bad tire as he pulls out his cell, I presume to either call Triple A or roadside assistance.

Sighing, I pull my pick-up into a newly-vacated spot. I'd prefer to watch him unravel, but I have my own place to be.

I eyeball him as I walk by but hesitate as he runs a hand through his hair, the frustration on his face apparent. His watch glints in the sun, which means it's expensive. Probably a Rolex, with cufflinks that cost more than my rent.

"Hey man, you need some help?" I throw my hand over my eyes like a visor. In return, he spins around in the direction of my voice. I'm fairly certain no one has ever called him anything less than his surname.

"Uh, hi." I say. "Thought you might need some help."

He's every bit as pretentious in person.

Dark hair, dark eyes, trim, athletic body, custom suit. He wears bright socks that scream, "I'm trying for fun in the only place I know how, my feet."

"Ah, yes, I do." He reaches out a hand to shake mine. "Darren."

"Brian." I return his firm grip. My callused hand probably feels weird to his soft one.

With a smirk, he asks, "You stop just for this?"

"It was a helluva good show watching you sweat, but I figured I'd help." I motion at the jack. "You can cancel whoever you called. I'll handle it."

"Uh, thanks." He stands back to consider me. "You do this a lot?"

"Stop for random men in parking lots?" With my tongue, I shove the chew deeper in my cheek. "Nah, only at truck stops."

He points his index finger at me. "You, sir, are funny." He shrugs. "I ask just because it's a luxury car..."

"I'm a mechanic," I offer, not wanting his boxer briefs to bunch into a tight wad.

"Then I'm in luck."

"I'll get to work and you can cancel your help."

"Thanks, Brad."

"Brian," I correct him.

"Brian." He repeats again and points to himself. "And I'm Darren."

"Got it."

Darren gets back on his phone and I inspect his spare tire for any damage. There are some tools in the back, and I grab the jack and lug wrench and get to work.

I keep one ear open as he talks on the phone. Judging by the convo, it's definitely roadside assistance. I can feel his eyes locked on my movements as I go through the motions of replacing his tire. When I finish, I sink back on my heels. "Make sure you don't drive this one for too long or travel at high rates of speed."

"I'll take it to the shop tomorrow," he promises, reaching into the driver's seat. Holding out his money clip, he asks, "How much?"

I peel the ball cap off my head, sweat dripping down my nose. "Nothing."

"Seriously, I can't let this go without payment."

"It's not a problem. Sometimes it's best to be a Good Samaritan."

He considers me for a moment, as if he expects me to change my mind. "Just pay it forward," I say.

"Thanks, Brian." He tries for a smile that doesn't reach his mouth. I have a feeling it's a rare occurrence for this man to look happy. It's not second-nature to him, and instead it appears like a half-smile, half-frown.

An aberration.

I replace the tools in the trunk and nod as he settles into the driver seat. He starts the engine and as he slowly passes me. I tip my hat to him and make my way back to my beat-up pick-up truck. It might not be new, or shiny, but I can change the tire.

I'm out of time, so my errand will have to wait until later.

I forget about the man until the next morning when I arrive at work.

A silver Jag's parked outside of my mechanic's garage with his custom plate.

The man, Darren, is waiting for me inside, clearly out of his element as he tries to fit his tall frame in the only chair available, a metal one.

We don't have a lavish waiting room since we're not a dealership and to keep our costs down, there isn't a place to hang out. I prefer it this way since it keeps the customers out of my hair. The small front room contains a cash register and shelves of motor oil and air fresheners that line the walls. There's no front desk person, and Chip and I ring up our own transactions.

"Brian." He hurriedly stands to address me.

"Darren, is it?"

He nods.

"How'd you find me?"

"I have my ways." A shark has a better demeanor. "You got time to replace my tire?"

"Sure thing."

He drums his fingers on the scratched counter, staring at the picture behind me. It's dog-eared and worn, but it hangs proudly with the American flag behind me.

"Is that your wife?"

I chuckle at his comment, which isn't surprising. I'm mid-thirties so it's unexpected that I have a daughter, let alone a senior in high school.

"No, that's my daughter."

I doubt he's embarrassed much, but he touches a hand to his forehead with a different watch, expressing his unease. "Oops, sorry."

"No, it's okay." I shrug. "I get that a lot. I had her young."

"You married?"

"Nah, never could find someone to take the plunge with."

"Her mom wasn't an option?" His question is more personal than I'd like to get with this man, and I need to deflect.

"She split when Madeline was a toddler." I gesture like I'm slitting my throat. "Which was for the best, she was a real piece of work." I don't bother to add she was the queen of manipulation and used it against me, every step of the way. We started dating when we were seniors in high school. I trusted her when she told me she was on birth control. It never crossed my mind she would stop taking it, especially after I made the mistake of telling her how I couldn't wait to skip town after we graduated.

I set my insulated coffee on the shelf behind the counter. "I'll check the pressure in your other tires."

The man nods at me but casually asks, "You raise her on your own?"

"Yes, sir." I nod. "There are no off days when it comes to being a parent." I realize I sound like a pompous dick from a self-help television show. "Just because teenagers are hormonal little shits," I add with a groan.

"You, sir, are preaching to the choir." Darren rolls his eyes. "I have a kid in high school, and it's always drama this and drama that." He lowers his voice conspiratorially even though no one else is in the office. "You ever wish kids didn't have an iPad and an iPhone and a laptop and every technological advance known to man?"

"Every day."

"Good talk." He slaps the counter, reaching in his back pocket. "Just call me when she's ready." Sliding a business card across the counter, he says. "You can reach me on my cell."

I stare down at it, trying not to let him see my wide-eyed look at his name and title.

Darren Atwater. CEO of Atwater Technologies.

That Darren Atwater. Drilling and blasting into impossible surfaces are their specialty. They use explosives to break rock for excavation so tunnels or roads can be built. Or on a personal level, their own mega-mansion.

"Certainly." I keep my voice level like I'm unimpressed. "I have some other vehicles coming in, but I'll give you a call this afternoon." I want him to know he doesn't get special treatment just because he might very well own this town. The bell chimes as Darren opens the door to leave. "Hey, Brian," he pauses, his shades in hand.

"Yeah?" I pocket his card.

"You ever need extra work?"

"Fixing vehicles?"

"Not necessarily. There's a variety..." His voice trails off.

"What do you have in mind?"

"Tell you what," he gives me a little wave. "We can talk about it when I retrieve my car tonight. Let's have a drink after. You know any good dive bars?"

Who does this man think I am? I don't know anything *but* dive bars. "You ever hear of the Roosevelt? It's got the best wings in town."

"I know of it. Sounds like a plan." He exits the shop with a bang.

And so it happens that prior to six PM, I'm sitting at a bar top with Darren Atwater, the richest man in the city, one of the wealthiest in the state, as he drinks an IPA and munches on stale pretzels while we wait for our wings.

We raise our glasses to cheer to his silver Jag, which is aptly named, "Your Highness."

"So," he drops his voice, "you ever need extra money?"

"Nah, I got all I need."

He doesn't expect this answer and I wait him out.

"I must've misread the situation."

I almost chuckle. Men like Darren Atwater don't get to their position in life by 'misreading' situations. They are calculated and cunning. Plus, I happen to know that he's self-made, which makes him tolerable.

"What situation?" I cock an eye at him.

"Thought you might want more income, that's all." He slaps a palm on the table. "But if not, I understand."

"Let's hear it." I shrug noncommittally. "I'm always down to hear about new opportunities."

"I always take an interest in people that are driven and hard-working." He wipes his mouth with a napkin. "And I'm looking for someone to help haul some extra loads," he says. "It pays well. Would you be interested?"

"Possibly." I rest my elbows on the table. "Need more details, though."

"I have a truck that needs to go close to the Mexican border."

"Is it for your regular business?"

"No. And yes." He swallows a swig of his beer. "It's a separate company, but not explosives or anything like that." I'm dying to know the price he's willing to pay, but I'm supposed to act like I don't need the money.

"Okay," I say.

"How about a round of shots?"

"Sure." I never turn down free alcohol.

"Oh, and payment." He runs his hand over the wet condensation from his beer on the table. "Five when you pick up the load, five when you return."

"A thousand dollars for one weekend?"

"No," He shakes his head. "Ten thousand dollars."

I choke on my pretzel and he's forced to thump my back. "Are you okay?"

"Wrong pipe," I stammer. "I thought you said ten thousand dollars."

"I did."

"What is it?" My heart starts to pound in my chest. I could really use the money, but he doesn't need to know that.

"Let's keep it simple." He runs a hand through his slightly-thinning hair. "You don't need to know a lot, you just need to drive."

I start to interrupt, but he stops me with a hand in the air. "It's nothing illegal. It's just that my right-hand guy, Joseph, quit. He had drama with his pregnant girlfriend and he was in charge of this load. It just has to have an on-time delivery."

"What am I delivering?" I'm curious. "Explosives?"

"Parts."

"Like car parts?" I ask, "automotive?"

He nods. "It would be a Friday thru Sunday trip, so all weekend. Think you can do the job?"

"Potentially." I act nonchalant. "Let me make sure my daughter doesn't have any activities or plans I need to attend with her."

"I'll put you in touch with Mickey, the man in charge. He handles all the details."

"Fair enough." I chug the rest of my beer, setting it down with a bang.

"Then consider yourself hired if you want the job."

We do a round of tequila shooters and the next morning, everything's a blur. If Mickey's number hadn't been written in black magic marker on my inner wrist, I'd think it were a dream.

Ten thousand dollars to drive?

For far less, I'd do just about anything.

10

BRIAN

I try not to act overeager when I dial the number and a man barks, "Yep?"

"Hi, uh, it's Brian. Brian Pruitt. Darren, ah, Darren gave me your number."

Silence.

"For driving a route. Said Joseph quit."

Another pregnant pause before the man I assume is Mickey responds. "You have a current license?"

"Yeah," I lie.

"And you can go Friday?"

"Guess so."

"Ask for Mickey when you come to the warehouse," he instructs. He tells me the address where I'm to meet him by six AM, sharp, on Friday morning. I look at the clock.

Shit. It's Thursday, I've got today and that's it.

"See you then." I disconnect just as the front door opens and Madeline strolls in, her jaw set in a hard line. She's a pain in the ass, a strong-willed and stubborn version of me. A spitfire, as my mother used to say.

I might be a drunk and let my tongue or hands lash out, but I also think Maddy deserves it. She doesn't know when to quit. I guess the same could be said for me, but she purposely twists the knife in deeper and pours salt in the wound.

She's been a ghost for the last couple days since our last blowout, and I've had it. If she did tell me where she went, I was either piss poor drunk or not listening. And being hypocritical, since I don't set the best example, I'm not going to tell Maddy where I'm going tomorrow.

I don't mean to be a shitty parent, but I am.

I didn't set out to be a drunk, but I am.

And isn't that the lesson in life? We develop bad habits without realizing them until it's too late.

And it's not like I care that Maddy left for a few days. What I *do* care about is drawing attention, *unnecessary* attention, negative attention, to my personal life.

Once they're in your shit, they're *in* your shit.

So, when CPS came knocking on my door, it didn't help the situation. It was made worse by the fact that I had no clue she hadn't been attending school.

"Shouldn't you be in class?" I pretend to glance at a watch that isn't there.

"Shouldn't you be at work?" she retorts.

I run a hand through my rumpled hair. "Enough." I try a different approach. "You want some breakfast?"

"We don't have anything," she grumbles.

I give her the dreaded, withering dad look.

"If you don't believe me, check the fridge."

"You wouldn't know since you've been gone," I say coldly. Her shoulders slump and she grabs a lone protein bar from a box. I couldn't even tell you where it came from. I'd bet it's expired, if that shit even spoils.

"Hey," Maddy settles on the couch next to me. "Do you mind if I go to a concert next week?"

"You disappeared for a couple days and CPS got called and now you want tickets to a show?"

"I try to stay out of your hair as much as possible."

"That's not the point." I reach down for an ashtray. "You haven't even been going to school, and the year just started."

"I don't like my classes."

"Again, not the way to become self-sufficient."

"So, what now?"

"You're grounded." I watch as she picks at the stuffing from the couch. "Stop that!" I stand. "You need to clean this place up, spend your weekend doing homework and chores."

"Why can't Dane take me to Taylor Swift?" she huffs.

"You're not going to that damn concert with that boy and that's final." I pull a cold beer from the fridge and pop the lid. "Any more questions?" My voice drips with sarcasm, since we both know that I won't be coherent in a short while.

"I'm not your punching bag," she argues.

"No one said you were."

"I'm tired of you never letting me do anything." Another withering dad look follows. It used to stop her in her tracks, but it's becoming less reliable as she gets older.

"You don't even give me an allowance to do chores," she snorts. "It's like I work for you for free."

"You live here for free, don't you?"

"Hardly," she mutters, "I have to deal with your bullshit."

"Keep that tone up, Madeline, and the next sip you take will be of soapy water as I wash your mouth out with it." I slam my chair back into the wall, already dented with scars from this same grand gesture.

I grab my car keys. "I'm out."

"Have fun getting drunk," she says over her shoulder before I hear her bedroom door slam with finality.

Blame is second nature and the truth is, I'm not lying when I tell Madeline she ruined my life. I shouldn't have had a child when I did. It's fair to say I didn't have a choice in the matter. Madeline's mom, my ex-girlfriend, was a sadistic bitch. I guess she thought there was no future for her without me, and she sure as hell wasn't letting me go. As soon as I was about to be free of our small town and her, she told me she was expecting.

We were eighteen.

This certainly wasn't the responsibility I had in mind.

She called me a baby killer for wanting her to have an abortion.

A deadbeat when I mentioned adoption.

A piece of shit for suggesting we break up.

And what I'm afraid of for Maddy, I'm scared to tell her. She reminds me so much of her mother, it scares me. I worry she'll get pregnant, under some guy's thumb, and mess up her whole life. Her boyfriend is some dumb hick that lives in our apartment complex, which has led to some explosive blow-outs between the two of us.

She thinks I hate her, but I don't. I just never wanted her. I still don't.

And now that I have someone I can see myself spending my life with, I resent Maddy even more. She's in the way. I'd like nothing more to move to another city and have a fresh start. It's something I've been planning for a long time.

My girlfriend also has a daughter, but that's different. She's not a single parent, the girl has a dad. Maddy doesn't have a mother.

And with that, I spend my evening getting shit-faced. Tomorrow's a new day. I'll be rich. And for once, I won't have to worry about how to pay my bills.

11

BRIAN

My alarm blares at five-thirty and I hit it with my palm as it rocks back and forth. Bleary-eyed and hungover, I take a quick shower, check that Maddy's sleeping soundly in her bed, and pack an overnight bag and some lunch. I leave her a strongly-worded note that she better be in class today.

The address Mickey gives me leads to an industrial warehouse outside of town. There's nothing special about it in the early morning hours, so I doubt it looks any more memorable in the daylight.

I ring a bell outside of a tan garage. In response, a metal door squeaks as it slowly rises. Behind it, two men load a truck. One is Hispanic and one is white. Both are shorter than I am, and both eye me warily while the white guy reaches in his waistband for something. Immediately, the Hispanic guy murmurs something and the white guy releases his hold on whatever it was.

Phew, I shake my head, assuming it's likely a gun.

Before I pass the concrete threshold of the garage, the door screeches to life as it maneuvers down towards my head. Mustering a cocky swagger I don't feel, I say in greeting, "I'm here for Mickey."

Both exchange glances but seem to relax. "He's in the office," they say in unison, not bothering to stop or hold their positions. The Hispanic one nods towards a back area with the shrug of his head. I can feel their eyes burn into the back of my skull as I walk down a dark hallway. A pounding headache matches my steps, a reminder of the copious amounts of alcohol that churn in my stomach.

The office is to my left and when I walk in, Mickey's not what I expected. I thought he would be some guy covered in tattoos, even on his face. Maybe even a teardrop one.

This man is muscular and dressed well, not like someone I'd expect to work or run a warehouse. He's dressed in jeans and a button-down, his jet-black hair is slicked back, and he's clean-shaven. His suede loafers rest on his desk as he motions for me to take the only metal chair in the small office. "You must be Brian."

"Yeah," I say, "and you're Mickey."

"Yep." He doesn't make a move to stand but stays seated. "Darren speaks highly of you."

"Good."

"The driver who usually makes this run is down for the count." He taps the metal top with his knuckle for emphasis. "This is last minute, but I think we can make it work."

I ask innocently. "What am I hauling?"

"We have some equipment for a rock cut in Mexico."

"Oh, I didn't know you dealt with Mexico." I kick my legs out. "Darren said auto parts."

He eyes me suspiciously and now when he talks, it's with a semi-twang, like he grew up in Mississippi or Louisiana. "We deal internationally, and they're parts for a blast site. Is that a problem?"

"No," I hastily add, "but I don't have a passport to get over the border."

Watching his shoulders visibly relax at my answer, he shakes his head. "Got it." He moves his feet from the desk and sits up straight. "Not a problem. You'll meet Vincent in Texas, close to the border, right near Nuevo Laredo, so that won't be necessary."

"Gotcha."

"Drive should take around eighteen hours. Vincent's expecting you in the morning."

"Okay."

"We have sleeping quarters at the ranch if you want to nap when you arrive or you can get a hotel before you head back. Makes no difference to me, but it's on you. We don't pay for it."

I nod my head in acknowledgment.

"Just contact me when you're an hour out from here on Sunday and I'll meet you back at the garage or have one of my guys let you in. I expect it'll be later that day or evening."

I lean my head back against the glass of the office. "Anything else I need to know?"

"Nope. You'll deliver the truck, Vincent and his guys will unload it, and you'll head back. Pretty straightforward."

"I'm ready." I slap my knee.

"Good. Let's get you paid. You'll get half right now." He swings his chair around to face a floor safe behind him. Entering a combination, he says, "And five thousand when you get back."

I hesitate. "Why so much?"

He pauses, and his eyes bulge in disbelief at my question. "It's expensive equipment. *Precious* cargo." He brings his gaze level to my face. "There is one stipulation."

Of course, there is.

I wait.

"You don't go through the items in the truck."

"Aren't they packaged?"

"You don't go through the cargo. Got it?"

"I hadn't planned on it."

"Sign this." He hands over a document. It states the compensation and how I'm receiving it. "Here's a pen." Asking for my driver's license, he makes a copy while I read the document and sign on the dotted line. My palms sweat since my license isn't exactly legit. I lost it after I hit a pole drunk driving one night. I haven't bothered to have it reinstated.

Mickey hands me a thick envelope. "Here's the first payment."

"Thanks."

"Okay, let me show you the truck." We walk back out to the garage stall. The other two men have disappeared from sight. I notice the large truck parked in front of us is advertised as *Office Pros, where we go the distance for our customers.* It's not an eighteen-wheeler, more like the size of a bigger U-Haul. Mickey goes over the equipment and outlines my job duties.

"What's Office Pro?" I ask.

"Another company we have." He throws the keys at me. "Any other questions?"

I start to open my mouth, but he cuts me off. "I didn't think so. You better get on the road so we don't piss Vincent off."

By 'we' he means 'me.'

I take that as my cue to leave.

He stands next to the garage door, pressing the button to open it as I slide in and get situated. I set my coffee thermos and lunch bag on the seat next to me. Turning the engine, I lower the window and slowly back out, relying heavily on the mirrors. I'm used to my tired pick-up, not something this heavy. When I'm completely backed out, Mickey reaches his hand through the window. "Oh, one more thing. I need your cell phone."

"You need my cell?" I repeat.

"Yeah."

"Uh, that's not convenient."

He gives me a hard look.

"I have a daughter," I explain.

"So," he shrugs. "I do, too."

"Then you understand emergencies?"

"It's a day and a half. Do you need me to go check on her?"

"Certainly not," I mutter to myself.

"Fine," he says with a snide smile as he pulls his hand back.

"Good." Sheepish, I give him a smile in return. That was easy, I think to myself.

"Put it in park."

"Huh?"

"Hand me the money."

"What?"

"If you can't turn over your phone, you can't drive for us." He leans forward to grab at the keys from the ignition.

"What about Vincent?"

He reaches into his pocket and pulls out a black phone. "This has his number programmed in. That's all you need. No other outgoing calls."

I hesitate before I hand my cell to him.

"You'll get it back when you return."

I nod.

"No other calls. Do I make myself clear? You drive,

deliver items, and come back. It's easy. You drive, get paid. Nothing else needs to be said or done."

"Okay."

"Don't make Atwater your enemy," he warns. "Directions are in the envelope I gave you. The phone is basic, so I printed these out for you."

I open the flap and pull out a sheaf of papers with the route marked. One is for going there, and one is for coming back.

"Oh, and no smoking in there."

"I won't." And with that, I salute him as I bounce out of the parking lot onto the gravel road. As I speed onto the freeway, my mind wanders as I consider this job that I find myself lucky to have.

If luck is involved...and this job is as straightforward as Darren and Mickey said.

But a feeling of nagging doubt sends a chill down my spine.

Just drive and stay out of trouble, I tell myself, already wanting a cold beer to quell my anxiety. Don't speed, don't draw attention to yourself from the highway patrol.

I pick a talk radio station to listen to. The paper instructs me to keep going straight for the next ninety-seven miles.

Eighteen hours there, eighteen hours back, add in breaks and unloading time, and some sleep. It'll be over before you know it, I think encouragingly to myself.

The envelope with five thousand dollars rests on the seat next to me and I touch it, ensuring it really does exist.

12

BRIAN

The drive to the border of Nuevo Laredo, Mexico, is more prolonged since I don't have my cell phone. I'd planned on making calls to pass the time. Usually I'm at the shop on Fridays, so there was no reason to tell my girlfriend I was going for a drive to make a delivery.

And if Chip happens to stop by the apartment, Madeline will figure out fast I'm gone. Except I didn't communicate to either of them I was leaving for the weekend.

My girlfriend's never been to our apartment yet, it's too risky. I contemplate how much longer I have to keep our relationship a secret before it gets out and becomes town gossip. In some ways, I want it to. I know she's married, but I don't care. I'm in love. Bring it on, judgmental city folk.

When I get hungry, I pull over at a rest stop and eat the lukewarm sandwich and chips I brought, chasing it down with a can of Coca-Cola. My hands quiver, tempting me to add some rum. A flask is tucked into my waistband, providing me comfort and security. I didn't know if Mickey would search me so I hid it out of sight.

Some people pop pills and need them as a placebo effect regardless if they take them.

I'm the same with my liquor. I know before long I'm going to drain it.

For this long haul, I'll need both alcohol and pills, the numbness and tingling in my nerves inevitable. Ever since I crashed my car in high school, my back has never been the same.

Just wait until you get closer, you don't want to get pulled over, I warn myself, especially since you're not exactly sure what you're hauling. And then there's the suspended license...

I pass the time by listening to old school country like Willie and Haggard. The new 'poppy' country shit drives me nuts.

The next time I stop to take a piss, I try not to focus on what's in the back, but curiosity gets the best of me. I justify sneaking a peek, telling myself I should know what I'm carrying in case I get stopped over by an overzealous cop.

Before I talk myself out of it, I release the locking clasp to haul the pull-up door open. Large boxes are stacked from floor to ceiling, and there's no walkway towards the back so I create a small path myself, zigzagging between the heavy cardboard.

All of the cartons are the same until I reach the very back, or the front, depending on how you consider it. A container sits in the corner, a different shape and color than the rest, what I guess to be a fifty-five-gallon blue drum.

Something's caught in the lid.

At first, I think it's a piece of fabric, but upon closer inspection, I realize that the material is practically see-through. Taking a step back, I let out a cuss word as the box behind me scrapes against my tailbone.

It's not material caught in the lid, it's strands of hair, so fine they seem translucent.

I tell myself that whoever closed the steel drum got a chunk of hair entangled in it. That must've hurt, I muse.

My hand grazes the drum and it's surprisingly cool, as if it had been frozen and is now thawing. When I lean down to inspect the bottom, I notice a pool of liquid has darkened the floorboards. I lower my face to smell the liquid, but it doesn't give off any type of noxious odor.

Darting my eyes, I look for something to open it up with, but there aren't any tools.

When I check the glove compartment, all I can find is a flashlight.

Exiting the truck, I tug the door down, lock it up, and head to a hardware store. The phone Mickey gave me is elementary, it doesn't have internet, and it's a good thing because I don't dare research hardware stores in the vicinity.

A few miles up, I see a road sign that mentions points of interest ahead. A big box home store is mentioned, and I take it as a sign to pull off.

The salesperson points me in the direction of aisle six, after I asked what I could use to remove the head of a steel drum. I grab a couple items and a drum deheader, using some of the cash in hand to pay for it, not wanting a paper trail.

I stop and peer at the outside of the trailer for a moment, deliberating on what to do as I chain smoke, my hand trembling as I suck the comforting smell down my lungs.

Keep driving, I murmur, stay on schedule.

My heart thuds in my chest but I stay on the interstate until I come upon another rest stop, then I veer off, parking in an isolated spot.

With a sharp pounding in my chest, I repeat my earlier

steps of opening the trailer. Using the newly-purchased tool to yank the lid off the drum, I grunt as I apply pressure to remove the top and disengage it.

Flashlight in hand, I stare down into the dark chamber.

It takes a moment to realize I'm staring at bare skin, the shoulder of a folded-up body. First, I assume the female is alive, her features delicate and feminine, with blonde hair and pale skin. Eerily lifelike, I realize she's been frozen, and that's why the drum is so cold, her preserved body is now starting to defrost and will eventually decompose. A small scar on her cheek is the only flaw lining her face.

SINKING ONTO MY KNEES, I let out a loud yelp.

This explains perfectly why Darren and Mickey are paying me an exorbitant price to deliver a load of 'precious' cargo. Whoever did this is ready to get rid of her now.

I'll be damned.

Is this the end result for crossing an Atwater?

But the girl doesn't look very old. I can't see her entire body, but she's either a late teen or a young woman. What harm could she possibly have done? She looks innocent, unlike some punk you would kill for causing trouble.

Wait, is Darren part of the Mexican cartel? Are these boxes full of drugs or contraband? Maybe even weapons? Is this the child of someone who betrayed them?

Even with the cold drum next to me, sweat pours down my back as I consider my options. If I open the boxes to check their contents, it will be obvious if they've been resealed.

That was a big no-no according to Mickey.

In regards to the drum, I can replace the lid and hope for the best.

Or I can drive back home, drop off the truck, and feign sickness.

Which would make today's drive a waste.

I'd have to return the money, and it's not like I can 'unsee' a body.

My pulse quickens. If I don't deliver the cargo, I could end up like this. I think of the life I've been planning on and I swallow hard. My girlfriend and I are getting close to moving. Maddy will be graduating soon and starting her own life, and what if Darren or his crew came after her?

Stepping outside, I kick a tire, cursing the day I helped Darren Atwater by fixing his flat one. If I don't follow through, he'll become suspicious. Paranoid even. Someone could start following me. Darren knows where I work, what Maddy looks like, my driver's license number. Hell, they also have my phone.

I climb into the driver's seat and sit there, I don't know for how long, but long enough to chew a piece of skin off my finger until it bleeds in protest.

I keep driving through the night, my mind wandering all over the place.

Who is she? I wonder. I know Darren has a daughter, and she's blonde. There's no way, I murmur to myself. He wouldn't kill his own child and put a stranger up to it. Or would he? I only know of the man. I'm not sure what he's capable of.

My hands shake on the wheel and it's time to remove the flask from my waistband. I pour the liquid down my throat and finish it off with a piece of chew.

When I start to approach the steel gate with spikes, I swallow the lump building in my throat. My directive was to call Vincent when I arrived. I hit his number and wait for him to answer. I hear breathing as I announce my arrival before the phone disconnects.

I wait, drumming my fingers on the wheel.

It's probably a mere minute or two, but it stretches on. I have to look innocent and unafraid. A tough feat when you've found a discarded body in the load you're hauling.

Out of a cloud of dust, a newer Ford blue pick-up appears and the driver gets out.

Again, I'm surprised for the second time by an appearance, or a third, if you count the dead female. I had a preconceived notion stuck in my head of what Vincent would look like. I figured he'd be late twenties, early thirties, with a leather vest and a motorcycle. In reality, he's white-haired and pushing sixty-five, maybe seventy. A white mustache twirls up at the ends, a handlebar, I think they call it.

Vincent opens the gate with a remote and waves me in. I pause next to his window as he greets me with a toothless grin, shutting the automatic gate behind me.

"Hello." I start to introduce myself, but he stops me with a gravelly voice. "I've got a couple helpers that can unload this. Just follow me."

I remind myself to breathe, feeling trapped now that I'm stuck in this enclosure of some sort. We drive down a dirt road, barren fields on both sides. This is a huge stretch of property, acres upon acres, and the uncultivated land is soon replaced by cotton crops, bursts of white covering every square inch. Past a barn and a small farmhouse, we continue down the dirt road, the gravel from his truck spitting onto my hood.

I'm glad this vehicle isn't mine, I think.

On to a large workshop and warehouse where two men stand rigid, spitting images of each other, and I imagine they're twins. Both are medium build with dark hair and mustaches, wearing cowboy boots and Stetson hats. They point to a concrete slab in front of the warehouse and motion for me to park on it.

Unsure what to do next, if I'm supposed to stay in the vehicle or hop out, they answer the question for me. One uses his thumb to motion me out of the cab. The other opens a metal garage door and then jumps in my seat as I exit, driving the truck into the warehouse.

"Need helping unloading?" I offer.

The men stare at me but say nothing.

I didn't realize Vincent used a cane until he slowly maneuvers himself out of his truck. He hobbles up next to me. "They don't speak English."

"Need help with unloading?"

Vincent watches them carry the boxes down the ramp and shakes his head. "No, they will count 'em and verify the shipment's all there, put a call into the home base, and then you can either stay or go. Would you like to go upstairs to the apartment over the garage and rest?"

I act like I'm considering his offer for a moment before politely declining.

"My daughter," I start to say, then stop. Why am I telling a complete stranger who's involved in some serious shit about my child?

"She has a thing I have to go to," I mutter unintelligibly.

He gives me another grin and nods his head as if to say suit yourself.

"You need to use the restroom or want some water?"

"Yeah, that'd be great." I certainly don't want to watch the twins as they do their job, scared my fidgeting will give me away. Vincent leads me to a small bathroom in the workshop, which is nothing more than a pedestal sink and toilet where I take a leak.

He's waiting for me when I exit, holding a couple of chilled water bottles in hand.

The men are fast and thorough, unloading everything in the time it takes to gulp a bottle of water and smoke a couple of cigarettes while Vincent inhales a cigar. They wave Vincent over when they're finished. All three men exchange a few words and then Vincent appears back at my side. "Hand me your phone and follow me back to the gate."

With a nod, I climb back in the truck as he hands me a replacement phone. "This has the number for Mickey when you need to call him programmed in. You know the drill. No other calls."

I try not to leer at the men and the stack of boxes as I back out, the blue drum innocently sitting against the farthest wall.

When we reach the oppressive gate, Vincent pulls to the side and motions me forward. A toothpick hangs off his lips, replacing his cigar. As the gate opens, I manage a salute as I head the hell outta there, my only concern to find the nearest liquor store and get hammered.

I'm ready to get shit-faced and sleep before I get home. As much as I don't want to stop, my body is dead tired. I can't keep driving, my lids are heavy and my head keeps jerking, warning me it's about to nod off.

There's a motel up ahead and I exit, a gas station across the street where I grab a twelve-pack.

Originally, I thought I could just sleep in the trailer or rest my head against the front seat, but I want distance from what I discovered back there, the space now tainted.

From the phone in the motel, I dial the only person I can think of. "Something's wrong." I say before she can speak.

"What?" Valerie whispers.

"Something's not right."

I can tell she's busy by the way she's not saying much, just giving me short responses. "Where are you?" she asks.

"Doesn't matter," I say.

"I'm with my daughter. We're watching a movie," she mumbles. "I gotta go before she notices I'm on the phone."

"This can't wait. I need to see you. When can we meet?"

"I can sneak away late Sunday night."

"Not until then?"

"It's tomorrow," she sighs. "And I need to see you."

"Yeah." I slur, "Okay."

I try and sleep, but I toss and turn. Restless, I flip through channels to find something to watch. Not even basic cable, I snort. I pause on the news. A reporter is discussing a gravesite located near the Texas and Mexico border, and my hands crush an empty can in their grip. It seems to be a common theme in this area. Girls dumped in shallow graves like garbage. It sickens me. Just like the image of her body. As much as I try and tell myself it was a doll, her features were anything but artificial.

It takes me a couple more beers to relax enough for sleep.

When I wake, I'm cranky, and my back aches from my stationary position behind the wheel. I pop a muscle relaxer and rub my spastic muscles. After eating cold toast and filling up my coffee thermos, I hit the road again, my palms sweaty as I close the gap between the open stretch of highway and home. Perspiration drips down the back of my t-shirt as I drive. The time I have to reflect inevitably leads to different scenarios involving the unknown female.

Did Darren set me up, I wonder?

Could he have found out about my relationship with his

wife? I try not to let my mind consider all the possibilities, but who's to say he hasn't had someone watching Valerie?

If they ever split, their divorce will be contentious, that's for damn sure.

Gripping the wheel, my hands turn pink from exertion, and I squeeze the hard plastic with doubt. It doesn't help that my throat is dry, itching for a drop of alcohol, ready to crawl out of my skin, but I can't afford the smell of liquor on my breath when I return to the warehouse.

I need the drop-off to go smooth with minimal questions.

I'll get my remaining 5k, and then I'll be done with Darren and his goons.

But is one ever really done with them?

I doubt it.

I certainly haven't been able to untangle myself since Valerie and I found each other.

"An hour out," I tell Mickey when I hit the call button.

"Good," he says, "all good?"

"Yep."

"See you soon."

When I pull into the lot, it seems impossible I was just here on Friday morning, and now it's Sunday afternoon. Just as I thought, the building looks worse in the sunlight. It needs a fresh coat of paint and some TLC. The warehouse is run down, and for someone like Darren Atwater, this is a far cry from his usual lavish digs.

I ring the bell and the garage squeals to greet me.

The nameless white guy from the other day stands in the empty stall, motioning for me to drive in. He does a quick inspection of the truck when I wobble out and gives a thumbs-up sign. I'm hoping that I still get paid today. I don't want to have to come back here.

"Office," is all he says.

Sure enough, Mickey is perched with his suede loafers on the desk, my envelope already in hand. "Here you go." He slides a paper towards me. With a pen, he taps the blank signature line where I'm to sign. I try not to let my hand shake as I scrawl an unintelligible signature across the bottom. He's wearing cuff-links and a button-down, dressed like he came from church. I exchange the paper for the money. Relieved to end this exchange, I stand to leave. I've made it two steps when I'm

interrupted by Mickey's Southern drawl asking me politely, but firmly, to have a seat.

I hesitate, my arms stiff at my sides. Turning around, I exhale as I sink down into the metal chair, my butt on the very edge.

"Vincent said you seemed off. Everything okay?" Mickey asks conversationally.

My palms twitch, but I try and remain calm, careful to not fidget in my seat. Does he know about the drum?

Of course he knows, you idiot.

"Yeah, I'm tired from the long drive. I'm not used to sitting on my ass for that long." I give a nervous laugh before I ramble on. "I'm used to being under the hood of cars and moving around, not stuck in a seat."

He pins me to the chair with his icy gaze, and I swear he can see my soul and every piece of food I've digested in the last twenty-four hours and every thought I've ever had.

"Are you drunk?"

"No," I say. "Course not."

"I smell booze on you."

I shrug.

"Where's the flask?"

I dumped it before I drove into the parking lot. "I don't

have one." He motions for me to rise and show him the waistband of my jeans.

Satisfied, he folds his arms across his chest. "Is the money for Madeline?"

"What do you mean?" My hands clench around the envelope. Why is he bringing up my daughter?

"For college?"

"Uh, no," I lie, "she's a straight-A student, and she'll probably get a scholarship."

"What're you going to do with it?" He smirks. "Waste it on liquor and cigarettes?"

"I'm going to buy a new truck," I say defensively, settling back in the chair, anger overtaking my fear.

"Why did you stop at the hardware store?" Mickey reaches under his desk to remove a gun from its hiding place.

I shift my weight, my body tense as I stare back at him.

"And why did you lie to me?" He cocks the gun at my forehead like it's a bulls-eye.

The envelope rests in my hand, but it might as well be a pipe dream because from the set jaw and flared nostrils, Mickey doesn't look too happy with me.

13

ALLEGRA

The mall's pretty dead for a Sunday afternoon.

I'm thumbing through a rack of blouses, considering what would look the best for an editorial pic that screams 'professional' yet 'trendy.' It's for my high school E-newsletter, where I scored a guest editor spot. I haven't decided what path I want to pursue after my senior year's over, but I love being on camera. Maybe an anchorwoman? I know it's a competitive job with shitty hours and crappy starting pay, but money is of no concern. It's amazing when you don't have to worry about finances how much you can concentrate on what you're really passionate about.

My earbuds are in, and it takes a moment to realize a male voice is addressing me. "Excuse me, miss." I hear the words, expecting it to be a salesperson eager to start me a fitting room. They work on commission in this department store, so without even glimpsing over my shoulder, I thrust the hangers toward a hand behind me.

"I don't work here."

I spin around and come face-to-face with a male, probably late thirties or early forties. He's not bad looking, just older, wearing a pin-striped suit and tie. He has dark hair and a clean-shaven face. He's not tall, but he's not short, either. He reminds me of the actor, Gerard Butler. I wonder if he just came from church.

"Oh, sorry." I shrug, yanking my earbuds out. "They usually give exceptional and annoying customer service here."

"I know. I learned that the last time I shopped here." He gives me a small smile, revealing even and perfectly white teeth. "Look, this might be forward, but..."

"No, I'm not allowed to date." I return his small smile. "But thank you."

"Not what I was after." He chuckles, resting his hands on the rack nearest to him. "You must think I'm some sort of pervert."

I eye him curiously. "Not the first thing that crossed my mind."

"I'm looking for a birthday gift for my daughter." He seems embarrassed to confide this to me, his eyes trailing down to his feet. I follow his gaze down to the Gucci loafers he's wearing. "I just wanted your input."

"Okay."

"I'd ask the salesgirl, but as you said, they work on commission, so I want an unbiased opinion."

I nod, waiting for him to continue.

"Perfume? A handbag? Is there something hip I should be aware of?" he asks.

"How old is she?"

"Younger than you, I think. I'd guess you to be eighteen or nineteen?" He looks me up and down in an appraising manner. "By the way, you're beautiful, in a classic sense. Have you ever modeled?"

"Seventeen. And yeah, mostly local stuff," I say as my phone vibrates in my pocket. He looks like he's waiting for me to accept his compliment. "And thank you."

"My daughter's fourteen," he offers. "She likes clothes and make-up, but I guess most girls do."

"What's her vibe?"

"I don't know how to answer that." He fiddles with his tie. "She lives with her mother most of the time."

"Does she have social media or anything I can look up?" He gives me her Instagram account, her name is Cassidy, and I see a girl that seems older than fourteen in every sense of the word. She has darker hair than her father and a punk rock vibe. A silver stud's in both her ears and nose, and her hair's streaked with burgundy red.

"I'd suggest you get her a pair of Doc Martens."

"What are those?"

I giggle. "Shoes. Or to be specific, boots."

He repeats the brand name out loud. "Done. Shoes are on the first floor?"

"Yes."

"Thanks for your help. I really appreciate it." He gives me a winning smile, one I'm sure has helped him out in life. The small lines around his green eyes crinkle. "And here, I'd like to give you my card if that's all right."

I notice the Louis Vuitton wallet as he pulls out a thick, creamy white card with shiny gold lettering. "I'm Pierce Arden, by the way."

"I'm Allegra." I examine the card he hands over before sliding it into my back pocket. "Nice to meet you." He politely shakes my hand, offering up a firm handshake. "Please call me sometime if you'd be interested in a lunch or coffee meeting. Bring a parent, whatever makes you feel comfortable. I'm in town for a few more days."

I nod, my face burning with pleasure.

"Do you have an agent?"

"No."

"I'm not local. Just happen to be here for a business meeting." He flashes me that smile again. "Los Angeles. You might've heard of it."

Rolling my eyes, I grin. "I *might've* seen it on television once or twice."

"Then you're probably thinking of the right place." He winks before he turns on his expensive loafers. Over his shoulder, he murmurs, "Talk to your parents and call me." I try to contain my excitement as he disappears down the escalator.

I almost forget the reason I came to the department store and have to retrace my steps back to the rack to pick something out. I'm about to call my mom when the salesgirl approaches me. "Can I start a fitting room for you?"

"Sure," I stammer, momentarily forgetting about anything else but the grand visions in my head. Me opening a glossy magazine and seeing my picture splashed all over it, modeling the latest Milan fashions. Maybe this chance encounter with Pierce is the answer to getting out of here and getting closer to Coye Kauffman, my boyfriend, who lives in California.

The idea of signing with a real live agent gives me the chills. I can't wait to tell my mom. Scattered, I can't decide what I like and don't like, so I text a couple of pics to Coye for his advice. When he doesn't respond right away, I decide on a striped blouse before heading to the register. The salesgirl upsells me on a navy camisole and a pair of earrings when I check out. Holding my shopping bag to my chest, I continue to daydream, a rather annoying habit of mine, or at least that's what my father tells me.

Speaking of him, my excitement's dampened by the thought of his disapproval. There's no way in hell he'd let me move, school or modeling be damned. We had the conversation recently and it ended in tears.

I rehash the talk we had a few weeks ago when I broached the topic of colleges. My father barely glanced up from his laptop when I entered his study. It's not until he heard my request that he paid attention.

"I'd like to go to college in California."

His head jerked up fast enough to cause whiplash. "Absolutely not."

"What?" I'm caught off guard by his answer. "Why not?"

His forehead wrinkles as he stutters, trying to think of something to say that makes sense. "In-state tuition is much cheaper."

Narrowing my eyes at him, I murmur. "Since when did you become concerned with the cost?"

He returns my glare. "Your private school isn't cheap."

"I didn't think it was. I thought I went to an elitist school so I could get the best education money could buy so I could get into a top university."

"Exactly." He snaps his fingers. "Bingo."

"Then why would you want me to stay here instead of applying out of state? What if I get a scholarship?"

"It's not about the money, sugar."

"But you just said..."

Before I can finish, he interrupts. "You go ahead and apply in-state for freshman year. If it goes well, maybe you can transfer later on..." he adds, "or maybe not. Maybe you'll make a lot of friends and want to stay."

"I don't want to have to transfer in the middle of college."

"Young lady, I don't think this discussion needs to

continue." He seals it with his 'look.' The 'dad look' that usually causes me to shake underneath his firm tone. "That's final. You'll start in-state and get adjusted to college first. It's a big change, and you'll be glad later on that the transition wasn't worse than it had to be."

Rolling my eyes, I sarcastically salute him and am quickly rewarded with a warning glance. With a quick hand motion, he dismisses me, signaling the end of our little chat.

We've never discussed it since.

Annoyed at the memory, I bite my lip as tears prick my eyelids.

My father tries to hold onto me, and I'm tired of being treated like a child. If my mother didn't secretly agree to my relationship with Coye, I'd have run away a long time ago. It's suffocating having a father that takes every decision so personally and makes them all about him. I don't understand how my mother can be married to him sometimes.

Speaking of my mother, I'm supposed to text her when I'm ready for a ride home. Another sensitive topic, my father's forbidden me from having my own car.

Feeling restless, I'm not ready to go back to the 'compound,' or what I call our sprawling mansion. It's isolated and matches how I feel most of the time. I relate to Rapunzel stuck in a tower with no way out. Instead, I decide I'll go across the street to the thrift store. Sometimes they have vintage pieces I love. One time, I got a worn leather jacket for Coye that he prefers to his expensive wardrobe.

I look both ways before I cross the street, except the sun hits me head-on. Stepping out into the road, a shrill honk blares in my direction, and I jump back in surprise. "Watch it," a man screams at me as he flips me off.

Stopping in my tracks, I turn my head as another loud

honk causes me to leap backward. I notice the metal grille on a late model sedan with the Mercedes emblem.

"Allegra." I hear a male voice yell through the barely-opened window before I connect the dots. It doesn't register at first until the tinted glass is all the way down.

It's the man from the department store, Pierce.

He's seated in the backseat and cupping his hand in a megaphone to greet me. I wave and just as I'm about to turn and start walking in the other direction, the vehicle slows to a stop.

"Freddy, mind waiting a second so I can talk to my friend?" He turns his head to address me. "You need to learn how to cross the street."

"I'll ask my parents for a lesson tonight," I say with a smile.

"Did you already ask them about meeting with me?"

I laugh. "Not yet."

He seems surprised. 'I thought that would be the first call you would make. I knew you wouldn't bother with a boyfriend, since you said you're not old enough to date." He taps the window. "But I understand it. My daughter's locked in a room until she's twenty-one."

"Whatever." I giggle. "I don't get why parents act like we're the ones making poor decisions. I know plenty of adults who make bad ones."

"Do you need a ride home?"

"No." It's automatic. He might be charming, but he's still a stranger. If I showed up at the Atwater compound with him, even my mother would shit a brick.

"Okay." He starts to raise his window then lowers it again. "Wait, do you have a sec?"

I shrug.

"I'd like to show you some of my clients so you'll keep our agency in mind."

"There's no need. It's already up here." I tap my forehead.

He gives me a wink. "I'd really like you to consider us."

"I have your card," I say. "I'll give you a call next week."

"I'll be back in LA on Wednesday, shooting a movie." He whistles through his teeth. "You like Gosling?"

"Who doesn't?"

"True." He reaches for his tie and gives it a small tug. "Everyone likes him, men and women." Pierce sticks his head fully out the window. "Come on, let us give you a ride," he jokes. "I'm concerned you don't know how to take care of yourself."

"I'm just going across the street. I think I can manage."

He holds up a shopping bag. "I actually need you to do me another favor, so it's not solely about giving you a ride."

"You bought the Doc Martens?"

"Not quite." He runs a hand through his hair. "That's why I need your expertise now. So pretty please," he rubs his hands together as if he's begging. "Will you jump in so I can show you what I got instead?"

I hesitate and internally list the facts.

He's the dad of a teenager, I have his card, and we're not even alone. What's the harm? In fact, I tell myself, I'll just have him drop me off at the movie theatre attached to the mall instead of taking me to the thrift store.

"Freddy," he leans forward and taps the African-American man on the shoulder. "Am I a scary person?"

I hear a loud chuckle as Pierce sits back in his seat. "See?"

"It's not that."

"What is it?"

"I'm late," I lie.

"For?"

"The movies."

"Shit. At least they have previews. Are you meeting a friend?" He stares at me intently.

"Yeah."

"Is it the one on the other side of the mall?"

I nod.

"Okay, how about this. We'll give you a ride there and you can look through my client book on the way over. If you like what you see, I'll arrange a meeting with some of my colleagues."

He adds, "in LA."

My first thought is of Coye. This would give me the perfect opportunity to go out and see him. I'm sure my mom would lie to my father for me to meet with an agent. When she was younger, she dipped her own toes in the modeling biz and loved it.

Plus, having a long-distance relationship is killing me. I imagine him all the time with other girls. Coye could have anyone. As much as I know how great we are together, I know he has his pick in Cali.

Especially with college girls that have more

experience than me.

The black passenger side door opens an inch, and Pierce waves me in.

As I settle in the backseat, I ask, "You drove all the way here?"

"Nah, but Freddy takes care of me when I'm in town. We go way back." He rests his hand on Freddy's shoulder. He has salt and pepper hair and is also wearing a suit, which seems a little excessive, but whatever.

"Why so dressed up? Did you go to church?"

"Yes, ma'am." Freddy meets my eyes in the rearview mirror. He looks like my grandpa's age. "Or at least I did. Pierce isn't a fan."

"Oh, I'm spiritual. Just not into the organized religion piece." Turning to me, he shoves the client book in my hand. "You know where to go, Fred?"

"Yep." He tips his hand in a salute.

I open the black book and inside is a laminated list of companies.

"I work with all of 'em," he says without airs. His tone is matter-of-fact. Handing me another binder, it's a bunch of headshots of models and actors he's worked with. "And these are clients of mine. I think you'd photograph nicely. I'd like to do a test session."

We pull up next to the theatre. "Do you feel comfortable giving me your contact information?"

"Sure." He hands me a pen and turns the page to a media release form. It asks for my name, address, phone, email and clothing sizes, shoe size, bra size, and measurements.

"Don't worry about what you don't know. My assistant can measure when your mom or dad bring you."

"Sounds good." I hand it back to him.

"I'll need a parental signature at some point, but I'm assuming that won't be a problem."

"Nope." I'll cross that hurdle with my mother.

"Oh, and before you go, can you show me the Doc Martens you think are the best for Cassidy?"

"You mean like on the actual website?"

He nods.

"Yeah, sure." I pull my phone out of my small handbag. "You didn't find any you liked?"

"That's the problem. I didn't know there were so many

styles. I should've had you come to the shoe department with me. I don't want to mess up since it's Cassidy's birthday and her mother has already made her hate me." He sighs. "We are going through a divorce, and it's turning out to be nasty. I hate that she feels caught in the middle." He seems genuinely sad.

"No problem." I suck on my lip as I scroll through the Doc Martens website. "What about these?" A pair of burgundy leather boots with black laces seem to be a good fit with her style.

"Those look hip. Wait, is that the right word?"

"Sure." I give him a small grin.

"Mind if I see that?" He reaches for my phone. "I thought I saw another pair that caught my eye." He presses on a suggested link for a white pair of pleather-looking boots with black laces. "These cool enough?"

I nod my head in agreement. "Sure."

"Okay. Done." He

looks up from my phone screen. "Thank you for your help."

"No problem." I wait for him to hand me back my phone, but instead, I watch as he reads my text messages.

I start to protest, and in return, he puts my phone in his pocket.

"Why did you take my phone?"

"There's the theatre." He points up ahead to the Cineplex. I'm relieved we've arrived and I can get out. He's starting to act like a real creep. "What movie are you seeing?"

"Answer my question first."

"In a moment. What movie?"

I scan the movie posters, unsure of what's out since I'm not really seeing a movie today. I pick one and mention it.

"And who are you meeting?"

"My phone..." My voice trails off. "Can I have it back?" I plead. "Please."

"Freddy?" He ignores my question to speak to the driver. "Would you turn around and look at Ms. Allegra, please?"

"Sure thing, boss." Freddy's face turns to consider me. At first, he gives me a smile and locks eyes, and then just as suddenly, it turns into a sneer.

"Ms. Atwater's side profile. What do you think?"

"I don't think so, boss." He tilts his head. "Her nose isn't right, her face is chubby, not angular enough. Babyface, I'd say, it's like she needs..."

Interjecting, I stammer. "What do you mean?"

"Shh...just a second." Pierce shoots me a pointed look. "Let Freddy finish his appraisal of your worth."

"She's not right for acting or modeling," Freddy finishes flatly. "Maybe something else."

Dismissive now, Pierce's voice is no longer kind but brisk. "You can go." He motions with his head towards the passenger door.

"What about my phone?"

Snidely, he says, "Would you just go already?"

My face burns as I try to exit the vehicle. The only problem is, I can't get the door to open, it's locked. I pull on the handle, frantically trying to unlock it before I turn back to Pierce.

"Well, go on." Pierce stares at me like I'm dumb.

"It's locked." I yank on it again. "Can you hit the locks? Maybe you have the child safety on?"

Puzzled, I look at Pierce.

"Freddy, care to unlock the door so Ms. Atwater can get to her afternoon matinee?"

"No, it displeases me to say I can't, sir." Freddy presses hard on the gas, and we lurch forward.

"Why not?" Pierce asks.

"I do not care to do so." And with that, we speed off, the theatre sign getting smaller and smaller behind us.

"But...Pierce..." I stutter, "can you please have Freddy pull over and let me out?"

"Sit back, buckle up, and shut up." Freddy glances in the mirror at me and shakes his head in annoyance.

"Please," I beg. "*Please* just let me out."

"You heard the man." Pierce instructs me, "You better buckle up and do what he says. You don't want to see Freddy angry."

Tears start to run down my cheeks while my mind races.

"Allegra," Pierce's voice softens, "would you like your phone back?"

I don't know what kind of a sick game this man is playing, so I only nod.

"Hold your hand out," he instructs.

I reach my hand towards him, and in the next instant, what I think is my worst nightmare occurs. Except I don't know how deep nightmares can go or how bad it can get, at least not right now.

Because instead of being reunited with my phone, I watch as he reaches down in the seat cushion for something. Before I know what's happening, something metal flashes, and I hear a click as my wrists are secured with a pair of handcuffs.

14

ALLEGRA

"What the hell?" I scream as I stare in horror at my bound wrists.

"You need to be a good girl." Pierce nods his head slowly. "I'm not getting the sense that you can follow instructions."

Closing my eyes, I shriek, clawing at everything in sight - the leather seats, the door frame, the window. I feel Pierce grab at my knee, his nails digging in my skin until I yelp.

"Be quiet." His voice brooks no argument, but I'm not done fighting. I twist my body so I can start pummeling him with my fists. Because of my shackled hands, I'm unable to hit him with full-force anything, not to mention he's almost double my body weight.

I'm rewarded with a slap across my cheek.

Momentarily stunned, I fall back against the leather seat, my back drenched in sweat. "Why are you doing this?" I sob, my skinny wrists now clasped together in my lap.

"I thought you wanted to be a model?"

"No, I'd like to go home. Please take me home," I beg.

"Is that what you'd like?"

"Yes, yes, yes, please just drop me off." I watch as the landscape turns to suburbia with housing developments and the usual chain fast-food restaurants. We're on the highway heading out of town. Before long, I will have never been this far east.

My voice and eyes both plead, "I *promise*, promise, promise, I won't say a word."

"You would keep silent?" Pierce jabs a finger at my cheek, twisting my chin so our eyes are level. "You would just let us get away?"

I nod, tears streaking down my face.

"You aren't pretty when you cry." He taps my nose. "You shouldn't cry. You ugly cry." Snot runs down as the sticky wetness drips onto my lips, the taste of my salty tears enveloped by my mouth.

"Please," I say. "Please!"

"You would just let us drop you off in a field and forget the whole mess?"

"Of course," I whisper. "A misunderstanding."

He smacks the back of the headrest. "Okay, then. Freddy, mind finding somewhere we can drop Ms. Allegra off at?"

"Not a problem, boss."

I rest my head against the buttery leather, breathing a sigh of relief.

This has taught me an important lesson. Never get into cars with strangers no matter how nice or responsible they seem. I'll tell Coye about this, and one day we can laugh about it, and I'll use this as a scare tactic with my own children.

Don't get into cars with strangers.

Even if they seem like they can help you.

Freddy drives for a few more miles, and nothing is on except talk radio. I don't know who the host is, and I don't care. My mind is wandering all over. I try and hold my knees, which are shaking.

We pass a green sign that announces the next town is sixty-two miles away.

Holy shit.

Will Freddy drive that far before we stop?

It's okay, even if he does, you can call someone. If it's a gas station or restaurant, I'm sure they will let you use their phone. My jaw tightens as I think about my father. He's going to kill me. I will never be allowed out of the house again if he finds out about this. What am I going to tell my parents?

As if Pierce read my mind, he asks, "So what will you tell your parents you've been doing all afternoon?"

"The movie."

"You hadn't planned on going."

I don't argue this.

"But don't worry." He gives my shoulder a gentle squeeze. "I texted your mom and told her you were at the matinee."

"*You* texted my mom?"

"Yep. So, she's not expecting you home anytime soon."

Smug, I say, "She'd never believe I was going to a movie by myself."

"You didn't go alone." His tone drips acid. "You went with Julie."

"Julie?"

"I saw a girl on your social media account and used her name. Julie Canto or Cantro or something like that." I don't bother to tell him I don't hang out with Julie Cambrero. We are classmates, but we aren't friends. When I get home, my mom will ask who she is, and I'll tell her it was our first time hanging out.

I stare down at the handcuffs and say nothing.

Pierce points up ahead and directs Freddy on where to pull over. "Up ahead, to the left looks like a good spot."

I cram my neck to see what Pierce is referring to. It's an old gas station, the windows now boarded up, the gas pumps rusted. What was once a parking lot's now overgrown weeds that are probably as high as my waist.

My heart skips a beat. I was hoping for a more public place, but this will do.

The turn signal blinks as we slow to a crawl.

Maybe I can walk, or even hitchhike. I know people in the seventies did a lot of that. A nice family will drive by in a minivan and take pity on me, wondering why I'm stuck out here in the middle of nowhere. I ignore the lack of traffic lights and the few cars we passed. Maybe there were more, and I didn't notice because I was in shock.

Except my mind drifts to Ted Bundy and the special I saw on Netflix about the deranged serial killer, and how he would pick up girls. Look what happened to them, I internally scream, they're all *dead*.

But you've already been kidnapped, I remind myself.

Holy shit, *kidnapped*.

A word that's not supposed to be in my vocabulary when it concerns me. You read about it and comment on it, but it doesn't happen to *you*. It doesn't happen to girls like me that live in small cities and are shopping at the mall on a Sunday.

My palms sweat as I think about that Elizabeth Smart girl. Or the one that lived in the backyard in a tent for most of her life. She was raped by some psycho for years.

Didn't she give birth to his child?

Fuck.

A shred of doubt invades my hopeful thoughts. Kidnappers don't let their victims just go when they can identify them. No one is that stupid.

Stop it, I command my brain. Stop being a downer. You must stay positive, yet my breathing intensifies. It's almost over, I keep telling myself, repeating it in my head like a mantra as I squeeze my fingers into small fists.

How did they catch Elizabeth Smart's kidnappers?

Didn't she escape? The police were able to catch them because she memorized her surroundings and everything she could about their identities.

Frantic, my eyes dart around the car as I try to memorize everything I can. My parents will ask, the cops will ask. I need to focus on what's in front of me.

Mercedes. Four-door. Black exterior and black interior. Tinted windows. Freddy has a mole behind his right ear and a gold wedding band. Pierce isn't wearing one.

And his business card.

I doubt it's legit, but there's gotta be fingerprints on it.

Freddy makes a left turn onto a gravel road that leads to the ugly gas station. It's unclear where the concrete and the field next to it start and end, the prairie grass has overtaken the empty lot as if they've fused into one.

Behind the sad-looking eyesore, Freddy puts the car in park.

We are hidden from the highway and anyone that might spot us.

A metal dumpster is up ahead, barely visible behind the weeds. An old payphone stands tall next to the building, and though I've never used one, I do notice that the actual phone and metal cord are missing.

I try not to get ahead of myself and worry about how I'll get back to the city. My focus needs to be on how to get away from these two men.

But I still can't shake the thought - why me?

My blood freezes in my veins.

Is this about money? Do they know I'm rich? But they aren't even from around here, are they? Well, maybe Freddy is, since he's the driver.

Pierce leans forward to whisper something in his ear.

Freddy responds by pressing a button, and I hear the pop of the trunk.

Then my window shoots halfway down.

Pierce retrieves my phone from his pocket, and my jaw drops as he hands it to Freddy. Instead of unlocking my door, I watch as Freddy exits his.

I don't dare turn around as Freddy moves to the back of the sedan.

By the loud thud, I can hear something roll in the trunk. In a moment, Freddy reappears and stands directly in front of my window. With a glance in my direction, I watch as he holds my phone out in the palm of his hand. He keeps his gaze locked on my horrified one as he drops it.

Then he starts jumping up and down, stomping on it.

Then he picks up a metal bar, I think it's called a crowbar, and in a grand finale, whacks it over and over before holding broken pieces up to show me through the window.

Pierce leans over and whispers in my ear. "Guess you'll have to figure out how to get that payphone to work." My stomach does flip-flops as I watch Freddy discard my broken phone in the dumpster.

Pierce reaches into his pocket and pulls out a key fob and hits the locks.

"Get out."

He doesn't have to tell me twice.

Holding my wrists out to him, he shakes his head. "Nope. Those aren't coming off."

My hands shake as I reach for the handle. It's awkward with my hands bound, but I don't care, I just want out of the car. I try not to let him see how excited I am, fighting to keep my voice even. "Thank you."

"Of course."

I practically fall out of the backseat, my fingers grazing the gravel underneath.

Freddy holds up the metal bar and points to me.

"What? No, no, please," Terror forces me backward and I half-crawl, half-run behind the vehicle as Freddy lunges forward with the weapon.

"You didn't think we could just let you go?"

Pierce hasn't exited the vehicle but watches, a look of boredom on his face as he checks his watch. "Hurry up, Freddy." Pierce complains, "or we're going to be late for our next appointment. Take care of it."

I'm hysterical as I stumble over the uneven concrete, my eyes locked on Freddy and the crazed look in his eyes. I keep my bound hands in front of me, using them as a shield against him.

"Don't run too far, girl."

"Please don't hurt me." I take a giant step back as he crouches forward, the metal bar in hand.

"It'll be over before you know it."

Pierce hollers from the backseat. "Hurry the fuck up and kill the damn girl."

I don't need another warning.

With one last glance at Freddy and his weapon of destruction, I run towards the highway, crashing through tall grass that does nothing but hinder my ability to run. I get tangled in it, batting my hands to separate it, which is made tough by the fact they're handcuffed together. I feel like I'm in one of those cornfield mazes they have in the fall.

Adrenaline propels me forward, and I manage to break through to the front of the abandoned gas station. I'm relieved I'm in wedges and not heels, which would make my ability to run difficult.

What if I miss my chance and Freddy and Pierce murder me out here and throw me in that dumpster?

No. That's not how this is going to end.

My heart races as I hear a vehicle getting closer, the tires on the pavement appearing like a figment of my imagination as it rises from a dip in the road.

I see a blur of white.

At first, I can't tell if it's a semi or a truck, but it looks taller and heavier than a regular car.

Raising my hands in the air, I lunge onto the pavement, the sun beating down on my head. It barrels towards me, and it's an SUV, some type of Suburban or Yukon, and I notice two passengers in the front, but I can't make out more than that.

I stomp up and down as if I've just won the lottery.

But this is better. This is my life.

They will either swerve to miss me, hit me, or slam on their brakes.

I'll take my chances.

They aren't slowing their speed, so I jump up and down with more emphasis, waving my hands. The metal cuffs catch the glint of the sunlight, which is gradually starting to fade behind the clouds.

Huffing, I watch as they dart to the other side of the yellow lines, giving me space as they pass.

From the passenger side, a look of surprise flashes on a female's face. The driver hits the brakes and the giant hunk of metal skids as it slows to a stop. I smell burning rubber as they pull off the road and reverse, their tires crunching over the gravel. They back up until they're directly across the road from me.

I have never been so happy to see a stranger. And not only that, a woman.

Tears of joy stream down my face as I run across the road, further distancing myself from the men in the Mercedes. The vehicle is large enough to block me from the view of Freddy or Pierce, so I run straight to the driver's side.

The window rolls down immediately. A man with sunglasses and a ball cap stares at me. He looks like he's in his thirties, but it might be because his arms and face are covered in freckles, which make him seem young.

He has a reddish goatee he strokes as he squints at me. "You need some help, young lady?" His eyes dart up and down, making judgments about why I'm wearing handcuffs, probably thinking I'm an escaped convict.

"Yes, yes, I need help." I pant. "Please help me." I lean forward to rest my hands on my knees. I feel like I'm going to throw up.

The woman sitting next to him leans over to ask what happened. All I can do is point to the abandoned gas station. "We need to call the police. They tried to kidnap me," I keep saying over and over.

"Did someone hurt you?"

I nod.

The man pulls out his phone, and without a word, I hear him speak to someone. "Hi, I've got an emergency on Highway 90, past Mile Marker 126. A young girl has been hurt. No, not a car accident. Possible kidnapping. She's safe though, my wife and I found her on the road."

The woman flings open her door and rushes around to where I'm standing. She's short and stout, with black hair pulled back into a tight ponytail. She's wearing black jeans and dark sunglasses.

"Are you injured?" she asks. "Are you bleeding anywhere?"

"Please," I stammer, "they might still be there."

"Where do you live, honey?"

I point towards the direction I think I came from. "In the city." I scream, "They took me from the mall."

"Who?" Puzzled, she examines my face. "*Who* took you?"

"Two men in a black Mercedes," I point again to the gas station. "They're behind there. Parked. Please help. I need help."

I burst into tears. "I want my mom, take me to my mom."

Heaving, I fall forward as the woman catches me. She runs a hand down each of my arms, focused on the cuffs. "Oh my God, sweetie," the woman gasps. "They did this to you? You poor thing."

"Come on." Holding one of my arms, the other one she uses to tug the passenger door open. "We've got the air conditioning running. Hop in." Guiding me up into the back seat, she helps me sit since it's weird with my wrists restrained.

"The police can remove these," she says reassuringly, patting my knee.

The man disconnects. "They're on their way now." He turns to give me a small smile. "They will be here soon. Just take a couple deep breaths. What's your name, honey?"

"Allegra."

"I'm Jeff, and this is Eva."

I nod. "Can I use your phone? I need to call my mom."

Eva settles back in the passenger seat. She turns to him, "Jeff, can you hand her a bottle of water? I think there's one in the side of your door."

She turns to me and smiles. "Don't worry, it's unopened."

I stare at her in shock. As if I care at this moment if I'm drinking out of a shared water bottle. I was about to be killed at the hands of two men that are still out there.

Jeff reaches for the water, uncaps it, and hands it to me. The need to speak to my mom and let her know I'm safe overrides my thirst. "Can I call her, like now?" My voice starts to rise. "I need to tell her where I am."

"Yeah, but first," Jeff tilts his head towards the gas station. "You said they might still be there?"

"If we hurry, maybe we can catch them," Eva states the obvious.

I nod, taking a long sip of the water as Jeff puts the SUV in drive and we amble towards the back of the station.

"I didn't do anything wrong," I cry.

The woman glances over her shoulder at me. "No one said you did, honey." She points to the man. "He's got a gun. Don't worry, honey."

It's like deja vu as we come face-to-face with the metal dumpster and the payphone, the overgrown and unkempt weeds standing at attention.

They all remain, but the black Mercedes is gone, the only evidence a few tire tracks in the gravel.

"Oh my God, they got away." I lean back in the seat, closing my eyes. A headache is pounding behind my temples, and my cheek is sore to the touch where Pierce clocked me with his hand.

"Eva," I ask as Jeff hops out of the driver side, his footprints ruining the earlier tracks of the sedan. "Can I call my mom now?" I'm hysterical. "I need to let her know I'm safe."

"Oh, sweetie, I wish you could." She twists in her seat to consider me. Her sunglasses prevent me from seeing her eyes, but she gives me a tight smile. "I don't think that's such a good idea right now."

"Why not?"

She reaches back to wipe a tear running down my cheek.

"Because you're not safe."

In one fluid motion, her other hand lunges towards me, a dirty rag in hand.

I scream as she stuffs it in my mouth. It's soaked in something, whatever it is tastes vile and I choke on the fumes as my eyes burn. Something pierces my arm, a stabbing at my vein, like when I get my blood drawn.

"That's too much," I hear Jeff hiss.

"Well, she's small," Eva mutters. "I don't know the exact dosage."

I flail, but I can't compete with her strength. With full force, her hand presses down as I gag, the rough material scratching my throat. All my words are swallowed as my eyes flutter shut, and I slide down in my seat.

Eva's voice is the last thing I hear before I pass out. "Jeff, honey, she'll be dead in no time."

15

VALERIE

Like a caged animal, I pace back and forth over the carpeting in our living room, sure that I'm wearing the fibers down with every footfall. I force myself back to the kitchen, where I rest my elbows on the island and figure out my next steps.

Where the hell is she?

Why isn't she answering any of her goddamn texts or phone calls?

Staring at my phone, I silently command my seventeen-year-old daughter Allegra to call me.

Right now.

Right this second, young lady.

So far, the three voicemails I've left haven't been accusatory or laced with anger. They have been that of a concerned parent. But I'm about to flip my switch if she doesn't respond soon.

Picking my phone up, I automatically put it back down, a nervous habit that's starting to annoy even me. I've checked our cell service to make sure that up here on the mountain nothing's happened to it, that a wire wasn't inadvertently cut or that our reception somehow became spotty.

Not only do I keep grasping for my cell, I can't decide if I want to sit or stand. I head into my office, a large room that's covered in framed photos of our family. I stare at a newspaper article that caught Allegra mid-split on the football field during cheer practice. Her beaming smile and confidence, something most teenagers try to emulate, but most can only fake. She has the drive and determination of someone much older. The positive outlook and self-worth that I instilled in her is evident every day.

Pushing back the curtains, I glance out the French doors that lead onto a private patio. Our house is tucked into the side of a blasted-out cliff, the stone facade blending into the landscape. There are multi-layered decks and an outdoor infinity swimming pool tucked into an alcove. Behind the main ten-thousand square foot house, there are other outbuildings. A stable, guest house, warehouse, and a gym with a sauna and indoor lap pool.

Out of habit, I look over my shoulder to check that my office door is closed before I sneak outside. I guess it's not technically 'sneaking' since this is my home, and I'm not doing anything wrong. But I equate my nasty tendency to smoke with something shameful that I have to hide, especially from Allegra and my husband, Darren.

I used to smoke to quell my anxiety, and what was once a weekly habit has become a daily one. It's now an ingrained ritual that if I'm feeling stressed, I light up.

I'm barefoot, and I let out a yelp when the cold concrete meets my skin. Reaching down in one of the planters, I wipe the soil off my pack of cigarettes. A lighter is hidden in a decorative lantern. Our landscaper, Raoul, replaces both for me in our agreed-upon hiding place. It's a shared habit and a shared secret between us.

Puffing on my first one of the day, I inhale, the comforting smell of nicotine and tar envelopes me in a warm embrace. I realize this is an unpopular opinion, most abhor the pungency of it.

Not me. I yearn for it. People don't call it a craving for nothing.

Exhaling, I stare down at the valley below, pretending like I used to that I'm a queen in my castle, the peasants beneath me. It's not from a place of contempt for those that don't have my life, because mine isn't all it's cracked up to be. It's solitary up here.

Even the loneliness I experienced growing up was different. There were always people around, but no one to confide in. I grew up poor on public assistance, bouncing around to different foster homes and overzealous parents. There were two kinds of families and no happy medium. They either tried to be my best friend in a disingenuous way, or they felt I was 'damaged goods' and needed firm discipline and rules. Because of this, I fought every family tooth and nail, and it didn't work out in my favor. I bounced around until I turned eighteen and was on the street. I lost a relationship and a child shortly before I met Darren.

Fast forward over seventeen years later, and here we are.

I take a long drag before I stub out my cigarette, drifting to my own child's bout of temporary insanity. Allegra is her father's daughter.

Deciding to light another, I check my phone, just in case Allegra's decided to re-surface. She sent her last text to me this afternoon. Instead of picking her up at the mall, she said she was going to a movie with Julie.

And then I heard nothing. Not a peep. As Allegra would say, crickets.

It's now after six.

Since it's Sunday, the mall is already closed, so there'd be no reason for her to be walking around and goofing off in stores.

And who is this Julie girl she said she was going to the matinee with?

I can do two things at once, so I smoke while scrolling through Allegra's Instagram account. Nothing new pops up on her stories today. Snapchat is also void of her usual antics. She barely uses Facebook, but I double-check just in case.

Sucking in a deep breath, I've already confirmed the length of the movie she supposedly saw today. It's 102 minutes. It should've been over a little after 4:45.

Before I started nervously treading over our carpet, I called the theatre to confirm the movie let out and that there were no incidents to speak of. The man who answered couldn't tell me if Allegra and Julie were there because he didn't arrive until four for his shift, and he was in the office working on payroll until five.

I nervously tap my fingers on the wrought iron railing that borders the patio. Maybe I should drive to the theatre. I toss my cigarette butt into the planter, knowing Raoul will discreetly discard the remnants of my tasteless but necessary habit.

I'm tempted to call Darren, but a bead of sweat crawls down my back. Darren is overprotective to put it nicely. The term 'helicopter parent' doesn't do him justice. I've fulfilled my obligations of trying to be Switzerland and act as a neutral third party between daddy and daughter, but it gets harder as she gets older, and the opposite sex becomes involved.

Not to mention drinking. Drugs. Parties. Allegra's life during and after high school.

And dammit, I used to humor him because he'd lost a toddler. I'd make excuses for his controlling behavior. I'd go along with some of his antics because he was my husband, and I wanted Allegra to view us as a team, a solid parental unit.

Dread overcomes me as I settle back against the overstuffed chair. I chew a nail as I think about my husband. He's become more and more unavailable, distant, combative, and absent. Even when we are in the same room, he's on his phone or laptop, the focus never on me. He spends some time with Allegra, but mainly it's him pestering her and putting stipulations on her time and how she spends it.

To me, he's become elusive, the man I married like a stranger to me. Yet I'd hate to ever give this up.

This life I've built one year at a time.

I wasn't his first wife, but I'll be damn sure I'm his last.

Settling a decorative pillow on my lap, I unlock my phone for the umpteenth time and scroll through Allegra's social media accounts, searching for girls named Julie or Julia. I find three - Julie Cambrero, Julia Larsen, and Juliette Jefferson. If I had to guess, it would be one of the first two. I negate the third one since she lives in another state.

I send the first two a message.

Then I wait.

But I can't sit still while I'm impatient and scared, wondering why she's put me in this position.

I should call her boyfriend, Coye Kauffman.

Would she have flown to California to see him without asking me first?

No. I gouge the skin around my nailbed with my teeth. Allegra wouldn't do that to me. We have an implicit understanding that if we are to disobey her father together in the worst way possible, there can be no secrets between us.

I cover for her and obscure the fact she has a boyfriend. Darren has no clue, and right now, I'm not sure he'd notice since he's preoccupied. In return, Allegra and I don't have the usual mother and daughter teen issues that stem from secrecy and distrust. I'm not going to lie, it's worked out in my favor. I can keep her safe because I know when she is with Coye, and it forces her to involve me in every relationship or personal decision she makes. A win-win if you ask me.

I'm the only reason she gets to communicate and even see Coye, considering he doesn't live in the same city, let alone the same state. He's a sophomore in college in California.

But no one can know how high the stakes are to keep Darren from finding out.

Because he *can't* find out.

He'd kill me with his bare hands if he knew Allegra not only had a boyfriend after he'd banned it, but that Coye's twenty, and I've let her visit him multiple times. I've accompanied her on the trips, but I've acted as a co-conspirator with our daughter.

I try Coye, but it goes straight to voicemail.

Pushing myself out of my chair, I can't stand it, this inaction. I'm going to drive to the movie theatre. It's a good twenty-five minutes, but at least I'll have to focus on something besides the fear twisting a knife in my chest.

Paying no attention to the fact I'm taking up two parking spots in the almost-empty lot, I waste no time with niceties, jumping straight into my predicament with the twenty-something pierced and tatted-up manager. He's got blond dreadlocks and a faraway look in his eyes. Maybe it's from smoking weed or his illustrious desire to prove to me he's the manager, since that's what he keeps dropping into our short but succinct conversation.

"I'm Andy, the *manager*."

"Okay. Hi Andy. I'm Valerie." I rarely drop our last name. This time it seems appropriate. "Valerie Atwater."

He doesn't flinch at the last name.

"How can I help you, Valerie?"

I explain that I'm having a hard time locating my daughter.

"Well, I'm the *manager* in charge."

"Have you been here all day?"

"Since our first show at noon, yes."

"My daughter and her friend, a girlfriend, came to the movies at three. She hasn't returned any calls or texts since then, and I'm worried."

"What would you think would've happened?"

"I don't know." I shrug, gripping my purse strap. "I just thought I'd ask to speak to someone who might remember the girls."

"Well, I'm the *manager,* and it's been a slow day." He shrugs. "Sunday matinees aren't as busy as you'd think."

"Then there's a good chance you'd recognize her."

"Maybe she just decided to stay out later, grab a bite to eat. It's not even eight yet." He gives me a withering stare. "How old is she?"

"Seventeen." I show him my screen saver. "Do you recognize her?"

"Can't say I do."

"Then maybe you or someone on your staff can help."

I attempt to show him a few more pictures of her. "Nope. I'd remember that pretty face," he adds.

"Who was taking tickets?" I can tell he's bored of our conversation by the way his eyes drift to the screen playing movie trailers behind us. He wants me to leave.

"We can ask the few people still here." He points to the snack counter. "I'm not sure it will help, I'm the *manager* and if I don't remember..."

No one remembers seeing Allegra. And Allegra doesn't have a forgettable face. Yes, I'm her mother, yes, I'm partial. But Allegra is tall and beautiful. A rail-thin blonde with high cheekbones and aquamarine eyes. You don't forget a girl like her. I bite my nails as I drive around the mall, looking for some sign that my daughter was legitimately here earlier.

Panicked, I start to call Darren but disconnect. I don't want to alert him, at least not yet.

I try Coye again, saying a silent prayer as he answers on the third ring. "Coye, hi, it's Valerie." I stammer, "Valerie Atwater."

"Yeah, duh." He snickers. "Your number's in my phone, Valerie, I know it's you." I feel stupid for a moment, but the seriousness of my call replaces my discomfiture.

I don't waste time. "Have you talked to Allegra today?" Wherever he's at is loud and noisy, and I struggle to hear what he says next.

"What was that?"

"Hold on a moment. Let me go outside." There's loud chattering and then a slam in the background, as if a door's shutting. It's now silent except for his voice. "Okay, I went somewhere quiet. I'm at a bar celebrating."

I don't bother to ask what for. I repeat my question. "Have you talked to Allegra today?"

"By text. Not on the phone." He adds, "I had a soccer game this afternoon. We won, so the team is eating wings and having a couple of beers."

"And you haven't heard from her this afternoon?"

"No. Allegra asked for my opinion when she was at the mall trying on outfits, but I didn't get a chance to respond until a few hours later. I haven't heard from her tonight."

There's a long pause as my stomach churns acid, and it's Coye who breaks the silence. "Why, what's up?"

"Coye, she's been unreachable since she texted to tell me she was going to a movie at three."

"A movie?" Nonchalant, he asks, "With who?"

As scared as Allegra is of losing him to another girl based on the fact he's in college and has access to a plethora of them, I point out how undeniably in love Coye is with her. There's no denying his affection toward her. When it comes to Allegra, he sees what the rest of the world does.

What a catch she is.

How beautiful she is. And intelligent. And talented. Allegra is a straight-A student, captain of the cheerleading squad, a talented dancer, and an aspiring editor.

"Her friend Julie," I offer.

"Are you sure they weren't grabbing dinner or something after?"

"No. I was supposed to pick her up. We have family dinner on Sundays." I don't bother to mention we *used* to have family dinner every night until recently. And that Darren didn't bother to come home last night, or the night before, nor has he set foot in the house all day.

I live with his shadow.

"That's right." Coye murmurs. "Yeah, it's weird she didn't reply back to me. I'll keep trying to call her."

"You promise she didn't hop on a flight to see you?" As

much as I'd be pissed, right now, I'd welcome it. In fact, the word 'hopeful' comes to mind. At least I'd know where she went, and it wouldn't be a mystery. "I promise I'm not mad," I add.

"No, Valerie, unless it was a surprise I didn't know about. Plus, how would she get to the airport?" He can poke holes in my stories all day long, but I'm going to keep coming up with scenarios until I know my daughter is safe.

"Okay, Coye, please call me if you hear from her, will you?"

"Sure thing. You got it."

We disconnect, and I rap my knuckles on the steering wheel in frustration.

When I drive up the winding road and punch in the gate code, I notice Darren's silver Jag is parked crooked in front of the six-car garage. Weird. Why didn't he move it into a stall?

I notice it's still running.

What is he doing now?

"Darren," I call out when I enter the house. Storming into the foyer, I try to keep my voice from betraying my anger at him. He's either in his office or his man-cave, except I find him in neither.

That leaves our first-floor master.

Sure enough, he's buried in his walk-in closet, which is the size of most people's apartments. Our bedroom has a his and hers, one on each side.

His back faces me, and I watch in surprise as he unpacks his overnight bag, only to replace his outfit with a fresh change of clothes.

I murmur his name.

He doesn't turn, his focus on his sock drawer, as he greets me lethargically. "Hi, Val."

Coward, I want to scream. Instead, I say, "What're you doing?"

"Grabbing a change of clothes."

"Are you leaving?"

"I am."

16

VALERIE

I lean against the doorjamb. "Where to tonight?

"Does it matter?"

I shake my head, but he doesn't see my nonverbal communication. Out loud, I say, "Our daughter is missing."

This gets his attention and swinging around, he glares at me. Funny, those eyes used to look at me with such respect and admiration. Now they loathe me. "What do you mean, *missing*?"

"Do I need to refer you to the dictionary for a definition?"

"Allegra being out is *not* the same as missing."

"She's not here and not at our agreed-upon pick-up spot."

"Why aren't you with her?" He peers at me angrily. "You had one task today. Get her an outfit for that school thing."

"She did go get an outfit."

"But you weren't with her?"

"No. We had brunch and then she went to the mall alone."

"By herself?" Incredulous, Darren pins me to the wall

with his scowl. He thrusts a belt angrily into his duffel bag. You would've thought I admitted to leaving a toddler in a hot car with the windows up.

"She's seventeen, Darren. Seventeen. She's not a child."

"Are you an idiot?" he asks coldly.

"Are you a sociopath?" I retort. "You have to stop treating her like a baby." I'm tempted to lob a pair of six-inch Louboutin heels at him. Or better yet, stab him with the pointed spike of the heel. But why ruin a perfectly good pair of shoes on this prick?

"Then why the fuck don't you know where she is?"

I shrug.

"Have you tried her cell?"

"Of course."

He puffs his chest up. "She'll answer if I call."

I roll my eyes. "Then, by all means, call Allegra so I can hear her voice since she'll answer *only* your calls."

I swallow my next words. They won't help, only hinder the tenuous situation. His daughter won't answer for the boyfriend he doesn't know about.

Seething, he yanks his phone out of his pocket. I watch as Darren angrily punches a couple of buttons before tapping the speakerphone as we lock eyes in hatred.

Immediately, Allegra's voice echoes through the line. 'Hi, you've reached Allegra, you know what to do, leave me a message. Unless you're my parents, then obsessively keep calling." She laughs cheekily before it beeps.

"When did she change it to this nonsense?"

"No idea." I could care less about what her message says right now. "Have you talked to her today?"

"No."

"Actually," I tap my fingers against the wood. "You're lucky she isn't home yet because she thought we'd have our usual Sunday dinner together tonight, except her father didn't show up." I give a final thud to the paneling. "And it looks like he's leaving again."

"Don't put this on me, Valerie." He thrusts a finger in my direction. "You made this choice for both of us."

"Oh, did I?"

"You thought your past wouldn't catch up with you."

"Oh, piss off."

"As much as I'd love to dive into our marital problems, I'm exhausted."

"Which hotel?" I sneer at him. "Since you like to claim you're at a 'hotel' when you're really with *her*?"

"Does it make you feel good to try and control me?"

I sigh. "There's no controlling you, Darren."

"Finally, you understand. It's taken you a long time to come to terms with the reality of the situation."

He pushes past me out of the closet and into the master. Flinging his hands up in the air, he hisses at me. "You better start putting your affairs in order because I'm not going to be tied to this sinking ship any longer."

I watch as he zips his bag and exits the bedroom.

Abruptly he stops, as if he had a sudden change of heart, but it's only to shoot a dirty look over his shoulder at me. His voice is low and controlled, but the threat is very much embedded in his words.

"If anything, and I mean *anything*, happens to Allegra, if one hair on her head is so much as disturbed, I will fucking destroy you, Valerie. *Destroy* you. I'll murder you and throw you off the fucking cliff up here. I won't bother to pretend it's an accident because I'll do it with my bare hands. Do you understand me?"

We both stand facing each other. My arms crossed over my chest, his gesticulating every word. "You are an incompetent mother. I told you that you would never succeed at this. You are the most selfish person I know, and Allegra is a product of you. She needs structure and rules. She's a teenager hell-bent on fucking up her life, because her own mother was a whore before she met me. You can't seem to fathom that *she,* at seventeen, shouldn't be in control right now. But why would you? You ran around and fucked your life up, so why shouldn't she?"

He mutters, "There's a bastard child out there somewhere with your DNA."

It takes all of my resolve not to close the separation between us and give him a hard smack across the cheek. I'd like to see him bleed some of the pain he inflicts on me on a day-to day basis.

Instead, in a calm voice that doesn't relay any of the anger I feel, I say, "Allegra is not seven, she's seventeen. She will be an adult in six months. You want to control her because you can't control me. Well, guess what, dickhead, you're going to lose both of us. She can't live up to your expectations, no one can. It's fucking impossible. And if she ran away because she got tired of living in your prison, I wouldn't blame her one bit. I blame you."

"Good," he shakes his head, pitifully, "because I want a divorce." He strides out of the room, his footsteps treading across the plush carpeting.

"Darren," I yell after him.

"What?" He turns around to face me once again, like a head-on collision.

"If I find out the woman you're fucking is messing with our daughter, you will never see either of us again."

"What the hell are you talking about?"

"This." I grab a red envelope drenched in annoyingly sweet perfume out of my tote. Inside is a card from Sandra, his secretary, and the current mistress. There might be more than just one, but this I have proof of. Frozen to the spot, I read out loud what Sandra wrote to him. His face turns cherry red as I emphasize each word.

"Darren, my love, I can't wait until we can wake up every day in the same bed. I know I'm the most important woman in your life. Soon your daughter will be in college, and you'll be divorced, and we can be together. That's all that matters, and I will do anything to make this happen."

"So," I close the card. "Tell me, Darren, *my love*, how far would you and your lover go to get rid of Allegra and I? And what about the other girl, the former one, Alyssa? Do they have to share you on certain days of the week?"

A fist comes pummeling towards my face. Expertly, I step to the left as he barrels it into the wall behind me.

Stunned, I glower at his beet-red face. "A man on the brink of insanity," I mutter.

Screaming expletives, he yanks his fist out of the crumbled drywall. His knuckles didn't fare so well, and they stare at me, crimson and bloody.

"You better have Sandy take you to the ER." I point to the door. "But for now, get the hell out of my house."

"Enjoy it because you'll lose it in the divorce." He cradles his injured hand in his other arm. "Remember when you were my secretary?"

I stare at him, hands on my hips.

"You were in the same position once. It must be hard to know that I've moved on to a better and younger version of you. They always say karma comes back around." He narrows his lids at me. "Once a cheater, always a cheater. You should've picked better."

"Have a nice evening," I say sweetly. "Give my best to Sandy. Or Alyssa."

17

ALLEGRA

When my eyes flicker open, all I see is black.

Pitch black.

At first, I think I'm blind, that whatever they injected me with caused vision loss. As my eyes adjust, I rock back and forth, my knees hugged tightly to my chest. I assume it's my weight shifting, but really, I'm in motion. I can feel the tension in my muscles from the awkward position I'm twisted in. I must be in a van or something with a higher roofline. If I were in a trunk, the roof would be directly above my head.

When I move my hand up to rub my tired eyes, I realize I'm still handcuffed. Using my palm, I massage my other wrist. They're sore from being shackled, and I can feel the rope cutting into my ankles, cutting off circulation. Even though the rag is no longer shoved down my throat, it might as well be, my mouth bone dry. Nothing but a hollow 'eek' comes out, as if my vocal cords are also strained.

My senses are heightened, but the only sound is the thud of the pavement beneath the tires. I hear nothing else - no chatter, no music, no bass from the speakers. I try and focus on noises, but my head feels like someone dropped a brick on it. The massive headache only increases in intensity. These are different than the ones I have a few times a week, the pain overtakes my entire head instead of just my temples.

I struggle to sit up and carefully, I move my arms in front of me to see what, if anything, I can touch. My hands sweep over the rough carpet of the floor but come up with nothing.

Tears prick my eyes as I think of my family and Coye.

How could this happen to me, and why?

The sobs torment me as unchecked tears drip down my cheeks.

Shutting my eyes, I keep them closed, trying to focus on taking small, shallow breaths. We lurch over what must be a pothole in the road. My stomach tumbles along with it. The next bump I'm not so lucky on. My tears mix with the contents of my earlier brunch. As it comes spewing out, I shiver, uncomfortable and miserable, in a tight ball.

Liquid drenches my hair as the rest of the runny bile runs down my cheek. A knot's tightly wound in my stomach as I smack the floor underneath me in anger. I have no more energy to fight or even sit up.

I drift back into a painful, restless sleep, and when I wake, I expect today to be a nightmare that I can remove myself from.

Unfortunately, that's not the case.

When I manage to flicker my eyes open, again, I wonder if I'm temporarily blinded, a dull gray the only color in my peripheral vision. It stares at me from the concrete walls and bare floors. No window filters in light, and I'm surrounded on all four sides by the monotony. The entire room's void of furniture, save for a tiny light bulb in the ceiling.

When I jerk my head against the wall, it smacks the hard cement surface.

Ouch, I cry out in pain.

Raising my hands to the back of my head, I'm now free of the handcuffs. Yet, I shiver uncontrollably. My hair, though long, covers my shoulders but little else. A fleeting glance down confirms why I have goosebumps.

I'm naked, my feet shackled to some kind of restraint in the wall.

Nostrils flared, an unbearable stench permeates the air, and I sniff. It takes me a second to realize it's from me. My stringy hair is crusted with dried throw-up.

Disgusted, I flip it over my shoulder and turn away.

A small shriek escapes my lips when I feel a tickle. I watch in horror as a giant cockroach crawls across my foot. I kick it off, my skin prickling at the touch.

This must be what prison is like. Maybe worse. And I'm in it without my consent, guilty of what, I don't know.

I stare at my feet, memorizing the small mole I have on the big toe of my right foot. I try not to focus on my basic needs. In addition to being naked and cold, I'm hungry and tired and scared and sore. I've never wanted a shower so badly. I've never wanted to hug my parents so tightly. They can ground me to my room for a month and keep me trapped in our compound that used to feel stifling. I long for it.

My mind wanders in and out of lucid dreaming. The thought of curling up in Coye's arms, wearing his favorite sweatshirt, makes me tingly inside.

I don't know how much longer I wait, tied to the wall like an abandoned pet.

As if the universe is listening, I smile as a warm touch

embraces my cold flesh. I relax, that is, until my eyes connect with the source. Then I scream.

It's not Coye, it's not anyone I know. It's a tall, muscular man with a tan face and dark hair. His eyes are slits as they consider me, and he looks pissed off at the world. This expression seems permanent and not mood-related.

A fitted tee stretches across his chest, busting at the seams. I think of Superman and his uniform hidden underneath his street clothes until he surges out of it. The giggle dies in my throat when my eyes drift past the tattoo wrapped around his bulging muscle. It looks like some type of tribal ink.

I notice what he's holding in his hand.

A knife. A long and shiny one. Definitely not the kind you carry in your pocket.

I yell at the same time liquid seeps down my bare thighs.

"What the fuck?" He stares at me in shock. "I didn't ask to buy a girl that's not potty-trained." He takes a step backward as a small puddle forms underneath me.

"Buy?"

He reaches towards my ankles and unwinds the shackles, releasing my legs from the chains. The muscles in them feel stretched, like a piece of taffy that's been pulled apart in every direction.

I cross my arms across my chest, both to cover my nakedness and also to rub the goosebumps. My teeth chatter as he murmurs, "Are you thirsty?"

I nod.

"First lesson."

I stare at him with wide eyes.

"You need to learn to address me as sir. Everything from now on is, 'Yes, sir.' Do you understand?"

I don't, but I can tell you don't mess with this man.

He waits until I reluctantly whisper my agreement. I must not be loud enough to hear because he kicks my bare ankle with his sneaker.

"Yes, sir." I yelp.

A tap of heels echoes through the room and expecting a woman, I peer in surprise at the man that appears. He's short, bald, and fat, his belly hanging over his enormous belt buckle. The clicking is caused by his reptilian cowboy boots. I wonder if they are made out of real alligator.

He speaks. "Is she what you expected?"

"I don't know. She just pissed all over the floor."

The man throws his hands in the air. "Fucking pig." Disgusted, he also kicks me, but his boots leave a sharp sting, and the spur claws through my skin, leaving a gash behind.

"Stand up," the dark-haired man commands me. "Let me see you."

The bald man yanks on the string of the light bulb, which doesn't help with the lighting situation. A small glow doesn't reach the corner where I'm being held. It's still dim in the room, which further intensifies the dark-haired man's wrath. He grabs my wrist and drags me to my feet. Unable to avoid the puddle, I step in my own urine as I stumble towards the middle of the room.

Once when I was a child, my grandparents took me to a county fair. We walked through a barn full of animals, and I stared with curiosity as a man inspected each one. In this case, cattle, as he carried around a clipboard and wrote down notes. He examined every scar, every crevice, as if the animals were nothing more than a slab of meat, which they were. Covering my eyes with my fingers, I watched as a hot iron was pressed directly into their flesh, a permanent mark, branding them for life.

This is no different.

The dark-haired man holds one arm up, which I can barely lift myself, as he stares at the red welts on my wrist and works his way up. He does the same with my other arm before twisting me around to inspect my back.

His commands are short and clipped. "Now, spread your legs."

"No."

"What did you say?"

"No, sir."

A hand wraps around my neck. "The word "*no*" is not in your vocabulary when it comes to me." He squeezes harder. "Do you understand?"

I blink.

"I need verbal reassurance."

"Yes," I manage to whisper. He jams his thumb into my clavicle. "What was that?"

"Yes, sir."

"Spread your legs."

Closing my eyes, my sticky thighs went from sweaty to now streaked with urine. The last thing I want is some strange man examining my private parts. Or worse yet...

I try not to let my mind drift as hot tears slide down my cheeks. Ashamed, I force my knees to lock, which does nothing, he just prods them open with his fingers, smacking my inner thigh as I resist. I let them buckle before I exhale, my eyes trained on the bare wall behind him.

The bald cowboy stands there, sweat pouring down his forehead, while I tremble.

"Turn around." The dark-haired man runs his hands through my tangled hair, his breath hot on my neck as he glides a finger down my spine, his palms pausing on my butt before he travels down the back of my legs.

My cheeks burn as I try to stay calm, anger and resentment threatening to bubble to the surface.

"Okay, she'll do." The dark-haired man stands back, a finger on his chin.

"You want me to clean her up?"

"No, I will." He shakes his head. "But at least give me something to cover her up with. I have a feeling she'll be my new prized possession."

The bald man licks his lips in agreement.

"She'll make me a lot of money, that's for sure."

Pressing my eyes together, I'm afraid to learn how I'll make him money. I don't allow my mind to travel to the dark chambers of what's going to happen to me. All I can do is shut out the small voice that tells me I might have been dealt a fate worse than death.

Someone has to come for me, they have to. It's been at least twenty-four hours. For once, the fact I have an overbearing mother and a controlling father is on my side. The police are surely involved, scoping out the mall and talking to witnesses. Did the driver who honked before he almost ran me over admit he saw me trying to cross the street?

I soothe myself with the fact that the saleswoman at Cazal's Department Store saw the man, who said he was Pierce, approach me. He also bought something for his daughter there. They will trace his receipt to his credit card, and then the police will contact him and arrest him. He'll have no choice but to lead the authorities to me. It'll be over soon, I give myself a pep talk, just be brave.

Except Pierce Arden's nowhere in sight, and where are the people that took me? Where is Freddy and the couple - Jeff and Eva?

And what if Pierce doesn't know what happened to me?

Could this be an awful coincidence?

My eyes release a fresh string of tears as I realize I have no control over my fate. This agitated, dark-haired man with the tattoo is the one in charge now. He makes this absolutely clear as he twists my hair into a ponytail with his hand and yanks it.

"Follow me." He pulls again, using my hair as leverage.

His mouth twists into a scowl, and I decide then and there to name him Muscleman because of his bulging biceps and his resentful demeanor.

18

VALERIE

After I watch Darren peel out in his Jag on our security cameras, I pour myself a glass of Merlot, twisting the stem of the glassware as the liquid dances at the bottom.

For a minute, I'm lost in a trance, the dark burgundy makes me think of blood and destruction in the form of my marriage. It's a dead carcass with nothing left but vital fluids, the organs permanently stopped working.

We are getting worse, and this is disconcerting news to me. We swore we'd never get to this point, where we can no longer stand to be in the same room, let alone the same house. Our fights are becoming tedious and destructive. As much as I haven't wanted to say it out loud, I'm relieved Darren mentioned the dreaded 'D' word. I'd hoped we could hide our problems until Allegra went to college. Obviously not.

Draining the wine in a long sip, I refill my glass before I snatch up my laptop and head outside on the patio, which has become my sanctuary, at least while it's not too cold. I rest it on the patio table as I locate my lighter. My hands tremble as they illuminate another cigarette, and I lean on the railing. The bulbous moon hangs above, the clouds offer little in the way of cover.

"Baby girl, where are you?" I whisper, gazing at the moon. Flicking ash into an empty bottle that I left out here to cover my tracks, I remember when she was little, probably five or six, and she'd ask questions about outer space. She'd want to know about the stars and the sun and moon. When she used to go stay at Darren's parents, her grandparents' house, she'd be scared to sleep in another bed and be away from us. To calm her fears, I would put her in front of the window of our old two-story rambler and point up at the sky. "Just remember, baby girl," I told her, "the moon watches over us all. No matter where you are, where I am, where Daddy is, we all stare up at the same sky. It's the same space above us, so when you're afraid, just look up and know we can see what you see."

Tonight, I take my own advice and direct a prayer at the moon. I hope she's staring up at it and can somehow feel my love wherever she is.

Phone in hand, I weep as I send a text.

We love you, Allegra.

Then I send one more.

Your father and I aren't mad. Not even a little. Just please call us. Better yet, come home. You aren't in trouble, we just want you home. I end it with some heart emojis.

Everyone leaves a trail, including my daughter.

I settle into a chair and sip my second glass of Merlot as I log into Allegra's bank account to check her debit card transactions. A pending charge from Cazal's Department Store was the last purchase made in the amount of $173.81. The movie theatre isn't showing, either because it's not yet pending or because she didn't go.

My heart skips a beat.

Allegra could've used cash, I chide myself. But she *never* carries cash. This girl has grown up on apps like Venmo or PayPal to transfer money between friends if needed.

My phone beeps, and I breathe a sigh of relief. Allegra got the text and knows we're not mad, and now she's replied. She was scared, is all. A hand goes to my chest, and I relax for a moment against the seat cushion.

Except it's not her. It's a notification from Julia Larsen. She sent a message saying she didn't see Allegra today.

I feel sick as I bury my head in my hands.

Think, Val, *think*. What else can you do?

The other Julie, the Cambrero one.

Pulling up her Facebook, I look at Julie Cambrero's profile picture. She's a short, petite girl, but I can't fathom what the two girls have in common. They aren't in any of the same activities or groups, and I'd never heard her name before today. Doing a quick search, I'm able to find a home phone number for her. I dial it, and after a couple of rings, a breathless female voice answers. "Hello?"

"Hi, is this Julie?"

"Uh-huh."

"Hi, this is Valerie. Valerie Atwater." I pause, since I've never heard of her, she's probably never heard of me. "Allegra's mom."

"Oh, yes, hi, Mrs. Atwater. I saw you sent me a message, but I haven't had a chance to respond. I just walked in the door from work."

My tone betrays my disappointment. "Oh, you had to work today?"

"Yeah, I'm a hostess at the Grille on Second Avenue. My shift started at noon, so no matinee, though that sounds better than dealing with cranky customers."

"I'm curious though..." her voice trails off. "Why would you call me?"

"What do you mean?"

"Allegra and I aren't friends." She quickly adds, "We don't hang out with the same people. I do have the locker next to her, though."

"That's a fair question." I go for blunt. "I'm trying all avenues. A 'Julie' was mentioned in her text to me. The last text she sent me this afternoon."

"I see. Did something happen to her?"

"Of course not, she just hasn't come home yet."

"So, something could have happened?"

"No." I sigh, wishing I could reach through the telephone line and shake this Julie Cambrero. "Are there any other Julies' that Allegra might've hung out with?"

She names the other one I already reached out to.

"And you're positive she said my name?"

"She just said Julie."

"I don't know why Allegra would say she was with me if she wasn't?" Julie asserts. "I'd think she would mention someone she's good friends with if she needed an alibi."

"Do you know what she would need an alibi for?

She inhales sharply through the line. "Uh, I don't know."

"Are you sure?"

"Uh-huh." She doesn't sound sure, but I let it go for now.

After I smoke one more cancer stick, I head back inside, throwing a cardigan over my chilled frame. I'm not sure if it's the fear or the outside temperature causing my skin to explode in goosebumps.

Catatonic, I sit on our couch in the living room, fiddling with the television remote. I have no intention of watching TV, but I need the background noise.

I add a throw over my lap, a biting cold permeating my bones.

I check the news reports to make sure there are no car accidents. I contact the local hospitals to make sure no teenagers have been brought in. Would Allegra blatantly ignore me? Maybe she's trying to teach me a lesson by asserting her independence. She's become tempestuous and moodier lately. I've just chalked it up to hormones, but maybe it's more than that.

"Are you and Coye having problems I don't know about?" I whisper.

My hands fly over the keyboard as I occupy my time messaging classmates and friends through various channels, both on my computer and on my cell. Allegra is going to be pissed when she finds out I caused this much of a stir.

Tough. That'll teach her to disappear without so much as a text.

My phone rings, and before screening the call, I automatically answer.

"Valerie?" It's Coye, his voice laced with concern.

I grip my phone. "Please tell me Allegra showed up in California."

"No," he mutters. "I wish. I haven't heard from her. It goes straight to voicemail."

A sharp exhale of breath on my part is followed by silence. Neither of us speaks for a moment. I twist the frayed edges of the blanket as I wait for him to inundate me with ideas of where she could be. They never come. Instead, he asks, "Did you tell her father?"

"That she hasn't come home, yes."

"And?"

"He seems to think his voice will magically make her appear," I mutter. "Father of the year award."

"Are you okay, Valerie?"

No, I'm not, but I have to rein myself in. I can't project my marital problems on this young man who is starting to worry about his girlfriend.

Keeping my voice even, I apologize. "I'm sorry, Coye. I'm just worried about her. Allegra's never been uncommunicative this long."

His voice suddenly sounds small, and it's no longer that of a twenty-year-old, but reminiscent of a young boy. "Tell me nothing's happened to our girl."

In a voice that conveys a confidence I don't feel, I say, "She's going to walk in the door any minute. She probably dropped her phone, and it's now busted, and there'll be a funny story when she gets back."

But deep down, I know there's nothing humorous about her absence.

After we disconnect, I sit back and close my eyes. My heart flutters as I realize I got the last text. It should comfort me, but in actuality, it terrifies me, because it forces me to consider the fact that she didn't plan on being out of touch.

I respond to messages on various social media accounts, all with the same outcome. No one's talked or heard from Allegra today. Every minute feels like an hour, yet when I look at the clock and realize its now past midnight, a sense of dread wraps me in its embrace.

If it were just Darren missing from the Atwater residence, I could tolerate it. It would be welcome. But not *both* of them, not my daughter.

Calling the police weighs heavily on me. It's admitting there's a problem, something sinister that involves an outside authority beyond parents. As much as I'm worried about Allegra, I'm frightened of what the police could uncover if they hunt in our past, the dark corners we've kept hidden. They will find out our secrets, and there's a lot I don't want to be unveiled, and for a good reason.

I fidget, biting my nails as I scroll through my contacts.

Dammit. I have to call Darren. It's time.

Hesitating, I needn't worry, the bastard sends me straight to voicemail. My message is a question, but it's a crucial one. "She still isn't home. Should we call the police?"

As much as he wants to cut me from all angles, Darren would throttle me if I called the police without discussing it first with him.

An hour later, a text pops up from him.

Do what you have to do.

I sigh at his flippancy.

Unable to sit still any longer and anxious to be near where she slept less than twenty-four hours ago, I tiptoe my way up to her living quarters. It sounds old-fashioned to say it like that, but Allegra has her own wing of the house, which is practically an apartment. A private staircase goes to her bedroom, bathroom, study, and living room. There's even her own individual laundry area.

My hand pauses on the doorknob of her bedroom. When I open it, I'm overwhelmed by the fragrance of everything '*Allegra.*' Smothered by the perfume she wears, the vanilla candles she sometimes forgets to blow out which I swear will start a fire one day, the leftover scent of her laundry detergent. All of her smells.

Her queen bed is made, the colorful throw pillows in their rightful place. She takes after me in orderliness and cleanliness. Same with privacy and space. Allegra isn't a big fan of people in her actual bedroom. She'd even asked that the maid not tidy up in here. We agreed that as long as she kept it clean, we'd respect that.

We've both kept our end of the bargain.

At least with that one.

But did she stop confiding in me when it comes to relationships?

With all the online dating that goes on, could she have met someone else? Or was someone harassing her online?

Was she afraid to tell me? Or afraid to break up with Coye?

I glance at the wall made of corkboard, a surprise I had installed so she could hang pictures of friends and her pom-poms from cheerleading. My fingers touch a snapshot of Coye and her taken at the beach. Allegra's wearing oversized sunglasses and Coye's grinning from ear-to-ear as they pose in the sand, her legs draped over his chest as she sits on his shoulders.

My throat constricts.

It's not merely the fact they smile adoringly at each other, both attractive enough to pass for models straight out of a commercial for suntan oil or sunscreen. It's the weekend this picture was taken that has me reflecting in stunned silence.

Sinking onto the edge of Allegra's bed, I rest my head in my hands, recalling our four-day trip to Manhattan Beach, California. I invited Darren, knowing he wouldn't go. He feigned disappointment, when really, he couldn't wait to have the compound to himself. With little disregard for our marriage, our cameras caught him screwing Alyssa, and then Sandy.

I told Allegra the beach house was a rental, except it wasn't. It was a little white lie, part of an intricate web of hyperbole, none of which she needs to know.

Allegra invited Coye, and I was solo until *he* came.

A friend had suggested the trip and the property, convenient because of his proximity next door. The house I brought Allegra and Coye was used as a rental. My friend would sneak to the top floor after Allegra and Coye were asleep, the master the only room on the third level. Because two staircases were leading up to the enormous suite, one hidden with a separate entrance, it was the perfect set-up.

On our last day, Coye and Allegra were on the beach, squishing sand beneath their toes and running into the waves while I sat on the deck, reading a summer romance. I didn't hear the man come onto the deck until I felt a hand caress my neck.

As if it were second nature, I lean back into his touch, but only for a moment. "We can't do this right now," I murmur. He pulls away, and where his hand was, a coldness tickles my skin. Inside, I'm screaming for him to keep going. His affection keeps me going.

I stand at the same time he tries to wrap an arm around my waist, where my see-through sarong hardly covers up the thin material of my bikini.

"Why not?"

"Because she might see." I giggle as I lower my hat. It's a 'fun hat,' I call it, a straw one, that begs to be worn on sandy beaches and near water.

He scoffs at this excuse. "She's not a child."

I can't argue this. He's not wrong. We watch as Allegra playfully kicks water at her boyfriend, Coye, who, in return, grabs her by the knee and pulls her into the ocean.

"Besides," I push my chair forward. "If you ever meet, you're the landlord renting the place out."

"I can pretend to fix something else." I feel his warm breath as he reaches down to taste my skin. "Maybe *you*, meaning *us*, broke the bed, and I need to reinforce the legs or something."

"I was awful clumsy when I lay down last night." I giggle. "Clearly, too much wine."

"Clearly." He pushes a tendril that escaped my loose ponytail off of my face. "You are so beautiful." He presses a thumb on my lip. "I want this so much."

"I know," I sigh.

He moves to lean against the deck railing. "Say you'll move here."

Caught off guard, I'm floored. "What?"

"Tell me you'll be mine. We can start a life together."

"I am yours." Staring at the book in my hand, then up at him, I wonder if this is insecurity talking. We've only been together a few months, and this is coming from out of nowhere.

"Are you jealous?" I prod. "You know that I'm still married."

"No." He lowers his Ray-Bans. "This is not about that."

"I can't. It would be a disaster."

"No, it wouldn't."

"Not to mention, *where* would I live?" I motion to the vast horizon, my daughter frolicking out there on the beach. "Where would *we* live?"

"Listen to my idea," he begs. "If we can make this work, then there's no problem with us building a life together."

"Sure, okay." I nod, unable to meet his eyes as I stare at the small tuft of chest hair escaping from his half-unbuttoned shirt.

I listen as he explains how this is a doable situation. First, with fascination, then with absolute horror, my expression froze in fear. Startled by this, he pauses mid-sentence. "Is this too much?" A gentle tap on my nose takes the heaviness of the talk down a notch. "Shit, baby, I should've known it would be a lot all at one time."

I give him a dirty look.

"Babe, Allegra will be much happier out here. I've got a place for us. And she's so happy, look at her," he motions to the beach. "You can see that glow from here."

"You're renting this place out to someone, you said."

"Yeah, but they'll be gone by the end of summer. Labor Day weekend is the last of my renters." He runs a hand through his tousled hair, "I don't plan to rent it out after that, so I can make this work for us."

Again, I can't argue this.

I stare at my only child, my only daughter, my lifeblood. I'd do anything for that girl. She has no idea how strong a mother's love can be.

"If I'm not bringing in rental income, I'm going to need some help with finances," he shrugs. "But I have some ideas." He reads my emotions to a T and watches a look of disdain twist my lips into a frown.

"Only for a short time," he promises. "Just until we get our own thing going. We can start over here. A new state, new beginning."

I slide my sunglasses up on my head. "I don't see this happening."

Crestfallen when I rebuke him, I give a string of excuses and reasons why it'll never work. It's too dangerous.

"Then I don't have any other thoughts right now."

"Please don't be like this," I plead.

"I'll think of other alternatives." He pushes away from the railing. "I'll make it happen." I don't have anything else to say, so I return to my book, opening up to the chapter I'm currently on. I hear his footsteps retreat and watch him return inside.

The words in my book swim in front of me. Did he really just say what I think he said? Sure, this is a reprieve from the monotony of my life, but he can't be serious. I'm so lost in my own thoughts I don't hear Allegra call my name.

"Mom," she hollers. "Earth to Mom." She's standing on the sidewalk beneath me.

Startled, I shift my gaze down towards her. "Hi, honey."

"We're going for a walk," She peers up at me, "Coye saw a wetsuit he wants to check out. Be back in a couple of hours."

"Don't go far."

"Is this too far?" she teases, taking a giant step back toward the sand.

I stick my tongue out at her as she mimics me.

Shaking my head, I grin as Coye runs up and grabs her, tossing her over his shoulder.

Young love, I think, smiling at them.

I'm obsessed with my daughter, somewhat of a voyeur, but harmless. I'm her mother, and it's my job to watch out for her. It's a change to see her relaxed and happy. Back home, she's anxious and has constant stomachaches, headaches, and fatigue. She has a lot going on, and I hate that she feels so much pressure to do and be everything to everyone.

Snapping out of my thoughts, I sniff,

my hand brushing across my watery eyes as I raise my head to the ceiling in her room. *Oh, Allegra, where are you?*

Shakily, I stand up, smoothing the comforter so as not to leave evidence that I sat on the edge of her bed, concerned. She's going to roast me for this, I just know it. Making a big deal out of nothing, she'll say. With a roll of those aquamarine eyes, she'll tell me I'm acting like an overdramatic teenager.

Unable to resist, I stand inside her walk-in closet, laden with clothes and shoes. I sort through her laundry basket, pretending it's innocent, like I'm going to throw in a load of wash. Instead, I check the pockets of her jeans and shirts. Sorting through her hangers, I separate each piece of clothing before turning my attention to her dresser. I rifle through the drawers, but nothing is out of place.

A row of wooden baskets lines the top shelf of her walk-in. Allegra uses them as storage for her accessories. All except the last one. That contains cards and romantic notes between her and Coye. It's the usual sentiments, nothing disturbing.

I nearly jump out of my skin as a beep disrupts my search. It continues, forcing an inevitable tension in my body. It's our security system, signaling someone is nearing the gate. Two beeps mean a vehicle is within twenty-five feet of the premises.

Taking the stairs two at a time, I expect it to be someone bringing Allegra home to me. My arms are outstretched, ready to fold her into a big hug.

19

BRIAN

"Lie to you about what?" I stammer.

"First, why did you stop?"

"A nail was in the tire."

"A nail?"

"Yes, I got a patch for it."

"You don't have a license," I say nothing as he holds the gun steady. "You realize the liability you created for Mr. Atwater? For the company? You could've cost me my job, my livelihood, all from your reckless decisions."

I have to swallow hard to avoid bringing up the cargo. *The body I found*. Mickey keeps the gun glued to my face as he picks up the phone and dials. He speaks Spanish to whoever is on the other end. Maybe it's the Hispanic guy that helped load boxes, or maybe it's Vincent and the twins.

After he hangs up, he lowers the gun to the desk. "You reek like a bar, and just because my men didn't confiscate anything from the truck, you show the classic signs of a drunk. Remind me of my old man."

I bite my lip.

"You'll never do another job for us."

With a solemn nod, he says, "You're free to go."

My legs wobble, but I manage to stand, stretching to my full height. Mickey doesn't follow me. Instead, he kicks his feet back up on the desk. I want to scream and bellow as I exit the side door, but I have to keep my steps slow and steady, the opposite of my heart palpitations.

Hands shaking, it takes a couple attempts to thrust the key in the rusted door handle of my Chevrolet.

I knew it, I knew Mickey and his crew were tracking my movements. That's why I kept moving forward, making sure I didn't backtrack. They knew every time and every place I stopped. Careful to avoid suspicion, I punctured the tire with a nail I found in the parking lot. When I was at the home improvement store, I bought a patch kit to secure the tear along with the drum deheader. At a gas station, I tossed the steel drum tool out on the way to Vincent's. The booze they smelled on me worked in my favor this time. Drinking and driving is a huge risk, and one this crew can't afford to take. Especially if they're transporting illegal substances or contraband.

Or dead bodies.

I shudder at the thought. Since I completed the job successfully, they can't fault me since the delivery was on-time and relatively smooth. They just won't hire me again.

Relieved, I take a deep breath as I exit the parking lot, the envelope tucked in my broken glovebox. I immediately dial Valerie's cell, incensed when it goes straight to voicemail. I don't want to be that guy, the one that repeatedly calls and has stalker vibes. However, this can't wait.

Heading to a dive bar, Harold's, I pound a few beers and then get lost in a game of pool. Or I should say, I lose money on a bet during the game of pool.

I'm bent over the felt green billiards table when his scent

overpowers me. I can smell him before I see him. Losing my concentration, I almost sink the cue ball. A whiff of expensive cologne follows him inside. It's out of place in this dump where cobwebs and dust are more visible than shots of whiskey.

Without another word, I settle my debts. Not bothering to stay or greet the man, I slink out of the back door.

This is why you should always adopt a bar to call your own. I liken it to a good woman. You memorize every curve of her body, the way she breathes, her scent. In the case of Harold's, I know where the bathroom is and where the exits are.

I'm tipsy, but my tolerance is built up, so I don't worry about driving. Depending on the source, some will say I'm a better driver when intoxicated, at least that's what Chip says. It might be a combination of wound-up emotions or liquid courage, but I have to see Valerie right now.

I groan as I'm sent to voicemail again.

Flustered, I toss my phone against the dashboard.

I know better than to go to her house. Valerie and I have a strict policy, which in my foggy state, I'm ignoring.

Common sense hasn't entirely left my slow-functioning brain. I don't dare enter the compound with my pick-up, so I ditch it on the side of the road a mile or so back from the Atwaters' gate. It's crooked, but hidden in the dense brush. As long as it's out of sight, no one seeks out this road unless they're pursuing an Atwater.

And in my case, I am.

My footsteps crunch on the silt underneath as I walk up the steep terrain to the massive gate that's more fitting of a prison. Isn't it the truth that even if you have the freedom to leave, you're still shackled to what holds you there in the first place, and in this case, Valerie to Darren.

The House Without A Key

I try not to think about it. The liquor burns fire in my stomach as my gut twists with worry. Fishing in my jacket pocket for my bottle of antacids, I swallow a handful.

Valerie's going to be upset.

Hopefully, what I have to tell her will lessen her anger.

Before I can buzz the gate, it opens, inviting me in.

Like a madwoman, I watch as Valerie's tall shadow darts down the drive. We meet in the middle, halfway between the house and the front gate.

Her mouth's drawn into a tight line. "What're you doing here?"

No greeting, this can't be good.

"I came to check on you." Shoving my hands again in my jacket pocket, this time for warmth from her steely gaze.

"Is that smart?" she murmurs. "That's a risk I didn't think we could take."

"Darren's at the bar, the one on Mountain View."

"Harold's?"

"Yeah. His Jag's in the lot." I shrug, "I guess I figured now was as good a time as any."

"Now's not a good time." She wraps her arms across her chest.

"Is something wrong?"

"Allegra hasn't come home."

"Shit," I say. "Is that why you haven't returned my calls?"

"Yes," she runs a hand through her chestnut hair. "It's been stressful."

"Did she say where she was going?"

"The mall. I dropped her off this afternoon."

"Is she with..."

"...no." Her hands shake as they rub at the thin fabric covering her bony elbows. "I already called and checked."

I reach forward to touch her arm, but she jerks out of my

grasp. "Not here. We need to go somewhere else." My eyes scan around the inky blackness. The only illumination comes from the small solar-powered LEDs that line the path up the driveway. "I can't see shit."

"Darren wants it to feel like we're secluded out here, which we are, living on the side of a mountain."

I don't add that he didn't have to try hard for that one.

Her eyes fill with tears. "I don't know what to do."

"Let's talk about it."

"Follow me," she whispers. "The guest house has an outdoor camera, but the storage room off the gym doesn't. I use it to hoard our holiday decorations." She leads me a roundabout way to the side of the gym, and it's clear we're staying off the concrete path for a reason.

I wait as she opens a side door and flicks on the light switch before motioning me in. She wasn't kidding about the storage, it looks like Christmas threw up in here. There are rolls of wrapping paper and box after box labeled 'ornaments.'

Facing each other, I notice her red-rimmed eyes and the small wrinkles tugging at the creases. "I'm worried she's not coming home," she cries. "What if she ran away because Darren is such a helicopter parent? I've tried to offset his restrictions, but Allegra has to feel like she's living in a fishbowl."

"Does she have any money?"

"She could easily get it. She's resourceful, and I'm sure Coye would help her."

"She turns eighteen soon?'

"Yeah. This year. Then she's free to do what she wants." She groans, "Unfortunately."

We're silent for a moment. Valerie's eyes hover over a box in the corner that advertises a realistic but fake nine-foot Christmas tree. "I wonder if Allegra has noticed the tension with Darren and me, if she knows about..."

I interrupt. "Would it cause her to run?"

"Darren is all but flaunting his latest affair."

"Another one?"

"Still Sandra Declan, his personal assistant," she shrugs, "but there have been others."

"She's what, like thirty, thirty-one?"

"Close. Thirty-two."

"And what about you?"

"I'm left to pick up the pieces."

I don't want to ask, but I do it anyway. "You upset?"

"Not that he left. I know it's time." She grabs my wrist. "I didn't think this would be so hard."

"Life is hard, Val," I grunt. "Even for people like you that make something out of themselves."

"And now I'll lose it all."

"Don't talk like that. You built it together. Fair is fair, and half is yours."

"Except it's not..."

"What do you mean?"

She snaps. "I need to focus on my daughter. Now's not the time for this."

"For what?"

"Should I call the police?"

"It depends," I chew my lip. "Are you sure she's not hiding out with her boyfriend or crashing with a friend?"

"I don't know." She drops her head in her hands. "Everyone claims they haven't seen her today. I'm worried about her..."

"Are you ready for them to come sniffing around?"

"I have no choice. The longer I wait, the more suspicious it looks," she sighs. "Maybe I'll talk to the press first.

See if we can draw attention to her disappearance that way."

"That'll get the police fired up," I warn. "They'll come a-knockin' sooner rather than later."

"I know. I have to prepare myself for that." Valerie tilts her chin, so my bleary eyes meet her tear-stained ones. "I just have to trust that our skeletons stay put in their closets."

20

ALLEGRA

"Come on," he tugs my wrist impatiently. I wince where he grabs, the angry red marks a reminder of the rope and handcuffs.

The cowboy comes back with a ratty men's t-shirt that's about five sizes too big. Grateful for the length, it reaches an inch above my wobbling knees.

Muscleman eyeballs the dirty room disgustedly. "We're going to get you out of here."

"And go where?" I ask timidly.

"Where you'll be staying when you're with us."

"Who is 'us'?"

"We can talk about it later."

"Why can't I go home? Please," I try to sink down to my knees, but he jerks my elbow up. "Please! My mother and father will give you anything you want. Money, cars, jewelry."

"You're rich, are you?" His eyebrow raises. "We can talk about compensation later."

I start to protest, but his grimace reminds me to tread

lightly. With a giant step towards me, I leap back. "Good, you're already learning. What do you say to me?"

"Sir."

"Better, but what is the answer?"

I lower my gaze to my dirty feet.

"What always comes first?"

"The word 'yes,'"

He waits, tapping his sneaker on the floor.

"Yes, sir."

"Good girl." He leans forward to pat my hair. "I've got something to cover you so we can go outside." Before I can respond, a piece of fabric is thrown over my head. I feel some type of string or cord tighten around my neck.

"You'll follow me," Muscleman instructs, "or I'll pull on this," he gives a tug as it clenches around my throat, "and you'll strangle yourself to death. Do you understand?"

There's no air inside the darkness, just fear I'm afraid I'll choke on.

"Yes, sir." My voice is muffled, and I'm unsure if he can make out my words underneath the fabric.

"Good girl." His callused hand grabs mine, and I feel the deep lines and indentations of his skin against my soft one. He wrenches me forward as I walk in total blindness. It's as if we're playing a game, except I don't know the rules, following him on blind faith alone. A couple of times, I crash into his rigid back, sturdy as a tree trunk. It's almost painful how solid he is.

The cover-up is immovable, the fabric stiff. My inability to fully take a breath of air frustrates me.

I hear metal scraping, and it sounds as if a lock's being unchained. There's a smack as it clatters against wood. Then the slam of a door. Instantly, the air changes as a gentle breeze tickles the bare skin of my arms and legs. "Now two steps going down," he cautions before we continue. "Next," he says. "I'm going to lift you up."

Unsure if this requires a verbal response, I say nothing. He launches me over his shoulder like a sack of potatoes, and I can feel a draft on my bare ass where my shirt rides up. He doesn't seem to notice my discomfort as I try to reach my hands behind me to yank down the cotton. There's a beep of a key fob, and then a thud of what I presume is a trunk hatch.

"You're going to stay back here and keep down." His voice gruff, "Understand?"

"Yes, sir."

I'm laid out on some type of cotton fabric, likely a sheet or blanket. Behind the dark cover and in a small, confined space, the stench of urine and vomit overpowers me. Not to mention the body odor and fear that seeps out of my pores.

As if he agrees, he says, "We'll get you cleaned up in just a bit. Are you hungry?"

"Yes, sir."

"Okay, we'll stop at a drive-thru." He lists off a couple of options on the value menu, and surprised, he asks me to choose what I want. I respond before he braces the cord around my neck. "I'm shutting this now. Don't you dare let me hear you scream, understand?"

Coughing, I sputter.

"What was that?"

"Uh, yes, sir."

"Good girl." There's a tap on my forehead. "Time to be quiet."

The metal bangs above my head, signaling the trunk has shut. This time, I can scrape the top with my hand, and I struggle to remain calm. Panic rises in me, my inability to see and breathe properly combined with the minimal airflow causes a queasiness in the pit of my stomach.

Breathe, Allegra, I command. *Count to twenty, focus.*

I do that, and then I count to a hundred.

I listen for confirmation of where we're going. The whirring of the tires on different types of pavement. The long pauses as we slow to a crawl and stop, an occasional honk or bass from a car stereo.

We idle for longer than normal, and I assume we must be at the drive-thru. I hear his muted voice, but I can't understand what he's saying. A woman's voice chimes in, same effect. Unable to comprehend, I wonder if he's ordering food. My stomach growls, and we creep forward. Before long, we're traveling at a higher speed, and I wonder if we're on the interstate. I have no idea how long I'm in the back of the vehicle. It feels like forever, but it's hard when you only have your senses to rely on for time.

Eventually, we grind to a stop as the engine cuts.

A door slams. Then another. I feel his strong hands on my shoulders. "We're here," he greets me. "I'm going to carry you again. Reach your arms up."

I forget to respond with "yes sir," but he doesn't seem to notice. Again I'm launched over his shoulder as I droop over his back. He smells like a mix of cologne and sweat, and I can feel his clammy perspiration through his shirt, where my arms and face rest.

He stops two times, once when I hear a beep and then a whoosh of air. Maybe a gate, judging from the shrill noise it makes as it clicks open. The second time I feel the sinewy muscles in his right arm tense as he reaches forward, followed by the sound of a bell.

I'm resettled onto some type of seat. It doesn't feel as

hard as metal, so maybe a couch or fabric chair. Before I can react, the cord's loosened, and the hood comes off.

I rapidly blink, relieved to be able to see again, even if the room is cramped and dark. A black-out curtain covers what must be a window to the right of me. I'm seated on a small navy couch with a brown leather recliner to my left. The furniture is mismatched and old, as if someone left it out at a junk sale, and it was adopted and brought here. A wooden coffee table rests in front of me, and the only item of value is the television mounted on the wall.

Muscleman pushes the coffee table closer to me. "We're going to eat and then get you washed up." He lays the bag of food down and arranges my burger, fries, and water in front of me.

I want to scarf it down, yearning to taste the salty fries and fill my empty stomach. Brunch with my mom was a long time ago. An image of her face comes to mind, but I force it away.

Instead, I concentrate on my fingernails, dirty, and ripped. Before I eat, I ask if I can wash my hands first. He responds with an automatic "no." I'm about to shovel the food down when he barks an order. "Hold up your hands." Afraid he's going to handcuff me again, I shove them in my lap.

"Little girl," he grits his teeth. "I wouldn't do that if I were you." Bringing them up slowly, one at a time, he examines them. "You're disgusting. Why did I even want you?" he mutters. "Let me grab some hand sanitizer. Don't move," he commands.

My mouth waters.

I concentrate on my surroundings instead of the food in front of me. The kitchen is a few feet away, and he starts rummaging through a couple of oak drawers before he finds what must be antibacterial wipes. A fridge and stove are in view, but I don't see a microwave or dishwasher. Everything looks like it's been there for decades, from the faded linoleum floor to the rusted sink.

I don't bother to ask why I can't stand up and wash my own hands, terrified he'll take my food away or restrain me.

He strides back over to me and hands me a couple of wipes. I try and clean my hands as best as possible, wishing I could erase the memories of all the people that have handled me since the mall.

"Eat," he points down to my food. "Then we can talk about rules and expectations."

He doesn't turn on the television. Instead, he pulls a phone out of his pocket to watch something that has sound, but I can't hear it because he puts earbuds in.

I notice multiple phones lying around, and I wonder if they are burner phones or whatever you call them - disposable ones that keep your location hidden.

Forcing myself to chew and swallow each tiny bite, I don't want to get sick from devouring it too fast.

As I take one small nibble after another, I search for a clock. With no clue on the day or time, I feel out of sorts in addition to every other emotion. I don't see one on the wall and the oven blinks, signaling the time is wrong.

I glance for a watch on his wrist, but it's bare, which is weird to me. I don't think I've ever seen my father *not* wearing one unless he was changing them out.

One phone buzzes to life, and he jumps up quickly. His eyes never leave my face as he takes a couple of steps back toward the hall. I ignore his fixated stare as he has a tense conversation with someone while I finish my meal. I can only hear his clipped tone in response to them. It goes like this, "What do you mean?"

"I did what I was supposed to."

"How much?"

"Let me know, because if not, she's going to earn her keep."

The fries gurgle in my stomach, and I instantly feel bloated. Is Muscleman talking about me? His voice lowers to an incoherent jumble before he disconnects.

"Are you done?" he chirps in my ear.

"Uh-huh." I suck down the last sip of water with a straw.

"What was that?" His hands twist in my hair. Grabbing a chunk, he yanks me sideways towards him.

Tears spring to my eyes. "Yes, sir."

Instantly he releases me and straightens up.

"Do you need money?" I ask.

His stare admonishes me, but I don't stop. "My family has money," I whisper, "they will pay you *lots* of money if you let me go." I sniff. "If it's about that, I promise my parents will come through on their end. We could pretend you rescued me, and you'd get a reward or something."

He glowers at me.

"I'd never tell, I just want to go home." I clasp my hands in my lap. It's unclear if he's angry or intrigued. "Do you know how to get in contact with them?"

The tension in the air is suffocating.

I shift my gaze to the wall behind him. Pierce took my phone and whether the two men know each other hasn't been established. I want to ask, but it doesn't seem like a good time. "I can give you my mom's number, and she will take care of everything."

"Are *you* the one with the money?"

"No. But I'm their only child." I shake my head sadly. "My father would do anything, as long as you promise not to hurt me."

"I didn't promise." He lowers himself back into his chair. "In the meantime, we should discuss our business plan."

I gulp. "Business plan?"

"Yes. You are going to provide a service."

The food I just swallowed rises in my throat. "What...what do you mean?"

"Until your parents pay for your return," he motions toward his chest. "You work for me."

"Work for you, how?"

He looks at me like I've asked the stupidest question in the world. "You provide pleasure to men."

"Ah," my voice comes out shaky. "Like prostitution?"

"I prefer to call it an 'escort service.' It's a trade, fair and square." He raises an eyebrow at me. "And *you* have all the control."

"How so?"

"You'll be a high-end escort."

"You don't look it now, but I've seen some pictures of you. You're pretty when you don't look like a slob."

Ignoring his backhanded compliment, I hesitate. "To whom?"

"You don't need to concern yourself with the details. I'll take care of that. In return, you'll have a roof over your head and a decent wardrobe."

"But what if I want to go home?"

"You'll stop asking that." Abruptly he stands, smacking his hands against his knees. "It's not time for you to go home."

His eyes never leave my face as he walks toward me. Bending over the coffee table, he gathers up our garbage as I watch the tribal symbol tattoo dance on his arm. "For the first couple of days, you'll shadow and get adjusted to the house you'll live in. There will be other girls with you."

"What girls?" My eyes glance around my meager surroundings.

"They don't live here. I'll take you to the house after you're presentable." He puts his hands on his hips. "Right now, you smell like shit, and your looks aren't much better."

Should I point out if I had a bathroom, a shower, and a bed, I might be passable?

Nah.

"What about if I leave?" I stammer. "My family won't want to reward you for forcing me to be...an escort."

"Let's choose our words." He lifts my chin up. "I'm not *making* you. I'm allowing you the opportunity to better your life."

"I already have a good one." We lock eyes, his narrowed, mine tear-filled.

"Tell you what, little girl. You do as I say, and get along with your sister-wives, and we will see how it plays out. If I don't get paid by your father, you'll be working off his debt. That's all there is to it."

"Sister-wives?"

"That's what we call the girls at the house." He rubs a hand over his mouth. "You all work together for the greater good, as a team."

My knees tremble with fear. I can't risk the sound of my own voice.

"Is that a 'yes'?"

My mind races with the thought of random men touching my private parts, their hands, and...without finishing my train of thought, I stumble forward to release the meal I just finished. Muscleman stares at the vomit on the floor, repulsed. Scared of an outburst, I stay down on the floor, my gaze trained on something other than the contents of my stomach. I don't dare meet Muscleman's stern-looking face.

The tears become full-on sobs. Before I can control myself, I'm huddled beneath his towering limbs. I shove a hand in my mouth in a useless attempt to be quiet.

What will I tell my boyfriend, Coye? He's the only person I've ever been with. He'll never want me again. Not to mention, what about diseases and pregnancy?

I tense, waiting for Muscleman to strike, but his feet don't move from his standing position. On the verge of hysteria, I slap my palm against the floor, swaying my body back and forth.

He says nothing for a minute, retreating to the kitchen. Wiping my nose with my hand, I sink back on my heels. "You're done," he says with finality. "Time to clean this up." A wet towel is shoved in my grasp, and he points at the watery bile. My nose drips with snot as I wipe up the mess, trying not to repeat the same reaction again.

Taking the dirty towel from me, Muscleman tosses it in the trash. "Let's get you cleaned up and to bed." My bare feet drag down the hall as he leads me to a bathroom. It matches the rest of the house, worn and outdated.

"Do you need to use the toilet?"

"Yes, sir." I expect him to shut the door and wait outside, but he doesn't. I hurriedly sit down to pee, unused to having to go on command or be watched by another person, let alone a male. It takes me a while to relax, and my face burns in humiliation.

Without a word, he ignores me as he turns on the shower. The sound of running water makes it possible for me to relieve myself, and I quickly finish and flush the toilet.

"Arms up," he instructs, yanking the extra-large shirt over my lanky frame. Pointing to the yellowed tub which has rust stains around the drain, he motions for me to step in. It looks like it's never been cleaned by the amount of soap scum and dirt. A bottle of shampoo and a half-used bar of soap are visible on the fiberglass sides.

He shuts the shower curtain so it's half-closed. I watch as he reaches underneath the sink and reappears with a clear plastic bag. "This will be yours. You'll take it to the sister-wives' house." It contains travel-size bottles of shampoo and conditioner, a new bar of soap, a razor, a box of tampons, and a miniature can of shaving cream. There's also floss, a toothbrush, and some toothpaste. Nodding as he unscrews the bottle of shampoo, I stand under the warm water. He roughly lathers up my hair and massages my scalp, then moves the bar of soap around my body, making sure to scour every crevice. My face flames as he leaves no part untouched. He scurries up and down my skin as if it's a chore, like a caretaker would. After he finishes, he flips the lid down on the toilet seat and sits. "I'm going to watch you shave."

I lick my lips nervously. "Watch me?"

"Yeah, from here." He motions toward the razor and shaving cream in the plastic bag. "I want to make sure you don't slit your wrists." It hadn't crossed my mind at this point to cut myself, and I doubt he'd take me to the hospital, anyway.

Staring at him in wide-eyed horror, "Has that happened?"

"Yes," he gives me an evil wink, "but the worst is when we have to kill a girl who disobeys." He shakes his head as I clumsily scrape the plastic pink disposable razor against my stubble. The blade feels rough against my skin, and I'm not used to the flimsy grip I have on it.

"Poor girl, if only she had listened. She was chopped up

into little pieces and buried in the garden out back." He points to the wall. "I'll show you myself."

At this mention, I yelp, cutting myself. I watch as a trail of red runs down my leg.

"And the closet incident..." His voice trails off.

"So," contempt laces his voice. "Not only are you *not* potty-trained, you're unable to handle the art of shaving?"

I glare at him with thinly-veiled disgust.

He drones on about another girl who didn't listen to his instructions. Her punishment didn't fit the crime when he strangled her with a necktie, or so he claims.

Tuning parts of his story out, my mind's on overdrive with thoughts of dead females whose only mistake was encountering him.

Since Muscleman hasn't killed me yet, he definitely has an intended purpose for me. To make him money. Lots of it.

If I don't, then I lose my value.

I shudder underneath the stream of water as it loses heat. It's impossible not to be afraid of my future if my parents don't rescue me soon.

21

ALLEGRA

"Will you at least tell me something?" I consider the top of his head as he focuses on his cell.

"What?"

"Do they know I'm here yet?"

"Who?" Muscleman is distracted with his phone, his eyes glued to the screen. He's playing a game of some sort, and since he warned me about keeping the thin shower curtain open, it's in view.

I'm able to glimpse the time. It's after seven pm.

"My parents."

"Of course."

"Then why am I still here?"

"You'd have to ask them."

"Certainly," I reach my dripping hand out of the shower. "Can I make a call?"

He smacks my hand away with a glare. "Time to get out." I shut the water off and wait for him to throw me a threadbare towel to dry off with. He doesn't leer at my body but keeps his head down.

My wet hair drips water droplets down my back, and I

uncontrollably shiver, from fear or cold, it's hard to say. My spine tenses as he runs a hand down it. "You're freezing."

I nod. "Yes, sir."

Handing me a thin robe from the back of the door, he motions for me to put it on. A pair of nondescript flip-flops are underneath it. "Try these on. I think they might be the right size." He shrugs. "They used to belong to Olive, except she's no longer with us."

I can tell he wants a reaction out of me, so I stay silent.

"Are you ready?"

Ready for what, I want to scream.

Instead, I say, "Yes, sir." My half-closed lids burn from a lack of sleep and the steam of the shower. My body has been in a constant state of fight or flight, and I can feel the adrenaline starting to subside, at least for the moment.

"Grab your belongings."

I tilt my head.

"The plastic bag. That's yours to take."

I'm tempted to respond with a sarcastic, "Oh, how kind," but I doubt it will be well-received. Biting my lip, I towel off the razor and shaving cream can and replace them in the bag.

I watch him stand behind me in the mirror, both of our faces and bodies blurred by the fog, and I lower my head, grateful I can't stare at my own reflection right now.

"You need a brush," he remarks, catching his hand in my tangled, wet hair. "They'll have one at the house." I'm against using other people's hair tools but realize this hardly matters anymore. If you're willing to run a prostitution ring, I doubt you give a shit about lice.

"Let's go," he yanks my wrist in command.

I assume the fabric hood will go back over my head to keep me from seeing where we're headed. Surprised when it doesn't, he leads me farther down the hall to a back door, a window shade tilted precariously off of it.

His hands move deftly over a deadbolt and another three locks beneath it. He's done this a million times, hasn't he? I gulp as I consider the answer.

"The sister-wives' house is across the road." He grabs my elbow and leads me out into the dusk. I take a moment to peer across the street and look left, then right. He's not lying, the house in question is directly across the street. We stand in an alley, and I realize the back door faces the rear of a rambling house. A tall, wooden fence with pointed stakes encloses the yard, and I can't see anything but the slanted roofline.

He snaps his fingers. "Follow me."

It's no more than ten steps to the fairly-hidden latched gate. A metal padlock is attached, and he uses a key to unlock it, ushering me in front of him.

I expect to see a large backyard, but the house sprawls across every open area, making it impossible to have much in the way of a lawn. It's like a Lego fortress, each piece connected from a clear starting point. In this case, the original house. You can tell what's authentic and what's been added with time because each section seems to have its own color scheme. The white paint peels on the initial home, yet other parts have more of an eggshell color or an off-white that doesn't match. Even the windows have distinct differences.

I stop dead in my tracks when I realize the one feature they all have in common.

Every window is covered by vertical bars - metal ones that leave a minimal amount of gap between each one, maybe a tiny hand could squeeze through if it belonged to a toddler.

I tremble involuntarily.

I grew up behind iron gates, but they were to protect me from outsiders.

Instead of keeping people out, I realize these bars have the opposite purpose - to keep people in.

This revelation terrifies me.

Crossing my arms across my chest, I hug myself, my legs rooted to the spot. I notice the abundance of security cameras that hang off the eaves, and I slow my steps as Muscleman lengthens his.

"This is it?" I whisper.

"This is where the girls live, the sister-wives." I want to ask if this is where bad things happen, where girls are forced to turn tricks, but I swallow my question. The less I know right now, the better.

Muscleman gives the back door three sharp taps before he flips open a panel. It's artfully hidden behind the doorbell. He enters a code, and it coos in acceptance.

"We are in," he says as a joke, "Mission Impossible-type shit."

I want to run, tilting my body to shy away from him, and as if he anticipates, even expects this reaction, he tightens his grip on my elbow.

Holding my breath as we enter, I'm now facing fears I never knew to have.

22

DETECTIVE DELANEY

"Delaney," Chief Bratton screams through the phone, and I imagine the spittle that's flying in the air through the gap in his front teeth. "Why the fuck haven't you followed up with the Atwater's?"

I say nothing for a moment because after ten years with the police chief, I know his train of thought isn't complete.

"They are currently on Channel 12 News having a pity party."

I roll my eyes, silently mouthing the next words verbatim as they come out of his mouth.

"You realize our public image is already under intense scrutiny?"

I'm well aware that we've had a couple, er, challenges, in our division, to put it nicely.

I am also aware that this is an Atwater child, so a high level of interest is an understatement.

"Yes, I do, Chief." I remain impassive. He's taught me a valuable lesson over the years. Stoicism. "They haven't been available for questioning."

"Horseshit," he growls. "Not what it looks like to me."

"I should clarify - they haven't been welcome to an interview with me." I don't bother to add the obvious. That Valerie and I go way back, and it's not shocking she chose the press first.

"Who's in charge of this investigation?"

"I will be."

"Then act like it." Before I can respond, the line goes dead.

The man is like a father to me. All I ever wanted was to be him, bringing the bad guys to justice. Especially insidious creatures that harm innocent children.

Sighing, I dial Valerie Atwater's cell number, which strangely enough is still programmed in my phone. Odd, she hasn't bothered to change it.

I'm sent straight to voicemail.

The same goes for Darren's phone and their business line.

If I were following up on a date, I'd feel outright rejected. Not bothering to leave a message, I grab the keys to my beat-up Land Rover, one that has been off-roading, tires deep in the mud, up in the mountains, and is now permanently covered in clumps of hair.

The fur kind.

My fur baby, a Great Pyrenees, is a big lover and a big shedder. He appeared on a trail before me when I was hiking a few years ago. He had seen better days, his matted fur covered in blood, dirt, and leaves. His face was scratched up, like he had been in a fight with prickly bushes or tree branches. Thirsty and emaciated, I knew I had to act fast. He was timid but earnest, an unspoken understanding I was his only shot at food. Keeping his distance in case it turned out I wasn't his savior, he followed me down the mountain.

I only had some fruit and a protein bar, and as he

scarfed that down and drank some water from my bottle, I waited to see if he would get in the Land Rover with me.

After a staring contest to decide if we could trust one another, he made the first move by launching himself into the backseat. I made the second by bringing him down to civilization so I could take him to the vet. Even though the circumstances in which I acquired him were heart-wrenching, it was comical to watch the gigantic furball try and fold his body underneath the waiting room chair. Weighing in at over a hundred pounds, he attempted to disappear behind four metal legs.

I'm sure he had a different name at one point, just like I did.

Except I didn't know what his given name was, so I renamed him Falkor after I noticed his tail wagged the hardest after ear rubs. He's the spitting image of the lion-like character in "The Never-ending Story." It's fitting because he's a fan of a good ear scratching. Minus the fact he can't fly, at least that I know of. He thumps along, his massive paws match me step for step.

We bonded over our love of hiking, long trail walks, and our ability to sniff out bullshit. This is why it's probably a good thing he's at home, and not with me right now as I drive to the Atwater's' gated mountain mansion.

They are not like the local folk, as people in this city like to say.

Darren and Valerie Atwater own a blasting, drilling, and explosives company that specializes in mining and construction projects. Because of Darren's unique skillset as a principal engineer and Valerie's business acumen, they were able to build the company from the two of them to a two-hundred employee enterprise. They contemplated moving their headquarters to another state, but after a bad publicity storm a few years back, they changed their mind.

I never understood the issue. They worked out of a fancy trailer and only have fifteen local employees. It wasn't like they were putting a chunk of their workforce out to starve. Most of their organization was located across the country.

The Atwater's are known for their altruism but also for their ostentatious nature. This meant they hadn't gotten to the top without making enemies.

Jealousy and envy are perfect words to describe how people feel when it comes to them.

The way Darren drives his silver Jag around town.

The lavish trips they go on when they travel abroad.

Their second and third homes in Puerto Vallarta, Mexico, and Florida.

The gossip's now drifted to their own daughter, a high school senior, an aspiring model, and supposed shoo-in for Prom Queen.

Reportedly she's missing. But I wouldn't know, because Valerie hasn't communicated this to the police department or me. Instead, she chose to flaunt her face and story on the news.

I rest my head in my hands. Some things never change.

23

DETECTIVE DELANEY

I park at the wrought iron gate in front of the massive mansion the Atwater's built on the outskirts of town. It looms across a mountain range, ginormous in its entirety and the way it's constructed, stretching out in a way that causes you to squint, as if it's an optical illusion, the way it peeks out from what you assume is just mountains in your line of sight.

Except you'd never know it was here unless you *knew* it was here. Hidden behind centuries-old evergreen and pine trees, the barely two-lane road was built specifically for them, their private sanctuary accessible by this one path up the mountain. I can see the garage stalls and acres of green spread out around the house, except the gate is closed to visitors, and I can't access it without a code.

I beep the call button on the intercom.

Surprisingly, it's Valerie Atwater who answers without hesitation, as if she expected someone from the police department to arrive after she stepped off of the television screen. "I'm coming down from the main house."

She's used to snapping her fingers and getting what she wants.

"Okay."

Expecting her to open the gates so I can drive forward, she doesn't.

Instead, I scan the natural surroundings. Even I can admit it blends in nicely with the backdrop of the outdoors. From the road below, it looks like a castle in the sky. That is, if you can find the right angle to see a sliver of the beauty between the Aspen trees. Up close, I see how pristine and manicured they keep their spread.

My thoughts are interrupted by the familiar appearance of a tall, chestnut-haired woman. Valerie's looks are opposite her daughter's, but not in an unattractive way. It's abundantly clear where Allegra Atwater got her height and figure. Valerie's no less stunning, just a different type of breed. In her mid-forties, she could pass for Allegra's older sister instead of her mother.

Six feet tall and unafraid to wear heels, dress in the latest fashion, or care if you abhor or adore her, Valerie Atwater strides out of a metal side gate, her perfume engulfing me as she opens the passenger door.

"Devon," she settles in the worn leather seat, "it's been a while." She has the nerve to act like its second nature to be in my vehicle.

But it was, once upon a time.

Today she's no less impressive, except for her puffy eyes and tear-streaked face. She's casual in jeans and a light jacket over a striped shirt. Clutched around her wrist are the straps of a tan handbag.

"It has." I agree. "And because of the ruckus you're making, it's *Detective* Delaney."

My icy stare meets her gaze head-on. We have history,

her and I. I like to keep it that way, a chapter in both of our books that reads like a romance but ends with a thrilling twist.

She tries to be cordial. "Thanks for coming."

"You didn't invite me," I point out.

"But I did," she shrugs. "In my own way."

"From the news?" I arch a brow at her. "Was this how you planned to get the authorities' attention?"

She dares to puff up her chest. "It worked."

"It was negative attention, at least in my corner."

"But here you are."

"Believe me, I like foreplay, and this isn't it," I growl. "I've been trying to reach you. This place is concealed, and the metal gates have you locked up pretty tight. The word 'stonewall' comes to mind in regards to you and your..."

I can't say the word 'husband.'

"Darren." I finish.

"That's absurd. Allegra's my only child!"

I give her a death glare. "Is that a fact?" She has the decency to peer down at her lap. I reprimand myself for even mentioning children.

Time to redirect. "Speaking of, we're going to want to search the premises. Will that be an issue?" I inquire. "Do you need an attorney present? Will we need a search warrant?"

Unflinching, she says. "No. I don't need my attorney present. He's expensive as fuck, and I have nothing to hide. By all means, search away."

"Any reason you didn't want to let me through now?"

"Besides the camera crews that will be heading up here shortly?"

"Again?" I shake my head in disgust. "For what? Another ploy for attention?"

Jutting her chin out, she snaps. "Channel Eight wants to film in Allegra's room."

"We need to establish a timeline of her disappearance and walk through the chain of events that led to now," I say through clenched teeth. "Our focus isn't creating a news story until we have the facts and can direct the narrative."

"Then let's talk," she muses. "Preferably somewhere else."

"The police station?"

"If you insist. I'd rather a coffee shop. Or park in the wilderness." She adjusts the visor, the sun hitting her in the eyes. "Look, I know I'm a suspect. You'll want to talk to our staff I'm sure, which is no problem."

I stay silent.

"Can we talk alone first?" She grabs my wrist. "I need to clear my head outside of the compound." My response is a three-point turn, so I'm straddling the road correctly, facing down the mountain.

"Any place in particular?" I know I sound like I'm catering to her, which is precisely what I want her to think, but I'm not. It's in my favor if she *believes* she has the upper hand.

"Can we grab a cup of coffee? I don't want to go inside, but I could use some caffeine."

"Sure. Pick a spot."

"How about Trudie's? It's where the old bagel shop used to be."

"Done." What I notice about Valerie beside her expensive watch is that she really is cut from a different cloth. She has no hang-ups about the dog hair on the seat or the dust accumulating on the dashboard. I knew her from before, and she didn't put on airs then, but people change, especially when money talks.

That, or maybe she's reached her exhaustion limit. Her

daughter has been missing since yesterday afternoon or evening, depending on your source.

I decide to start small and build on verifiable facts I already know. It's impossible to sit beside Valerie without concentrating on our past. This makes me nervous, so I rattle off easy questions, dipping my toe into the trenches. "What's Allegra's middle name?"

"Eleanor."

"She has a unique first name. Is it a family name, or how did you come up with it?"

"You really want to know?"

"I asked." It comes out gruff.

Grateful for the question, she elaborates. "Allegra's named after this woman I encountered as a teenager. She was drop-dead gorgeous. I used to do some modeling with her, but she was in another class entirely. Cheekbones up to her ears, beautiful blue eyes. The shyest, sweetest thing you'd ever met. A soft-spoken Midwesterner until she strutted on the runway. Then she had this confident alter-ego who could stomp all over you. But in a good way."

"I've seen pictures of your daughter. You share the same bone structure. She's got your cheekbones." It's a compliment, and she takes it as such. "The name suits her."

"Yes, it does. And thank you," Valerie murmurs. "But, I hate that."

"What?"

"Like what are you supposed to say when people compliment your kid's beauty? It sounds pompous to thank them just because genetically, it's your DNA."

"I have no idea. But Allegra's your daughter, so it's okay to take credit."

Slowly she nods. "I guess. Anyways, she was this happy

baby, and the name means 'lively,' so it was a perfect fit. Her middle name is Darren's mother's name."

"Speaking of mothers, how is yours?" Valerie drops her voice. "Is she still in remission?"

"Yeah, she is." I wring my hands. "And still as ornery as ever."

Valerie launches straight into a high school memory about my mother, and I tense up. Now is not the time to take a drive down memory lane.

I switch gears.

"You were living with the Ellis family when I knew you," I point out, "than that other foster family, the Hewitt's. You ever hear anything from your real mama?" I don't mean it to be condescending, but it sounds that way.

I can tell my words hurt Valerie because she clenches her jaw. "No, she's dead now." She cocks an eyebrow at me. "I figured since it's been profiled in multiple stories and magazine articles, you'd have read she reappeared in my life on her death bed. Of course, she didn't take any responsibility for my childhood."

"Don't worry. I know you grew up rags to riches." It comes out a bit smug. She's bringing out my worst today. In the interest of rebuilding our trust and keeping her ego inflated, I better tone down my acerbic commentary. She *did* just have a daughter go missing. "I think it's commendable how much you donate to the women's and domestic violence shelter."

She shoots me a barbed look. Flattery will get me nowhere with her, so I change direction. "My question is, could your success story have contributed to a situation where you might have gained some enemies? Namely, any that might want to harm your daughter?"

Valerie leans back against the seat. She bites her lip and

true to form, it means she's contemplating my words. I'll let her ponder this as we reach the drive-thru of Trudie's Coffee on Sullivan Street.

At the drive-thru, I break the silence. "Still iced black coffee with a splash of milk?"

She gives me a light tap on the shoulder. "I've evolved to iced lattes. Almond, please. Are you still plain old black coffee?"

"With one packet of Splenda."

"Creature of habit."

I order my coffee and her latte. The lot's relatively empty, but I don't want to draw attention to us, so for privacy's sake, I drive to the last corner space and park. We sit in companionable silence for a moment as we sip our drinks and gather our thoughts.

"Walk me through the weekend. Start with Friday."

"Umm...Friday night, she had a couple of girlfriends over after they had cheer practice." Valerie lists the names and scrolls through her phone for their contact information along with their parents. "All three stayed the night minus one girl who went out of town with her parents the next day."

"Enemies?" I unbuckle my seat belt and turn to her. "Any you know of? Maybe some you've thought about but haven't said out loud?"

Closing her eyes, she murmurs, "Yes, of course."

My briefcase, not as classic as the Givenchy that rests at her feet but just as durable, holds my notepad and a Montblanc pen I consider good luck. "I'm going to take notes."

"Certainly." She opens her eyes to stare at me. "There're a couple business associates we've had to sue. And we've been sued. All of those are public record, and I'm sure Darren can elaborate, or you can search them online."

"Okay." I tap my fountain pen against my notepad. "Allegra's obviously beautiful, wealthy, and as a high school senior, that can cause jealousy amongst her peers. Is there anyone she's been having issues with? A friend, boyfriend, or someone she's rejected?"

"No." Valerie is firm. "She's not allowed to date."

I keep my sentiments to myself. "Is that your rule?"

"I agreed to it," she twists the straw in her plastic cup. "It was Darren's suggestion, but to keep a united front, we both have to be on the same page, so I humor him."

She might've shut down my question, but I'm not going to let her skirt the issue. She keeps tugging her ear, as if hearing herself tell a lie out loud is painful.

"Okay, so without Darren here, let me ask again. Anyone she sees behind your back that you suspect or know about?"

"No." Another pull to the ear, her diamond stud catches the light. Valerie opens her mouth, and I wait her out. A brief pause follows. "We didn't have all the temptations of kids these days. Cell phones, laptops, iPad, Tinder. Snapchat. It's possible she met someone through an app or online."

"Fair enough." I taste the last drop of my coffee. I can't decide if it tastes bitter or if my mood has infected it.

"Do you monitor Allegra's accounts and social media?"

She grimaces. "Not as much as I should."

"Are you opposed to me pulling phone records for not only Allegra but you and Darren as well?"

I watch a sliver of fear settle on her face. "No. I guess that would be okay. Darren isn't going to be thrilled about that, but if you think it'll help the investigation..."

"It certainly won't hinder it." My jaw clenches. I don't want to ask, but I have to. "How is your marriage?"

"Hanging on by a thread." She's forthright. "We've been

married a long time, seventeen years now, have a successful company, have a child, but something always has to give."

"Any reason to suspect Darren would hurt your daughter?"

"Absolutely not. He's a great father to our daughter."

There's that acrid taste again. I swallow it. "But *not* husband?"

"A great father," she echoes. "Devon, humor me. I know you will inspect every facet of our decades plus-marriage. Do not put words in my mouth."

"It's what you *didn't* say that has me worried."

"That's awfully assumptive." She slumps against the seat. "You're right, of course. We've been struggling, but nothing financial, and nothing with Allegra. She has no idea about our marital problems. We hide them well."

"Everyone says that."

"We don't sleep in separate rooms. We go on vacation together as a family. We don't bad mouth each other to her. We are in survival mode right now, but I'm confident we will get back to a good place..." She sighs. "If only Allegra could be found safe, I know we'd resolve to try harder."

"Would she have run away?"

Valerie fidgets when I ask this. "I don't know."

"Pivoting back to the rest of the weekend, what did she do Saturday and Sunday?"

"She hung out at the house and watched a movie with me. We watched that funny Bridesmaids movie with Melissa McCarthy."

"Where was Darren?"

"He was out."

"Where?"

A hardness appears in her green eyes. "You'd have to ask him."

"You don't know?"

She grits her teeth. "I know what he told me."

"Which is?"

"Poker night."

"Where?"

"One of his friends, Lloyd Saffell. He has a house on the outskirts of town. Think they played there."

"And you don't believe your husband was at poker night?" She doesn't respond, choosing instead to pick at her once-manicured nails. I can tell she's been chewing them by how ragged they are.

"He has a lot of secrets lately."

I interrupt, but she holds up a hand to stop me. "It doesn't mean they're connected to Allegra's disappearance. I think he's having a mid-life crisis."

I drop that line of questioning. For now. "Did he come home over the weekend?"

"No."

"The day in question, Sunday. What happened Sunday?"

"Allegra asked to go to the mall. She wanted to get something to wear for pictures next week. She was chosen to be the spotlight editor of the e-newsletter that goes out to the high school." Tears stream unchecked into the collar of her shirt. "The school planned to post a profile picture up with her bio."

"Mall meaning Sheffield? How did she get there?"

"I dropped her off."

"The mall opens at noon on Sunday. What time?"

"Close to one. Probably a quarter till one. We stopped and had brunch beforehand."

"Where?"

"The Marketplace across the street."

"What entrance did you drop her off at, and what was

your agreement on pick-up?" Valerie goes through the timeline, which I've already memorized, but I want to make sure she's consistent.

She is.

"Why doesn't Allegra have a car?"

"Her father's decision," she sighs. "He doesn't think it's necessary until she goes to college. She borrows our vehicles, or I give her a ride."

I'm glad I'm not at Darren's poker table because I make a face.

Defensive, she retorts. "I actually like that she doesn't have a car. It might sound weird, but it's nice for me. We spend a lot of time driving to activities, and it forces us to talk." Her voice catches in her throat, "Or so I thought." Her knuckle moves into her mouth to cover a sob.

"Do her friends drive her places?"

"Only if Darren doesn't find out. I try and pick my battles. Darren thinks every teen is distracted, high, or drunk driving."

"Did you see Darren on Sunday?"

"Not until later. He stopped home that evening after Allegra still hadn't come home."

"Did he stay on Sunday at the house?"

A pained expression crosses her face. "No."

I hide my astonishment at how irretrievably broken her marriage is and my triumphant satisfaction behind it. I can tell she's done with the questions. Just like when we were younger and in a heated discussion, her body is unyielding, her shoulders tight and her jaw set.

"That's all," I say.

Valerie visibly relaxes, collapsing back against the headrest.

"I'll drop you off. Make sure Darren knows I want to talk to him ASAP."

The silence, once amicable, seems fraught with tension, and I don't know how to fix it at this moment. There's a lot she's not saying, and it's that elusive behavior that makes me wonder what's going on behind that beautiful face of hers.

As we drive back to the Atwater compound, I don't know about her, but all I can see are the places in the city we used to go together. My face flames with heat as we pass the once-empty field we lost our virginity together in. I want to mention it, but considering the circumstances, it's inappropriate and likely unwelcome.

24

DETECTIVE DELANEY

When I pull the Atwater's' phone records, I begin with out-of-state numbers. There are two different California numbers Valerie called on Sunday, the day Allegra went missing. There are pages to sort through, but first, I address these.

The first account belongs to Mark Kauffman. His son, Coye, is the owner of the number Valerie called. Suspicious, since Coye is in college, I almost fall out of my desk chair when he explains he's Allegra's boyfriend.

Coye's alibi is rock solid. He had a pick-up soccer game that afternoon. He provided the field he played on, the names of the guys on his team, and the Facebook group he's a part of that organizes the Sunday league. He definitely was over three hundred miles away in California, no doubt about it.

Interesting enough, the second number is disconnected. It's a different area code, so it wasn't a misdial. I'll have to do some checking.

Next, I talk to Julie Cambrero, the classmate who's confused as to why she's a part of this investigation. She confirms she goes to school with Allegra but that they aren't close friends. I ask her about Coye.

"Tell me about Allegra's boyfriend."

"She's not allowed to have one."

"She does, though, doesn't she?" It's like I've stunned her into silence, the only sound is the blare of speakers in another dumpy office.

"I don't know," she hesitates.

"Yes, you do. Look, Julie, we want to find Allegra. She's not in trouble with us, she's not in trouble with her parents, she's not in trouble, period. And you aren't, either. Bottom line, we want to make sure she's safe. As you can imagine, her sudden disappearance is scaring people in the community, not to mention her family and friends. Are you afraid?"

"No."

"Why not?"

"I think she probably ran away."

"You do?" I tap my Montblanc on my blotter. "How come?"

"Because the guy she's in love with lives in California. She wanted to be with him. She thought he might cheat on her if she couldn't get out there fast enough."

"Allegra told you this?"

"No, not exactly. But I heard it."

"You mean, from gossip?"

"No, not gossip. I heard Allegra say it at her locker. It's next to mine, and I listened to her complain to her friend Monica. She thought Coye, her boyfriend, might dump her for another girl."

"Did she have proof of that?"

She shrugs her shoulders. "No idea."

"Did you meet him?"

"No. He doesn't visit here. Allegra's dad is like, psycho.

He'd probably kill her and the dude." Her face goes ashen. "Sorry. I shouldn't have said that."

I don't bother to add it might very well be the truth. "Have you seen any pictures of Coye Kauffman?"

"Yeah."

"How?" I ask. "Social media?"

"No. Allegra didn't dare post about her and Coye's relationship. Even when she and her mom went out at the beginning of summer to California, she didn't brag online about it." Her face reddens. "I might've eavesdropped as she told her friends about her vacay. All I do is work, and she lives a far more interesting life than me." She sounds envious of Allegra's life, which isn't surprising.

"A trip to see Coye?"

"Yeah. Her mom rented them a beach house at the beginning of June."

"Where did you see pics of him?"

"Coye's on her cell. Her home screen. He's the picture when she enters her passcode."

"On her cell?"

"Uh-huh."

This isn't adding up for me. If Allegra can't have a boyfriend, a car, or openly date, then I doubt she would parade an older, out-of-state guy on her cell, visible to anyone who picked up her phone.

Including her father, Darren Atwater.

Sure, she's a teenage girl. She's going to brag and talk about her boyfriend. But I doubt she would change her phone screen picture every time she came in contact with her father. That would be too tricky. And oddly enough, when I pull Allegra's cell records, there are hardly any calls between her and Coye's number.

Hmm...time to keep digging.

What I find out is enough to make me take a boxing class so I can take my frustration out on something else. Keeping my composure, I ask Valerie to come down to the station. I preface it like I need her to sign a form so I can legally pull Allegra's bank account statements.

When she arrives, I motion for her to take a seat in my office. I try not to stare at her usually shiny but lackluster hair or tired eyes, keeping my empathy bottled up. I'm frustrated with her, I remind myself.

Even in the short period since I've seen her, she looks like she's lost weight. Her gray slacks bunch around her legs, and her belted Burberry trench swallows her up.

I begin quietly. "You lied to me."

"What?" Her response is terse. Her eyes are redder than the other day, they look like someone rimmed them with fiery burgundy eyeshadow.

"I don't like being lied to."

"I don't understand," she shrugs helplessly.

"That makes two of us." I stroke my chin. "You took my virginity, and now you want to come after my career?"

A flash of light clouds her emerald eyes. I can't tell if it's from anger or recollection, but I'm hoping for the latter. "I beg your pardon?"

"I have more questions than answers."

"What're you saying?" she huffs. "Spit it out, Devon."

"Allegra has a second phone, does she not?" I keep my voice neutral. "Tied to Mark Kauffman's account? His son Coye, Allegra's not-so-secret boyfriend, is also on the family plan."

Her forehead tries to wrinkle. The fillers only let it move an inch. "What do you mean?"

"What do *I* mean?" I kick my foot out, thumping the metal desk. "I *mean*, you lied to me."

"Yes," She physically deflates in the chair. "Allegra has another cell."

"Is there a reason you didn't tell me?" I lean back in my chair when what I really want to do is yank her by her messy ponytail. "Or the police you have on a manhunt looking for your daughter?"

"Her father doesn't know."

"Darren doesn't know about what?" I intone, "the boyfriend or the phone?"

"Both." She fidgets nervously with the belt of her trench. "I shouldn't call him a boy, he's a young man and a sophomore in college."

"Is it serious between them?" At least with Valerie, who took the plunge at nineteen, she doesn't respond with some dumb shit parents usually say about high school romances. They dismiss it as "puppy love" or question how serious it can be.

Pretty serious, folks. I'm looking at my first love. Or more like breathing fire at her.

"I think so, but it's a crapshoot, you know? He's a good kid from what I've seen. She seems happy with him, and he treats her well. I've taken her to visit him a couple times in Cali."

"Are you referring to a trip in June?"

The color drains from her face. "We visited him in June, yes." She falters. "Allegra hopes to attend journalism school out there and model, but you never know what will happen between now and when she graduates high school."

"And Darren doesn't know about him?"

"No. He wouldn't approve. Coye is in college."

Valerie doesn't elaborate, so I have to pry. "Is there a reason he's so overprotective?"

She brushes a strand of hair that's escaped her limp

ponytail. "Imagine if you had a daughter." I wince at her words, pushing my chair back further from my desk to distance us. A slap would have hurt less.

"Shit," a hand swats her forehead. "I'm not trying to be insensitive."

I frown, "You aren't, are you?"

She decides to start chewing a fingernail.

I take a deep breath. "You know, it wasn't just *you* that lost *our* baby."

"I know," she whispers. "And I know I ran. I couldn't...I couldn't handle the disappointment in your eyes, the blame."

"Blame?" I sputter. "That's unfair. I didn't hold you responsible then, and I certainly don't now. It was nature taking its course."

She shuts down, her body rigid. Back to the question at hand, she gives me her perspective. "Darren and his first wife, Elizabeth, had a daughter." Wringing her hands in her lap, she adds, "She died from an accidental drowning as a toddler. Darren's always been overprotective of Allegra, of her image. He's a strict father, a controlling one, but it's born out of love."

Isn't that what they all say, I murmur in my head.

"So many of us feel like we have no control over what our kids are exposed to these days. We can only limit their exposure to a degree. Darren doesn't like what she wears, and he hates she's growing up. He's a typical dad that fears he's losing his hold on his little girl who's not so little anymore."

My emotions are back in check. "And what about you?"

"I don't want to lose her by keeping her on a tight leash. That breeds resentment. I think it's more hazardous to tell Allegra she can't date and then have her secretly hide it from us. The last thing I want to do is drive a wedge between us during her teen years."

"That sounds reasonable."

She starts to sob. "So many of her friends have waged war with their parents. I'd rather her be honest about who she's with and where she's going."

I'm not in the mood to personally hand her a tissue, so I do the next best thing and throw her the box.

"In regards to Coye, I'm assuming this secret is no longer private?" Her voice is muted behind the tissue, "That Darren will find out?"

"This is an open police investigation. Nothing should be classified. Your daughter is missing," I say with emphasis, "and *you* want to keep things from *me* because Darren didn't know? Grow the fuck up, Valerie." I add her maiden name, which fires her up.

Jaw set, she sulks. "It's been Atwater for seventeen years, Devon."

"Who cares?" I say. "I knew you before you became a fucking Atwater and you'll always be that girl to me." I run a frustrated hand through my silver hair. "You're fucking impossible."

"You can't talk to me like this," she seethes. "I'll lodge a complaint with the Chief of Police."

"Oh, really," I snort. "Go ahead. He'll pull you and your shit husband into his office, and we can discuss every little detail you lied about. In fact, I welcome it. Maybe I'll be the one to file a formal complaint so the Atwater's can be interrogated for hindering our investigation."

Now it's her turn to flinch.

Slapping my palm on the metal surface, I say. "I am trying to help you. I have a police force trying to help you. This is all for *and* because of Allegra." I swipe my hand across my desk, piled high with loose papers and files. "All of this. If you have anything to hide, I swear to God, Valerie, you better lay your cards on the table right now.

Her hands clasp together in her lap.

"I mean it. It will all come out in the wash." I continue, "and what then? It might be too late to save her. Money can't solve everything, Valerie."

Quiet for a moment, I strain to hear her next words. "I never understood that expression."

"Excuse me?"

"'It all comes out in the 'wash.' What does that even mean?"

"When we start digging, nothing is off-limits. Everything leaves a permanent stain no matter how thorough you are in cleaning it up.

A blight or some type of residual is always leftover."

"So nothing is a clean slate? Even with us?"

"Exactly."

"Don't you dare bring our past into this," she hisses. "Just because I didn't want to be stuck with you doesn't give you the right to verbally attack me."

I whistle through my teeth. "I forgot how tiring it is to deal with people like you."

"Oh, a jab at the rich person?"

"Actually, no. You and I go way back before you had a dime. I've seen you at your worst. I don't hate people because they have money. I hate individuals that think their positions of power put them above my call of duty, especially when a minor's involved."

I twist the knife in deeper. "It's your daughter. You should be ashamed." I rise to stand. "Now get out of my office."

Surprised she doesn't follow my lead, I lean against my desk, impatiently waiting.

Instead of hurrying to her feet, she settles back in her chair. "I'm sorry. You're absolutely right. I'm..."

I walk to my closed office door. "No need to apologize. And *we* will wipe the slate clean, Valerie, regardless of how you feel about the expression. Right here and right now. But you forget, we are on the same team. Regardless of our history, I want your daughter back safe."

"I know." Her lower lip trembles.

I clench my hands, wanting nothing more than to hold her. Her public persona is a façade, and I watch it crumble and become unvarnished, like her demeanor.

Matter-of-factly, she states, "Darren is having an affair."

A second ago, I wanted her out of my office. Now I sag against the door. "Care to tell me about it?"

"Not really, but I will." Squarely looking me in the eye, she continues, "There have been a few." I peruse my notes, pretending I don't know the name of the latest off the top of my head. "Sandra Declan?"

"Yes, Sandy."

"She's not married?"

"No." She crosses her legs. "She's young, early thirties."

"And she's worked for you both for how long?"

"Five years. I found out about it a couple years ago, but I assume it's been going on longer."

"And you want to divorce him?"

"He asked me first," she sighs.

"Could be a motive."

"If you think Darren leaving is motivation to hurt my daughter, you're crazy."

"What about to hurt him? Or ruin his relationship with Sandy?"

"I don't have a motive for either. I don't care if he has a mistress."

"Wow. How things have changed," I point out. "You didn't used to value open relationships."

Now it's time for her to wield the sharp knife. "Just because I don't like being cheated on while someone's away at basic training doesn't mean I feel the same about my marriage."

And plunging in deeper, she goes for the kill. "It also doesn't help when you're pregnant with their child, the father is nowhere to be found. Probably why both the unborn baby and the relationship died."

The words are cold enough to send a chill down my spine.

I own it. I deserved that.

Crouching down beside her chair, I wrap my fingers around her wrist. "I'm sorry." I'm tempted to bury my head in her lap, but I know it's wrong, so I don't. I have more self-control in my old age.

"I know," she whispers.

"I can't take back what happened." My own eyes burn with regret and possibly tears. "I was selfish, but I didn't cheat on you. That was an ill-timed rumor. I swear on our unborn child's life that I didn't. Not that it matters now."

"Just find Allegra." She runs her other hand over my cheek, "and I'll consider it a wash."

I soften my tone. "Are you upset about Darren's affair?"

"*Affairs*," she corrects me. "I used to feel unlovable. That I was somehow a lesser person because my own husband didn't find me desirable. But when Darren and his first wife, Elizabeth, lost their little girl, the two of them never recovered. She turned to pills and self-help books, and Darren turned to me. I was his secretary, and I guess his wandering eye couldn't be tamed, then or now."

"Why didn't you tell me when it happened?" I ask. "Why did you isolate yourself?"

"Because you were a shell of a person," she says simply. "You were lost, and I couldn't save you. Hell, I couldn't save myself."

Valerie's phone vibrates, and it's her turn to hurriedly stand. "Thanks for the chat, but I've got to get going."

Before I can open my mouth to speak, she disappears out of my office. No backward glance or mention again of the past.

She's gone.

Just like she was back then. When at Atwater is finished with you, there's no time for sentiments.

25

ALLEGRA

The dilapidated house is not what I expect inside.

It's decorated, but like Muscleman's house, it reminds me of a thrift store, where nothing seems to belong together. Dusty fake potted plants are next to a glass fish aquarium that has no water and no sign of life.

When we step directly into a large kitchen and dining area, I notice the appliances first. They aren't as outdated as the ones in the last house, but upon closer inspection, I spot a metal lock latched to the refrigerator. The cabinets are also padlocked.

Weird.

The only furniture in the kitchen is the corner table, a built-in, made of pale stained wood, like oak.

It's noisy in here, but for different reasons than television or radio sound. The voices belong to females, one wails, another has a high-pitched squeak that echoes down the small hallway and grates on my nerves.

A narrow hallway leads straight to the front door, visible from where I stand in the kitchen. My heart pounds in my chest as a glimmer of hope makes me antsy. I shift from foot to foot as Muscleman strides farther into the house, clearly at ease here.

"Sir," a female screeches before a face appears. This woman has long, dark hair that looks like it could use a wash. When she's near, I note the purple streak in her locks that adds a punk rock vibe. She's wearing a tank-top and terry cloth shorts, nothing on her feet but chipped yellow toenail polish.

"Ruby," he greets her with a kiss on the cheek. "How're you?"

"The same." She gives him a tired smile. "Just trying to keep everyone in line."

"Well, I have someone who won't trouble you a bit." Poking me, "Will ya, newbie?"

I say nothing at first until he elbows me cruelly in the ribs. "No, sir." I hug the plastic bag of items to my chest, unsure what to say or do. The woman, Ruby, has large, red lips. I wonder if this is how she got her name.

With a welcoming smile, she leans forward to pat my shoulder. "Nice to meet you." I glance at her with interest. Maybe she will be the one to help me escape. But if she hasn't left, then why would I be afforded the opportunity?

My heart sinks.

"Where'd you find her? She's a pretty one."

He seems uncomfortable, his eyes twitching. "A friend of a friend."

"What's she going to be doing?"

"TBD." He shrugs, "I'm waiting on more information. I have some ideas, but we can't do anything with her until I hear from him."

My ears perk up at this, and he pauses. "Never mind," he touches Ruby's shoulder. "We can talk about it after..."

"Certainly."

He moves a finger to her lips. "Are you ready for our anniversary?"

"Yes," she claps her hands in front of her. "Can you believe it's been three years?"

"Oh, you've been together that long?" I say, "Congratulations!"

Peering at me in confusion, Ruby nervously taps her foot while Muscleman fixes me with a steely gaze.

She waits for him to address me, and when he doesn't, she offers. "Uh, no, not a couple, at least in the traditional sense. Three years as a sister-wife in the house."

When I'm nervous, I sometimes giggle, so in response, I cover my discomfort with anxious laughter.

He's unimpressed. "That was stupid," Muscleman snarls. "Don't speak unless spoken to."

I keep my mouth shut as they continue their conversation.

"Wait," he snaps his fingers. "What was that? Someone's missing something." He turns to me, and I realize he's waiting for me to address him.

"Yes, sir," I say as he mutters something under his breath.

"Whatever," he scowls. "Ruby, how many girls we got right now?"

"Four now with her." She crosses her arms. "It's too bad about..."

He clenches his fists. "Don't you dare mention her or..."

I interrupt. "What happened to Olive?" Clasping a hand over my mouth, I've spoken without permission. To hide my distress, I lower my eyes to the tile floor.

I keep my head down, but it's not enough to escape his wrath.

"Where can I take her?" Muscleman grabs me the elbow.

"I need to tend to something."

"She can have Olive's old room, number four." Ruby sighs. "I still need to burn her sheets."

What happened on that bed, I wonder as dread covers me like a heavy blanket.

I'm dragged by my elbow down a hallway off the kitchen. I can tell by the uneven step that this must be one of the multiple additions to the house. There are two doors on one side of the hall, both closed, and another door's ajar to my right. The rooms are labeled with a bold number written in black marker.

Muscleman grips my arm, his fingernails sinking deep into my skin. Jerking a set of keys out of his pocket with the other hand, I watch in horrid fascination as he shoves a key in the lock. I have no idea how he keeps them all straight. Various colors and sizes occupy a full keyring.

Letting go, he pushes me over the threshold, causing me to lose my balance. I stumble toward a pair of dark curtains on the opposite wall of the narrow room.

"Take your robe off," he commands.

"What, why?" I spin around, alarm in my eyes.

In one motion, he yanks the fabric belt off my waist and replaces it around my neck, tightening his hold on me. "Take it off."

Wordlessly, I let the robe drop off my shoulders and fall to the ground.

Venom drips from his voice. "Look at me."

I shake in fear as I move my gaze up to his hardened eyes. "You do not talk unless you are asked a question. *Ever.* Then you respectfully answer after you're given the go-ahead. Do you understand me?"

"Yes, Muscleman."

This is the wrong name to call him, and he responds by

slapping my cheek.

"You are never to call me anything else," he thunders. "I am *sir* to you."

"Yes, sir," I reply, but it's too late.

His hands are back around my neck. "You're getting whipped for this." My protests aggravate him further. "You will learn to control your emotions." He pinches my shoulder with his fingers, pressing them into my tender skin. "Do you understand me?"

"Yes, sir."

"I'll be right back," he says. "Don't you dare move."

Frantic, I dart my eyes around the little bedroom as soon as he leaves. I fling the curtains open, only to become tangled in the heavy fabric. There's no way out, I discover, finding myself face to face with a dirty window and metal bars.

Twirling around, I search the room for something I can try and break the glass with. There's a cramped metal bed. One pillow. A sheet. No lamp.

I tiptoe over to the open doorway he exited.

Scanning the hall, I wonder if I can find an escape route. I shove out of the flip-flops and notice the corridor to the left stops in a dead end. With no choice but to go back the way he brought me, I run towards the kitchen, praying I can make it to the back door we came in.

I don't get far.

Both Muscleman and Ruby with the big lips are standing in the kitchen, their backs turned to me. She removes something from a drawer to hand to him. Without pausing to consider what it is, I run full-speed ahead down the hallway that leads to the front door.

A large living room on my left-hand side is full of chatter, and three girls with three pairs of eyes stare at me.

One in admiration, one in disgust, one in concern - all with surprise. But none seem alarmed by my nakedness or my flailing arms.

Without speaking, I lunge for the front door. Of course, it's locked, dead-bolted, and chained. One of the girls lets out a yelp as the metal hits the door with a whack. This draws the attention of both the Muscleman and Ruby.

I jiggle the lock and steal a quick peek over my shoulder. The fury in his eyes tells me I'm in deep crap if I can't escape. Even the girls avert their gazes as if making eye contact with him will only provoke him further.

He closes the gap between us as he closes in on his intended target.

Me.

I stand at an angle so I can watch his movements. He rubs his hands together like he's gearing up to swoop in for the kill. I won't give up on the door, even though I know it's useless at this point. I know I'm in a pile of steaming shit. There's no question about that, which for some reason makes me want to fight harder.

So I do, to my detriment.

Behind me, his breath tickles my neck as my bare feet are lifted from the tile. He slings me over his shoulder, and his hands latch on to my bare knees like leeches, cementing me to him. Except I'm not ready to give up just yet. All of my pent-up anger, anxiety, and fear unleash themselves in a blinding rage as I scream, kick, and hit. My tiny fists fly as I hit him everywhere I can manage. His back muscles tense, but they don't yield to the blows.

"Show's over, ladies," he twists his body so I can see the girls from my draped position on his back. They stare in both awe and amusement. I hear one snicker behind the hand she claps over her mouth.

In full view of them, he smacks me directly on the ass with an open palm. "And let this be a lesson to you all. She's going to pay for this dearly, so you'd be smart to not follow her lead." They nod their heads in unison, human expressions on all their faces but one.

The one that yelped has a gleeful look in her eyes. She's got fiery red hair, blue eyes, and porcelain skin with freckles. I can tell at one time she used to be pretty. Now she looks washed-up. Even her emotions seem dulled.

Will this be me, too, I wonder?

Ruby stands with her back against the wall, out of the way, rolling her eyes as she commands the other girls to go to their rooms. I hear one whine, "Why are we being punished for what she did?"

"Yeah," another one grumbles, "she's clearly a newbie."

The other one remarks, "She'll learn fast."

Hopelessly, I kick as Muscleman carries me back to door number four.

When we enter, he doesn't bother setting me down, choosing instead to let go at the same time he shoves me over his shoulder. I have no choice but to tumble to the ground and land headfirst in a crumpled heap.

Gasping on my side, I try to catch my breath and contain my fear. He marches back to the door to lock it behind us. I examine my arm, scraped, and bleeding from where I hit the uncarpeted floor. A floor I wish I could sink through.

I'm afraid to look up at his massive frame as he towers over me. I hide my head in my hands when he takes a step forward. He stands, so one leg is on either side of me. If he sat, he'd be straddling me.

Sobbing, I scoot back until I hit the metal side of the bed.

"Don't you dare," he roars. "Don't you dare act like you

don't deserve what's coming to you." His bulging bicep yanks a chunk of my hair before he slams my head into the side of the bed. I scream in agony. He must like the sound because he repeats this a few more times. "You are a spoiled brat." He picks me up like I'm weightless and tosses me on the bed. It grunts underneath my body as I spring up in the air with force and back down. "Don't worry, it won't be long before you learn your place."

My voice doesn't belong to me anymore, I only hear a terrorized girl screaming bloody murder.

"And here I went to do something nice for you," he runs a hand through his hair. "I went and got you a new, unopened brush from Ruby."

I try to scoot off the opposite side of the bed, but he holds me in place.

Giving me an evil grin, he wickedly says, "You're lucky I don't cut all your hair off. Maybe even shave your head. I'm tempted. Very, *very* tempted."

This elicits another shriek from me.

"I'll make that stop," he says confidently, pushing me onto my stomach and pressing down on my back. Afraid he's going to rape me, my instincts are automatic, and my foot kicks out and catches him in the chin.

He loosens his grip in surprise, and I manage to flip over.

Outrage follows, and in return, he punches me so hard in the back of the head I see stars for a moment, my eyes unable to focus.

I slump down, unable to fight anymore, the pain unbearable.

"That's better," he murmurs, "Much, much better," as he flips me back onto my stomach.

26

ALLEGRA

Letting out a small shriek, Muscleman pulls me over his lap.

I tense, expecting him to take his pants off and violate me internally, but instead, he injures me differently - a brutal punishment he doles out superficially. The hairbrush is now being used as an implement, cracking against my bare skin.

Wriggling, I grip the bedsheets, trying to free myself from the sting of the bristles and the plastic handle. When that doesn't work, and I can't disentangle myself, I jerk my arms back to lessen the blows. This further irritates him, along with my gut-wrenching sobs.

He pauses for a moment as if he just lost his train of thought.

The next thing I know, he responds by binding my wrists in the fabric belt from the robe. Yanking me up by my armpits, he restricts me to a metal bar that hangs above the small, lumpy bed.

Each time I think he's at a stopping point, when he takes a moment to catch his breath, both of us panting from exertion, he continues with a renewed vengeance. The hard plastic of the brush is replaced by his open palm and vice-versa. He moves up and down my back, buttocks, and thighs, repeatedly following the same pattern.

Beyond limp by this point, even the energy to scream has left my body. The pain is like nothing I've experienced before. I twitch from the burning sensation that radiates from every fiber of my being. Convinced he's going to break my body in half, I shut my eyes to try to take my mind anywhere but here.

I picture my last vacation in June, the beach house my mom rented in California. Burying Coye in the sand and scouting for seashells on the beach, the romantic sunsets we made future promises on.

A shattering blow brings me back to reality as my head jerks forward from a thwack to my backside, hitting the wall. Suddenly, there's no more movement. His hand's no longer thrashing, my body's no longer jumping in response.

I hold my breath while he slackens his grip. He inhales, then exhales, and I feel both of our hearts racing, his from exertion, mine from agonizing pain.

I'm choking on tears and snot, coughing as I turn my head to the side while he moves to a side position beside me. A hand brushes over my cheek and his fingers lace through my hair. I cringe, expecting him to be rough.

My mouth gapes open as he picks up the hairbrush again. About to cry out, my breath gets caught in my throat, but instead of using it for further punishment, he gently brushes my hair, careful to delicately comb through the tangles.

I don't know how long I lay there while he brushes my hair. Long enough that I'm in a kind of trance, each stroke through my hair seems to have a sleep-like effect, the motion provides a type of soothing comfort. My mind tries to settle down, but my body can't after such a brutal punishment. I'm drained, both physically and mentally, from lack of sleep, fear, and pain.

With a final caress, he whispers in my ear, "You'll sleep restrained tonight." He seems sad about this, like he hadn't planned on this outcome, his brow furrowed. "But you'll turn over. I want you to lay on your back so you can feel the effects of your bad behavior."

Removing me from the metal bar, he repositions me on my back. My skin's tormented by this, the cotton sheets worn and cheap, abrasive against my marks. I'd give anything for my expensive satin sheets and comfy mattress at home.

I want my bed. I need my parents. I ache for Coye.

"Tomorrow is a new day, and hopefully, we can start over." He kisses my salty cheek, overrun with tears. "Goodnight."

I try and move my lips to ask for a glass of water or something to dull the pain, but my mouth is too dry to form the words. Wordlessly, I watch as he slips out, and the lock clicks shut behind him.

As lethargic as I feel, I'm restless, drifting in and out of unsettling dreams. Unable to find comfort in either the strange bed or my new reality, I'm haunted by nameless men with masked faces invading my space.

I can't tell if the voices and noises I hear are real or imagined, but the rattle of a carburetor and the squawking of animals must be. Life goes on outside of the barred window.

Sleep is futile at this point. When I open my grainy eyes, I'm stuck to the sheets in a layer of sweat. I'm forced to stare listlessly at the popcorn ceiling while tears run fast and furious. With no way to wipe them, they slide into my ears.

Feeling sorry for myself, I clench my fists, trying to wriggle out of my predicament.

Before this 'kidnapping' or 'torture,' I had a good life. I never tried to hurt anyone, and my outlook on life was mainly positive. It's surreal to think about how quickly it's been upended.

My thoughts are interrupted by a scraping sound.

It must be a key twisting in the lock. As much as I tense up, I hope it means I can move and stretch my sore muscles. I strain to hear who's speaking outside of room number four. It's the voice of Ruby. "What do you want me to do with her today?"

"Introduce her to the sister-wives," Muscleman grunts. "Go over the house rules."

"Should I get her ready for..."

"Not yet," and then, "I'm trying to figure it out."

"Are you sure you don't..."

"I said no," he rumbles before she can finish.

When he enters, Ruby is nowhere to be seen. Walking over to the bed, he sits down beside me. His tattoos are covered up today, and he's wearing a long-sleeve shirt and jeans.

"How are we feeling today?" He asks, "A little sore?"

"Yes, sir." A bottle of water rests in his hand, taunting me. I stare at it, parched.

"Would you like some water?"

I nod, my lips chapped.

"Yes..."

"Yes, sir."

"Let me have a look at you first." He unties me from the bar and positions me, so I'm back on my stomach. This time his fingertips start at my neck and trace down to my buttocks. Letting out a low whistle, he murmurs, "Wow, you are striped like a zebra." I wonder if he expects me to respond to his animal comparison.

My face burns at his comment, and I bite my tongue. "What did you learn yesterday?"

"To not run," is all I can muster.

"And?"

"To not question your authority."

"Good girl." He pats my shoulder. "I brought you some pain pills if you promise to be a good girl today." They don't look like regular aspirin, and when he drops them in my hand, I notice they're small and peach-colored. At this point, I could care less, as long as they dull the ache. He uncaps the water bottle and lets me drink greedily from it. My stomach growls at the same time I swallow, wiping a hand across my mouth. "Did you talk to them?"

"Who?"

"My parents."

He lifts my chin. "It's official. I own you."

"What do you mean, you *own* me?"

"I bought you," he shrugs his shoulders. "They declined to take you back."

"You mean, they won't pay you what you want?" I raise my voice. "That's not true. It can't be." My hands start to perspire, as even my sweat rejects the news.

He doesn't like my comment, and he expresses his distaste by pinching my chin and tilting my head back. "What did you say?"

I realize I need to change my tone or risk a repeat of last night. I don't think I can survive another beating.

Keeping my voice low, I murmur, "That can't be true, sir."

"You don't believe me?"

I choose silence instead of the truth.

"You'll learn to trust me." He says this with confidence,

brushing a strand of hair off my face. "We'll have to learn to trust each other."

"What happens now?" I whisper.

"You want to be part of the film industry, don't you?"

"Uh," I stammer, "I don't know."

"Oh." His shoulders slump. He seems dejected by my answer. "I thought it was going to make you happy when I told you we'd make you a star."

"What do you mean?"

"You'll get to be on film." He wipes away a tear that leaks out of my eye. "Don't cry, little one. You're going to be your own brand of famous in the adult world."

I shudder, and he ignores the angst in my eyes, his focus on the barred window of my prison. Thankfully, we're interrupted when his phone vibrates in his pocket. Immediately he stands and walks a couple of steps away from me.

Turning his back, he answers. "Everything's going to be just fine." And, "Uh-huh," in response to the person on the other end. "Okay, I'll make sure I have her there later." He disconnects and walks back to my side. "Ruby will be back in a little bit. I gotta go. Business to take care of."

Meekly I ask, "Can I go to the bathroom, please?"

"Of course." He acts as if my question is silly. "Let me walk you there." He takes my elbow and gently helps me off the bed. My nakedness is masked only by bruises and marks. Guiding me to the bathroom across the hall, I'm relieved he doesn't follow me in and more surprised when he shuts the door behind me. Of course, the knob has been removed, preventing anyone from locking or fully having privacy.

The bathroom is paltry but clean, the space half the size of my walk-in closet. A floral shower curtain covers the ugly

Pepto-Bismol pink bathtub. On top of the toilet, another bouquet of dusty fake flowers rests in a basket.

The sink is a beige color as if it were once a shade of white until rust discolored it over the years. I notice a sliver of light filter into the space. Excitedly, I fling the shower curtain open, only to discover the tiny window is impossible to climb out of and barred to prevent anyone from leaving. I doubt I could get more than a couple of fingers through the ugly metal.

As I settle on the toilet, I notice a small cabinet next to the sink has a supply of bathroom necessities and contains various soaps and lotions. Underneath, a shelf is filled with plastic bins, all clear and labeled with different names, or to be exact, shades of colors.

The labels have been scratched out, black lines covering the old print. I pull them out one by one, expecting products to be sorted by color, but instead, each has similar toiletry items. Oddly enough, I don't see one for Ruby.

My search is interrupted by a rap on the door.

"Yes, just a minute," I say, except the person doesn't hesitate to open the door. I'm face-to-face with Ruby, her hair now twisted into a loose bun. She's not wearing any makeup today, and I notice a discoloration on her left cheekbone, a bruise that's faded to a yellowish color.

"You gonna be long?"

"I'm done now," I try and hide my nakedness behind the shower curtain.

"No point," she smirks. "I can still see you."

She's right. I wash my hands in the chipped sink as she gawks at my injuries, but says nothing.

Uncomfortable, I ask, "Why are the bins labeled with colors?"

"You'll learn." She motions towards the kitchen. "Follow me."

"Can I please have something to wear?"

She shrugs, "Not until the girls see what happened to you."

We stop at door number three and Ruby knocks. "Violet," she shrieks, "family meeting in the living room. Now!"

The door opens and Violet appears, her big brown eyes clouded with confusion. She has limp brown hair and pale skin that's shiny, like she just finished running a marathon.

"Okay," Violet starts to shut the door in our faces.

Ruby catches the edge before it closes. "Tell Ivory, will ya?"

Violet nods.

Ruby waves a hand at me. "Let's go have a talk." We end up back in the living room. My eyes drift longingly to the front door as Ruby pretends not to notice. She squeezes my arm and directs me to the couch.

The room seems unfinished somehow, but more than just the poor decorating, it finally dawns on me. The absence of a television or entertainment system makes it look incomplete. The couch and chair are both leather but different colors. One is black, one is brown. A coffee table is jammed between them, and a piece of artwork hangs over the couch, a mass of colorful blobs. Just like the kitchen, it's as if nothing is part of a matching set.

We both settle on the creased leather while I wait for her to speak. "I'm Ruby," she rests a hand on her collarbone, "and I run the household. I used to do what the other girls did until I got promoted."

I don't ask how she came to be 'promoted.'

"This might seem, uh, unconventional to some, but I've

grown to like it here, and if you follow the rules, you will too."

Staring at my hands, I sit perfectly still. "You learned who was in charge. The only other man allowed in the house is John, his partner. We don't answer the doorbell for nobody. Any business we attend to, we go off-site, and we're never allowed to be alone in public."

She rambles on with more rules and advice. I learn that food is a privilege, hence the locks on the fridge and cupboards. So is the bathroom, sleep, and practically everything I take for granted on a day-to-day basis. Most teenagers would love school being erased from their vocabulary, but not me. I love class and being social, my afternoons spent on extracurricular activities like editing the school newspaper and cheerleading.

Ruby finishes explaining the backyard is off-limits unless she's with us when Ivory saunters in, followed by Violet.

Hands on her hips, Ivory looks more translucent in the daylight, her red hair wild and frizzy. Her blue eyes darken as she groans, "Does this dipshit that got us grounded last night have a name?"

"You hardly got grounded." Violet rolls her eyes, "You had to go to your room for what, like fifteen minutes?"

"So?"

"It was a nice break," Violet mutters under her breath.

"Girls!" Ruby interjects, "This is...well, we still have to come up with a name for her." She motions for me to fully reveal my marred skin. "Violet and Ivory, this is what happens when you try and leave. I doubt you need a reminder..."

Violet whistles at my marks while Ivory seems overjoyed I got the brunt of Muscleman's fists yesterday. Ashamedly, I

The House Without A Key 227

try to cover up my exposed body with my hands, but it's useless.

After the comment on my welts and bruises, Ruby reaches underneath the coffee table to toss me a blanket to cover up with.

"Ivory," Ruby gives her a warning, "don't think I forgot your first day a few months ago." She adds, "And what you did." I didn't think Ivory could turn a shade paler.

Curious if I'm allowed to talk, I raise my hand. I'm puzzled as to what Ivory did, but I don't want to ask that right now.

"When it's us girls, you can talk," Violet says matter-of-factly.

"How long have you all been here?" I question.

"A year for me and probably three-and-a-half months for her." Violet smirks at Ivory, "But it feels like longer, like *way* longer."

"Are there other girls?" I wrap the blanket around my trembling shoulders.

"Some come, and some go." Ruby jumps in before the other girls can respond. "Until Olive disappeared, it was the four of us."

Ivory raises her eyebrows while Violet twists her hands anxiously in her lap. I want to know about this Olive girl, but I'd rather question Violet when we're alone, if that's even an option. I can tell from Ivory's indignant attitude she's plain trouble. I'll have to watch out for her.

Ruby changes the subject to the chore wheel and how they rotate every week. "Right now, one handled kitchen duty, the other the bathrooms, and one the living room and bedrooms. We can add the outdoors, pulling weeds and watering the lawn. With supervision, of course."

"Of course," Violet and Ivory mutter.

"What about laundry?"

"It's divvied up by all of us," Violet says.

"Let me give you a tour." Ruby rises, and we all follow her as she walks me through the floor plan of the house. Across from the living room is a hall closet, stuffed with cleaning supplies and a vacuum. The first door on the right is the master bedroom and bathroom. It's where Ruby sleeps, and she quickly opens and shuts the door. Ivory's modest bedroom is next, followed by a half-bath.

"You've seen the kitchen," Ruby says. "And the pantry is back here." It's the size of a small closet and was clearly added to the house along with the laundry room.

"You and Violet are in the other two bedrooms." Ruby points down the other hall. "That about covers it. Any questions?"

"Does *he* live in the other house?"

"Yes," Ruby explains. "He stops in occasionally to see us and to give us our work schedule."

I stare at the refrigerator, picturing a breakfast of pancakes or waffles. My stomach grumbles at the lack of calories I've been eating lately.

"Sounds like someone is hungry." Violet giggles.

"Yes." I pat my stomach. "Very."

"Okay, it's time for breakfast then." Ruby heads to the pantry to unlock it. "You want cereal or oatmeal?"

"Oatmeal, please."

"Okay, come get a packet," Ruby orders. "Violet, show her the kitchen utensils and where the dishes and silverware are. I expect you to wash your own dishes after you've used them. We don't need flies or bugs."

I nod.

Eager to please, Violet leads me around the kitchen, pointing to every drawer and cupboard with a description of what they contain, except she can't open any of them on her own. Ruby instructs everyone to get their own food. Ivory doesn't need to be told twice before she stalks over to the fridge. "It'll be nice to have breakfast for once."

Ruby ignores her comment. "Sit down, and we'll all eat together."

Ivory and Violet tear into a box of cereal. It's not until it's poured into the bowls that they realize there's not enough milk for two. Improvising, I watch in disgust as they water down the milk like it's an everyday occurrence. Ruby eats oatmeal and a frozen waffle she found stuffed in the freezer, stiff with frostbite. I eat a package of microwaved oatmeal cooked with water and sip orange juice that's past its expiration date.

"We're getting low on food," Ivory mentions. "Who's running to the store next?"

"I'll tell John," Ruby says, "when he comes by later."

Violet swallows a spoonful of cereal. "Does anyone know about John and..."

With a loud clank, Ruby sets down her spoon. "Violet, please." Changing the subject, she turns to me, "So what would you like your new name to be?"

"It has to be a color." Ivory pushes her empty bowl across the table.

"What about something blue, like Aqua?" Violet stares at me. "You have such pretty eyes."

Ruby agrees. "Yours are the prettiest color."

I consider my watery oatmeal while Ivory mutters something rude about my appearance. I'm

grateful everyone ignores her.

I confirm. "Something with the color blue?"

"Absolutely," Violet says, "it fits you."

"What about *cerulean*, like cerulean blue?" I intone. "It's my favorite color."

"Sa-real-e-un." Ruby sounds it out, while Ivory spits it out like it's poison. "Aqua's a lot easier to say."

"I don't have a problem pronouncing it," I demur.

"I love it," Violet claps her hands. "It's perfect for you."

And that's how Cerulean was born, and Allegra Atwater died, at least in the house of sister-wives. I'm now a one-named moniker in a house of other colors.

"Anything else?" Ruby fixes me with a small smile.

"Why does Muscleman, I mean sir, refer to you as sister-wives?"

Ruby puts down her utensil, and the girls sit quietly as she explains. My knees wobble underneath the table, and I force myself to sit on my hands, so they don't see them shaking.

I regret my question as soon as I know the answer because I learn to become one, which they all have, there must be a ceremony.

The ceremony is scheduled after you have a new name, which now I do. It must be held before anyone else, meaning another man, has access to you. The other sister-wives bathe you for cleanliness, then you are dressed up in what they consider suitable garments. The color of the clothing matches your new name. The man who owns me, Muscleman, is now permitted to have his way with me. He will spend the night teaching me how to pleasure him and do what he likes. You're expressly forbidden to share details with anyone else about their preferences, though the girls snicker when Ruby says this.

The men do not share the sister-wives.

Each of them belongs to one man or the other. It's taboo for them to trade-off. I guess it's like your ex dating your best friend, or something like that.

Just like the other night, the food I swallowed refuses to settle in my tummy. I quickly stand and run to the bathroom, spewing the oatmeal and orange juice in the toilet. When I feel well enough to remove myself from the porcelain bowl, I meet Ruby's eyes in the mirror.

She's watching from the open doorway, a vague expression on her face. After disappearing, she comes back with my plastic bag from Muscleman, a toothbrush in hand. "You can store this in the bin labeled 'Emerald.'

After I brush my teeth, I'm instructed to get to work.

My first chore is to start his laundry, Muscleman's dirty clothes piled high in a laundry basket. I spend my afternoon washing, drying, and ironing. This was new for me, and when I asked how to iron, Ruby laughed like I told a funny joke before she walked away in disbelief. Ivory said she hoped I burned the house down, and Violet patiently walked me through a demonstration on how to use it.

Now my fingers are numb from the amount of clothes I've made wrinkle-free.

I slide the hot metal plate across another pair of his pants. As much as I despise the monotony, I'd rather be a seventeen-year-old housewife than one of the sister-wives. A shiver runs down my spine at the thought of him undressing me in some sadistic ritual.

Howling, something hot flicks against my finger.

I suck my thumb to lessen the burn.

Taking a deep breath, I watch as wetness drips onto the collared shirt. I assume it's from the water reservoir, so I press the button to spray again, but nothing comes out.

It's empty.

It's then I realize my tears are being ironed out on Muscleman's clothing.

27

BRIAN

It's one in the afternoon, and I've already downed a shot of whiskey and ordered my third rum and coke. I convinced myself I'll lose my nerve and balls if I don't order another. The trusty bartender, Al, sets another one in front of me.

I asked Valerie to meet me here. An overwhelming urge to talk to her outweighs my cold feet. This isn't a conversation I want to have, but if Darren's involved in something sinister like murder, he's not going to worry about hurting those around him. He's a dangerous man, and considering my relationship with his wife, if he gets wind of it, I might be in my own body bag.

Judging from the pain on Val's face when she enters, it's going to be a rough afternoon for both of us. Besides her sullen expression, she looks entirely out of place in this dive. Even ditching the heels and the expensive Givenchy tote she typically carries, she's forever bathed in riches. Even her scent is overpowering, like money.

Sinking onto the barstool next to me, she orders a vodka tonic, extra lime.

I stare straight ahead, not daring to look her in the face and see the hurt. "You still think she's in Cali?"

Al settles her drink in front of her, and she squeezes the second lime before taking a long sip. "No." She leans her elbows on the shiny mahogany counter.

"I have to tell you something," I stammer.

"Me too."

I open my mouth, but she interrupts. "I don't know how to tell you this." She buries her head in her hands. "I should've told you this before. When Darren and I got together, his ex-wife tried to convince him I was a gold-digging, psycho bitch who only got knocked up to be taken care of."

"That sounds like every ex-wife."

"Out of pride, I signed an ironclad prenup before we got married to show him it wasn't about the money."

"You did what?" I'm incredulous. "Why would you do that?"

"Now we have an empire, and I stand to lose a lot more than just him. Which could come crashing down at any minute with the erratic decisions Darren's been making lately."

"Speaking of," I take a deep breath and rush into my confession. "I uh...I don't know how to tell you this." I gulp the last of my drink down. It burns so good. "I found a..."

Grimly, she stares at her drink, "Why didn't we go to your shop? Why did you want to meet in public?"

I shrug. It's pretty dead, so I'm not worried we'll be spotted. Paranoid, she slips a pair of dark sunglasses on.

I don't have the right answer, except I needed a good buzz. She of all people should know this, so she drowns her vodka and orders a second round.

Waving at Al, she begs to smoke. He gives her a thumbs-up, and an ashtray magically appears between us as we light up. "Thanks." She rewards him with a forced smile, which he returns with a grin. Waiting until he retreats to the other end of the bar, she finally speaks. "What did you find?"

I move the chew to the inside of my cheek. "I drove a truck for him."

"You drove a truck for who?"

"Darren." I give her a pitiful glance. "I should've told you."

"You did *what*?" Anger strangles her voice. "That's *not* what we agreed to." She tries not to slam her fist on the counter, instead dropping a light fist bump. "You were supposed to flatten his tire to buy me some time."

"I did," I drum my fingers on the counter. "I did what you asked. But he showed up at the shop and asked me to replace the punctured one and then offered me a job."

"Oh my God," she hisses under her breath. "Tell me it wasn't a route to Nuevo Laredo."

I swallow. "I found something I shouldn't have." The mix of alcohol and nerves causes me to break down, and Valerie pokes me in the ribs.

She doesn't bother asking Al for the tab, she just slips a hundred-dollar bill on the table and stands.

I take that as our cue to leave.

As we head outside, I lean on her for support. We walk toward the edge of the lot and loiter behind the dumpster. She removes her shades. "What did you take to the border?"

"I was carrying," I whisper, pulling her shoulders toward me, forcing her green eyes to focus on mine. "A body. There was a body in the back. A *dead* fucking girl."

Gasping, she sinks to her knees, and I go down with her. We both sit behind the smelly metal bin in silence. I add, "It was a female with blonde hair."

"How old?"

"Late teens, early twenties. I didn't...I didn't want to touch her."

"How...was it..." she breaks down, and now it's my turn to comfort her. "Was it..." she can't even form the words. "When was this?"

"No. It wasn't Allegra. It was before she went missing."

Valerie replaces the glasses on her face. Muffled, she asks, "How could you do this to me?"

I watch the tears roll down her face.

"I called you the night I found her," I'm helpless as I try and fold her in my arms. Angrily, she swats me away. "I wanted to tell you sooner."

"How could you go behind my back and work for my husband?" She weeps. "You know what he's capable of."

"I needed the money."

"I offered you money." She snags my arm with her nails, digging in. I get the point. "You're supposed to work for me, *only* for me. We had a deal."

"Oh my God, oh my God. What if...?" Her mouth drops in horror.

I finish her unspoken thought. "What if Darren had something to do with her disappearance? Believe me, I've thought of that."

"Do you think he knows about..." A hand clamps over her mouth.

"No. He doesn't know about us."

She shakes her head. "I can't believe you did a run for him."

"What was I hauling?"

"You don't want to know."

"I do."

"No, you don't." With clenched teeth, "Whatever Darren told you it was, it wasn't." She stands and brushes herself off.

"Val," I say.

"Don't even." She pushes a hand against my chest. "I can't do this with you. I think it's best we have some space."

"Valerie, don't be like this."

Without a backward glance, shoulders trembling, she walks away from me. The fact I caused her pain and broke our trust kills me. It's more ammunition I didn't need to drink. I spend the afternoon getting shitfaced before I drive home. When I stumble upstairs to the apartment, I enter the wrong one, much to the dismay of the elderly woman staring at me. Her hand rests across her heart as if she expects me to harm her.

When I realize my mistake, I shake my head and turn around, steeling myself for a fight I want to have. Madeline's not home and eager to take my rage out on someone, I destroy most of the furnishings in the apartment.

28

VALERIE

I'm nauseous the whole way home about what Brian told me, the pit only hardens in my stomach. He shouldn't be working for my husband, and my husband shouldn't be transporting dead bodies.

We have a daughter. How could he so heartless when he has a child of his own? What if something happened to his own flesh and blood?

But it has. I clench my fists around my steering wheel.

Did Darren piss off the wrong people? A drug cartel?

Brian has no reason to lie to me, and even though he's an alcoholic, I love him. He's all I have right now. *Especially* now.

When I get to the house, I waste no time in opening my laptop. I have to know if it was all a lie. Since Allegra vanished, I have more questions than answers. The phone number I have has been disconnected. A delivery status notification alerts me it's no longer a valid email address. With no choice, I book a ticket to California. I have to see the truth for myself. The man couldn't have been lying about all of it, could he?

It's a short flight, and I'll be there by sunset.

I find an email from June with the address. Printing it out, I fold it in my tote, not bothering to pack an overnight bag.

This will be a quick trip.

What about Coye? Should I contact him?

No. I can't draw attention to myself. I have to go there and back.

When I land, I grab a taxi instead of using my preferred method of rideshare. I want to pay cash with no paper trail.

The sheet of paper now rests tattered in my hands. Unfolding and creasing it multiple times on the plane ride, it quells my apprehension.

When we arrive along the strand, I quickly exit the vehicle, much to the driver's dismay, since I forget to pay him. Sheepish, I hand him an extra twenty-dollar bill.

The boardwalk's not as busy as it usually is. The barrage of skateboarders and cyclists and tourists have thinned out now that Labor Day and the summer months have passed. Life has resumed for most people. Back to their corporate jobs and their sense of normalcy.

The walkway to the beach house is lined by orchids and rosebushes. I waste no time knocking on the door. Even the waves can't enthrall my attention like they usually do.

No one answers, so I peer in the small window and glimpse a bed, a couch, a television, and a kitchenette. There's no sign of anyone and no personal effects, which is not what I expect.

Numb, I walk back and ring the doorbell for the house we stayed in, the memories sweeping over me like the choppy water in the ocean today. I stare up at the third-floor deck, my body trembling. Allegra was relaxed and happy

The House Without A Key 239

here, the beach a place of tranquility. Not just for her, but for me too.

An elderly woman answers, and at first, I think I made a mistake. It's the wrong house. In my rush, I didn't bother to double-check the address. Out of sorts and shaking my head, I apologize. "Sorry, I wrote the house number down incorrectly."

She peers over her thick bifocals at me, leaning heavily on a cane. "What's the address?"

"Mortimer," I say.

"This is it, dear." She sags against the doorframe. "But I wasn't expecting any visitors for another week."

"I'm not here to stay."

"Really?" She lets out a breath. "Thank goodness! The last thing this old bag needs is to screw up my reviews."

"Reviews?"

"Guests book through a vacation rental site. You have to have everything just so."

"Oh," I'm at a loss for words. "I was looking for a friend of mine. Did you just buy these properties?"

"With the real estate prices here? Heavens no," she clutches her chest. "We'd never be able to afford it. No dear, I grew up here. My family invested in beach properties a long time ago. My husband and I live closer to Los Angeles, but we had a couple housekeeping items to take care of before the next visitors come."

She takes my gaping mouth for amazement. "Oh, I know what you're thinking, young lady. That we are much too old to be puttering around the house." With a twinkle in her rheumy eyes, she laughs. "My husband can't do much, but he can replace a couple of cabinet knobs."

I give her a shaky smile. "Do you by chance own the house next door?"

"Yes, we do," she tilts her head. "For twenty-seven years, actually."

"Wow, a long time."

The woman smiles at me, her tan face creased with wrinkles. "You say you're looking for a friend?"

"Yes."

"What were their scheduled dates?" She frowns. "Our last tenants in that house were from two weeks ago. We require at least a week's stay."

"Uh, it was actually this house."

"We don't rent this house out during the summer."

"You don't?"

"No," she shakes her head. "Our own family tends to stay here over the summer months."

I don't bother to tell her I stayed here in June. "Third-floor master, right?"

She nods. "I can't get up the stairs, but there's a bedroom on the first floor."

"Do you know a Mickey Sullivan?" I ask.

"The name sounds familiar. You can certainly check with Walt, my husband." Pointing to her cane, "Might be easier if you go next door. He should be there. He's hard of hearing. Holler his name when you enter so you don't give him a heart attack."

She starts to shut the door, but reconsiders. "Is there a problem I should know about?"

"No. Mr. Sullivan used this address as his place of residence for a loan," I lie.

"Oh wow, I didn't know bankers were that thorough. Thought you approved everyone and everything."

"Uh, well, not all of us," I say lamely. "Thanks for your help."

"I'm Joanne, by the way."

"Nice to meet you, Joanne." I nod. Picking the first name that comes to mind, I go with Jean. Turning to leave, Joanne watches me through the open window as I approach the other house.

I holler Walter's name as I enter. He's in the back of the house, fiddling with a cabinet in the bathroom. He looks surprised to see me, but not alarmed.

Explaining my predicament, I ask about a renter named Mickey Sullivan. His bushy eyebrows raise. "Hmm...I can look through our rental history, not a problem. What did you say your name was?"

"Jean. Jean Samuels."

"Can I give you a call?"

I hesitate. I need the information like yesterday. "How long do you think it will take?"

"I can pull it up tonight when Jo and I get home. I'm almost finished here."

"Thanks," I try not to let the disappointment show on my face. Forcing a small smile, I write down my phone number for him.

Dejectedly, I fly back home. The landmine I've stepped on has blown up in my face. As if this realization wasn't bad enough, I'm greeted at the gate by the likes of Detective Devon Delaney. He could pass for a corporate traveler, his dark suit and briefcase screams 'businessman.'

My heart stops beating in my chest, and I'm convinced by the scowl on his face he's about to deliver alarming news I don't want to hear about my daughter. I slow down to a crawl, tempted to turn in the other direction.

Trembling from head to toe, his hazel eyes bore into mine. He doesn't close the gap between us. Instead, he waits for my acknowledgment. This is a departure from his usual preference of being the hunter. He likes the chase, or at least he did when we were younger. I approach him like you would a wild animal, sluggish, and with distance between us. An exit strategy in mind, no doubt.

"Are you here because of Allegra?" I say sharply. "Did something happen?"

Not one to waste time or words, he stands. "When were you going to tell me?"

"About what?"

His clenched jaw signals his patience is running thin. "That you were going to California."

"I think Allegra ran away, and it's my fault." My face burns. "And if she did, she'd go there."

"Why would you think that?" He strokes his chin. "Is it because you like to control what information you disseminate to my department and me, regardless if it helps the investigation or not?"

I ignore this jab. "Allegra wants to be a model. I think she hooked up with someone shady in the industry, someone who lured her in. Probably from the internet."

Delaney doesn't disagree. "Possibly," he folds his arms across his chest. "Still doesn't answer why you flew there for a day trip."

"I wanted to check on Coye."

"Really? That's sweet, but implausible, since he hasn't seen you," Delaney hisses. I know his body language, and the way he's yanking at the tie around his throat sends me a subtle warning. "I called him. Do you have another lie you'd like to try on me?"

I keep my voice steady. "That was my intention."

"Then why, Valerie, did Coye say he hadn't spoken to you?" He shakes his head in disgust. "It's been a long time since we've acquainted ourselves with each other, but I didn't know time would turn you into a pathological liar, and a shitty one at that." He continues, "And another thing, you told me Allegra didn't have a vehicle, but I see a relatively new Jeep is registered in your name, and your name only. Care to discuss?"

I stare at the floor, burning a hole in the carpet. People are starting to take an interest in our conversation. A few raised brows and hushed voices turn in our direction.

"I'm going to arrest you," he says softly. If he's joking with me, his face doesn't reveal an ounce of humor.

"What?" My head snaps up. "What for? Going to California?"

Reaching into his pocket, he retrieves a pair of handcuffs.

"You can't be serious."

"Try me. You're on my last nerve."

"Devon..."

"Don't you 'Devon' me." He raises the cuffs. "We can do this the easy way or the hard way. Makes no difference to me."

"What do you want?" I moan.

"You either tell me what the fuck is going on, or I'm arresting you right here in the terminal. You want to parade around on the news like you're the victim? How about we show the world the other side of Valerie Atwater?"

I spew, "Fuck you, Delaney."

"Been there, done that." He reaches for my arm, but I jerk it out of his grasp.

"Your choice, Valerie. We can ride back to your house together and have a nice chat on the way, or I'm taking you down to the station."

"But my attorney," I start to interrupt.

"I don't give a shit about your attorney," he spits out. "I

work for the missing girl, and in case you forgot, it's *your* daughter."

I jeer at him.

"Either way, Darren is going to come home, and the three of us are sitting down to talk. Only you can decide if we're on the same side or if you want to be enemies." He tucks a strand of hair behind my ear. "And you don't want me as your enemy, Val."

29

DETECTIVE DELANEY

Valerie seethes as we walk to my Land Rover. When she sees my personal vehicle, she rolls her eyes. "Thought this was 'official' business?"

"Everything with you is on the record," I retort.

"I did need a ride home from the airport." She gives me a sickening sweet smile I want to remove from her face.

"Before we are stuck together in a vehicle, let's take a moment to do what we like to do." She's waiting for the punch line or a suggestive glance. I offer her neither. "I know you're dying to calm yourself with a cancer stick. By all means, please do. I'll ignore the disgusting smell of poison, and you can dismiss the dog fur." Her green eyes narrow, darkening to a moss color.

"You keep thinking you can hide habits and secrets from me. You can't, so stop trying." I slam the car door in her face as she stands on the other side, reaching for her lighter.

I flick on the radio while she inhales tar and nicotine, our chosen method of soothing ourselves. I can think of a much better idea, but she doesn't need to know what I have in mind.

When she slides in beside me, I start the engine. "Speak," I command.

"What do you want to know?"

"Let's start off with why you went to Cali for the day."

"To clear my head."

I give her a sideways glance.

"Here, if you don't believe me." She reaches into her purse and pulls out a piece of paper. "A receipt for a taxi. I went to the beach. Manhattan Beach, to be exact." The drumming of my fingers must tell her I'm unconvinced. "Allegra loves the beach. I wanted, *no,* I needed to feel close to her today. It was impulsive." She wrings her hands in her lap. "If you don't believe me, check when I bought the flight."

"I already did," I say. "

Where's the Jeep?"

"Parked in a garage."

"Where?" I smirk. "I'm assuming not at your house."

"No. A friend is keeping is for me."

"Must be a *good* friend."

"It's *our* mechanic, actually."

I whistle. "Are they prepared to lose your business when Darren finds out?"

She chews her lip.

"I'm gonna want to see it."

"Why?"

"So I know someone else isn't driving it." I snort. "Or that you gave it to Allegra, and you're assisting her in some hare-brained scheme."

Disgusted, she slams her hand on the glove box. "How could you even think that?"

The rest of the way up the mountain passes in an icy silence, battle lines clearly drawn. Tension mounts as we arrive at the 'gates of hell,' also known as the Atwater compound. I can tell Val's fit to be tied by the way she fidgets in her seat. She's itching for a cigarette, and most likely, to stub it out on my skin.

"Can you buzz us in?" I speak into the intercom.

"Our staff has left for the day, and I doubt Darren's here yet to let us through." Valerie sounds annoyed. "Let me enter the code."

Unbuckling her seatbelt, she leans over the console and my lap, stretching her long arms through the window. I smell her hair, and I try my hardest not to inhale. She taps in a code, mumbling that I'm an impatient dick or something to that effect.

Not making a move to sit upright, she asks. "Did you already talk to Darren?"

"I gave him a specific time." My tone brooks no argument, and Valerie says nothing else. "If you'll move off my lap, I'll drive us through the gate." I run a hand through her chestnut hair. "Or we can stay like this until Darren comes home."

She shoots up, glowering at me.

I chuckle. "By the way, does Darren know about us?" I pinch her cheek. "I'd love to tell him our history if he doesn't already know it. Does he know I took your virginity?"

"I hate you," she mutters.

"But remember when you used to love me?" I remind her haughtily.

Blowing her a kiss, I park in the driveway and let her lead us inside. The property's eerily dark, and I notice there's very little in the form of outside lights. I guess some people like their privacy shrouded in darkness. The Atwater's are the perfect couple for that.

Absentmindedly, she turns on lamps as we walk toward the kitchen. "Would you like something to drink?"

"After this day, I'd prefer hard liquor," I say pointedly. "But I'll stick with water." I can tell we're on the same page by the amount of Merlot she pours into a wineglass. She offers me some, but I decline. I'm not here to catch up.

Handing me a chilled bottle of water, I try to get her to relax. "I'm surprised you didn't ask if I wanted sparkling or tap."

"I know you better than that," she says. "Frankly, I'm surprised Darren agreed to be in the same house as me."

"He didn't have a choice. I told him he would be under arrest if he didn't." I give her a small smile to show her I'm facetious. "But yes, he said he'd be home."

I follow her into what must be a sitting room. A massive stone fireplace is the focal point. On the mantel, instead of a deer head, there's a sculpture made from recycled auto parts. Floor-to-ceiling windows line one wall, and in the morning, I bet this room is bathed in natural sunlight. An overstuffed couch, chair, and matching ottoman take up a majority of the space. An Oriental rug spans the length and polished hardwood peaks out from underneath.

We lock eyes as the squeal of tires in the drive signals Darren is home. His headlights illuminate the paned glass. A car door slams shut, followed by another thud. "Val," a harsh voice echoes through the hallway. "Where are you?"

Flinching, she yells. "Sitting room."

Motioning me to have a seat, I take the couch, and she sinks into the corner chair.

"Where is he?" Darren slurs as he strides into the room. "I see his piece of shit in the drive." Where Valerie stinks like smoke, he reeks of booze.

Darren Atwater is a little under six feet tall, medium build, light brown hair that's thinning. The quintessential tennis player. He has what people term a "dad bod." His expensive clothes hide the few extra pounds well, and his style shields him from being ubiquitous.

"This is *Detective* Devon Delaney," Valerie scoffs. "How nice of you to grace us with your drunken presence. Glad happy hour was a must while your daughter is missing."

And...we're off to the races.

She wasn't kidding about her marriage being in shambles.

I hate the prick, so I don't point out the hypocrisy of her flying to Cali today.

"That's my POS in the drive," I don't stand to shake his hand. "Are you okay, Mr. Atwater?"

"No. I'm not." There's a wet bar in the corner, and he reaches into the refrigerator for a bottle of San Pellegrino sparkling water. I try not to smirk as Valerie's gaze locks on mine. "I don't like the public spectacle this has become. Allegra is a child and should be treated as such," he sneers, "not as some sensational news story."

Valerie says nothing, twisting her hands in her lap.

Stony, I say. "Then maybe you both should stay off of the television."

He fixes me with a hostile stare.

"Perhaps you should locate my daughter, so it doesn't have to be news fodder," he shoots back.

Glad we know where we stand, it's time to dive in. Waiting for him to settle on the other side of the couch, I take this as my opportunity to drop the first bomb and see where it lands.

"If information was forthcoming, I'm assured you would feel differently."

"Like what?" he snarls.

"Darren, what do you know of Allegra's relationships?"

He shrugs. "She has lots of friends."

"I mean, with the opposite sex."

"She's seventeen. Some have crushes on her, but that's it."

"Allegra has been in a pretty serious relationship for the last eight months with a young man in California, Coye Kauffman. He's a college sophomore."

Boom.

His jaw drops, and it's almost worth it to see him not only confused but fighting for composure. If it weren't for the pained look on Valerie's face, or the fact she'll get the brunt of his anger, I'd thoroughly enjoy it.

Though come to think of it, she's part of the problem with her stilted answers and lies.

Darren breaks my concentration. "What are you talking about?" He swivels his head from me to his wife and then back as if we planned to release this bombshell together. "There's no way, absolutely no way. We have a zero dating policy in this household." He glances at Valerie with coldness. "Right, Val?"

I'll let them hash this out later. I continue. "Coye isn't under arrest and isn't considered a person of interest at this time," I explain. "He's fully cooperated with our investigation."

"Was this someone she met online?" Bewildered, he looks at Valerie, who stares with a deer-in-the-headlights expression at me. "Did you know about this, Val?"

Now it's my turn to feel uncomfortable. I yank on my tie as Valerie's face crumbles. "Yes." Her shoulders shake. "I took her out to California a few times, always supervised, to see him."

Speechless, which is a first for someone like him, Darren opens his mouth, then closes it, unsure how to react. He chooses anger. His eyes practically bulge out of his head.

"Which brings me to why I'm here." I claw at my neck. I hate these damn nooses around my throat. "We look at the family first and expand upon those connections. I've spoken to the household staff, and now I'd like a list of your business associates and employees."

I'm worried steam's going to follow out of Darren's ears soon. Ignoring his reaction, I say,

"I want to know who else you think I should take a closer look at."

"Isn't that your job?" Darren hisses, "to figure out the puzzle?"

"If you think this is some kind of jigsaw I'm supposed to fit together like a fucking game," I snap, "I'm going to punch you."

"Are you threatening me?"

"My job is to find out what happened to Allegra. The whole process goes smoother and is more efficient if the parents and last known people to see her alive are cooperative, just like Coye Kauffman was."

Darren gazes at his wife, his eyes bloodshot. "You were the last one to see her," he shoots daggers at Valerie. "Surely, you know something."

"I don't."

"What could've happened to her?" Darren slams his fist down on the glass table beside him, upending his sparkling water.

"A multitude of things," I tick off on my fingers. "Sex trafficking, kidnapping, murder." Both of them gasp in horror. Now that I have their undivided attention, I say. "That's why I'm trying to identify people that play a role in your lives. I can't help unless you both are honest with me and each other."

I watch as they sulk at each other.

Sternly, I say, "It's time to give up your secrets. It's only hindering this investigation. I need the good, the bad, and the ugly."

I mention Elizabeth, Darren's first, and up until now, only ex-wife.

"Harmless," he shrugs.

"Tell me about Sandy," I say.

His lips thin. "Sandy, my assistant?"

"Is there another?"

"I thought you came to talk about Allegra," he explodes. "I don't see how this is relevant."

We lock eyes. "Are you and Sandy involved in your daughter's disappearance?"

His face reddens. "Why would Sandy be involved in it?"

"Why are you repeating my questions back to me?" I chasten him. "Don't you know that's one of the first clues someone is lying?"

"It's an absurd question."

"Are you having an affair?" I ask him.

"Yes," he lets out a deep breath, his eyes refusing to meet Valerie's. "It's not like it's a secret, Val knows." It disgusts me how casual he is about the whole thing. As if he accidentally burned their dinner. Not fucked his secretary.

"What about you, Valerie, anyone I should take a closer look at?"

Darren points his finger at her. "Yes. I bet Valerie hasn't clued you into her own affair." He looks pleased with himself as he picks lint off his navy pants. "I'm sure Detective Delaney would be interested to hear about more than just mine."

Now it's my turn to see red.

30

VALERIE

A stormy look crosses Devon's face, and he's about to throttle me. In fact, they both are.

"My affair?" I let out a cackle. "That's hysterical."

"You think I don't know? That you were that cunning and clever?" Darren shakes his head in disgust. "You aren't, and you weren't. In fact, I hired him to do a job for me. I own his ass now, just like yours."

"Wow, that's a great impression to give Devon."

"Who's Devon?" Darren's eyes search around the room.

He's quick to jump in. "*Detective* Delaney."

"Just like you to be on a first-name basis with everyone you meet. No wonder our daughter is missing."

My eyes tear up as Delaney interjects, "Stop it, please." He stands to press some tissues in my hand.

Instead of sitting back down, he leans against the mantel. "Who is the affair with?" Unsure who he wants to question, his gaze drifts to Darren.

"Brian Pruitt," Darren says heatedly, "I don't know how

long it's been going on, but it's been at least eight or nine months."

"Is this true?" Delaney keeps his voice level, but he's about to choke himself with his tie.

"No, I am *not* having an affair with Brian Pruitt."

"Oh, really? I have proof," Darren says with a wicked smile. "You can't dispute cold, hard facts."

Delaney starts to speak, but I interrupt, raising my voice. "What do you think you have?" I roll my eyes. "*Seriously*, what do you think you have?"

Running a frustrated hand through my hair, I say. "I can't believe you. Our focus should be on our daughter, *not* my brother."

"Brother?" Darren snorts, "You don't have a brother. Unless now you want to consider every foster sibling you ever had a blood relative." He sneers at Delaney. "Can you believe this shit? This is a new low even for you, Val, pretending your lover is your brother."

"Brian is my half-brother, from my real, live, drug-addled birth mother," I spit out.

Delaney takes a second to digest this. "I'm assuming this is what you found out recently? A deathbed confession or gossip after she died?"

I nod, my shoulders trembling.

Puzzled, Darren glances between us, wondering how Delaney knows about my birth mother dying. "I knew she had had another child, a boy, and in the few remaining items she had, his name was listed, actually his father's name," I shrug. "I did a search and found him. He even has a daughter Allegra's age."

"Brian is your crack mother's son, and now you two are in a relationship?" Darren slaps his hands against his thighs.

"I can't wait to see that splashed across the front page of the newspaper."

"I don't understand what's so awful about connecting with my half-brother," I stiffen. "I'm not sure what kind of twisted relationship you think Brian and I have, but you're disgusting." I peek at Delaney for his reaction, but his face gives nothing away.

Frustrated that he's not coming to my defense, I rise. "Are we done? Did you get what you needed?"

Delaney shifts to his other foot. "Not exactly, but this was entertaining."

Darren sits there, inebriated, ready to fall asleep on the couch. "I'm going to spend the night here," he moans.

"Like hell you are," I stomp my foot. "I don't want his car here. Or him."

Delaney certainly agrees on this point. "Come on, Darren. I'll give you a ride." He touches my shoulder. "I'll make sure the Jag's picked up in the morning."

"Okay," I nod.

"I'm gonna want to talk to this half-brother of yours," Delaney sighs. "Let me know how to get in touch with Brian."

I watch as my first lover and soon-to-be-ex-husband exit my home. One stone-cold sober, the other a stumbling mess. If it were under different circumstances, it would be comical.

Instead, I shake my head in pity.

31

VALERIE

It's me that falls asleep on the couch, the hours pacing the carpet with my wine end up in confusion when I wake, red stains leaving a trail on my light-colored shirt.

Convinced Darren came back into the house to stab me, I scream. It takes a moment to realize it's Merlot and not my blood. Clutching my chest, I take a couple deep breaths.

My cell rings. It's Brian. "I'm here," he says.

I rub my eyes. "Where?"

"The gate."

"What?" I'm only half-listening when I hear the intercom beep twice.

Sighing, I groan. "Okay, I'll let you in."

Disconnecting, I slide my feet into furry slippers and stumble out in the early morning light. I click the electronic gate open, but not before my low-functioning brain realizes that it's Delaney entering, not Brian.

I cross my arms across my chest, watching from a hidden spot near the garage. He's not alone, and I squint at the other man.

Shit. Did he bring the Chief of Police?

It takes a second to realize it's Darren in the passenger seat. Delaney drops him off beside his car. Maybe they will both leave before spotting Brian walking up the drive.

Darren must want to go inside the house, but Delaney shakes his head. I watch Darren point at the door, but whatever Delaney says, it defuses the situation. I'm relieved when Darren climbs into his Jag and drives off, Delaney behind him.

Unfortunately, when Brian comes into view, Delaney grinds to a halt.

I watch Brian's shoulders slump as Delaney stops to speak with him, but I can't tell what's said. Delaney's going to wonder why Brian didn't park in the drive. A headache pounds in my temples. Heading back inside, I quickly freshen up and take some pain pills. They're going to want a fresh cup of coffee, so I turn on the pot.

The knock on the door startles me, even though I expect it.

Taking a deep breath, I find both men standing there when I open it. Delaney's going to expect surprise on my face, but I keep my cool. "Hi, gentlemen," I give them my biggest smile. "Come inside. I started a pot of coffee."

Grinning at Delaney, I add. "I see you met Brian." I pretend this was planned and not a coincidence. "Brian, Detective Delaney and I went to high school together." I don't mention we dated and he broke my heart along the way.

Brian turns to Delaney. "I grew up about twenty miles from here, but your last name rings a bell. I can't put my finger on it, though."

Neither Delaney or I say a word.

Brian is adamant. "I'm sure I'll think of it later."

"I was going to contact you, but Valerie clearly beat me to it," Delaney says. I invite them to have a seat at the table while I pour the coffee. Burning myself with the hot liquid while I strain to hear their conversation, Brian twitches nervously. He keeps tugging at his ear. I exchange an anxious look with him.

I'm relieved when the shrill ringing of the telephone interrupts their small talk.

Caller ID is unknown.

Hands shaking, I answer. A man sneers on the other end. "Why don't you want your daughter back?"

Quivering, I tap the speaker button. Both Delaney and Brian freeze as the man says. "I thought you loved your daughter."

"Excuse me?" I clench the phone in my hand. "Who is this?"

"Someone you don't wanna fuck with."

Wildly, I search Delaney's face for how to respond. In his haste, he knocks his chair over to reach me.

"Is this a sick joke?" I cry.

"She's missing, ain't she?"

I pause, unsure what to respond with as my mind races a mile a minute. Delaney mouths for me to keep the man talking. I know he'll want to trace the call later.

"What do you want? Money?" I whisper. "I can offer you money."

"We sent a request for funds for the safe return of Allegra Atwater," the man snickers. "But no one responded, so we took matters into our own hands."

"What did you do?" I scream.

"Ask your husband."

"You sick fuck," I holler. Delaney yanks the phone away

from me, slashing a hand across his throat as Brian pulls me backward.

I shriek. "She better be alive. Don't you dare touch her. Don't you dare hurt my baby."

A chill goes down my spine as the man says. "Then you better answer our demands."

"I want a picture showing she's alive," I wail. "Send me a picture!" I start to ask a question, but it's useless, the line goes dead.

Whoever the man is, he's gone.

32

DETECTIVE DELANEY

After calling my department for back-up to get a trace on the call, I console Valerie and write down Brian's contact information.

I have a list of questions for him, like why he hides his vehicle in the brush near the Atwater property. I saw him ditching his pick-up on the way up the mountain, but I didn't want to draw attention to him while Darren was messing around on his phone. He's so self-involved, I doubt he'd notice a bear unless it was on top, attacking him. I kept going, whistling as I paused at the gate.

Reluctantly, I leave Valerie, who's pacing the floor, her eyes crazed. I suggest she take a chair and catch her breath. The dirty look she shot me was enough to silence my useless input. As if handling one Atwater isn't enough, now I have to confront Darren for a second time today. Picking him up at a motel and driving him to their house like a chauffeur was terrible enough. I tell myself he'll let something slip, and it'll be time well-spent if it helps with Allegra's case.

When I show up at his office, a glorified trailer in the

middle of nowhere, he doesn't seem particularly shocked to see me. A dark-haired woman is filing papers when I walk in.

He nods in greeting from behind his desk. "Do I need my attorney?"

I don't ask to sit, but I do, in an uncomfortable folding chair. It's a vast difference to the Atwater's' lifestyle. "Not unless you have something to hide."

Darren goes for humor. "It's only been a few hours. Miss me already?"

Motioning behind me, I wink. "Is that Sandy?"

He smirks. "Uh-huh." Raising a brow, he mouths, "She's pretty hot, yeah?"

I prefer the other version, but I keep my opinion to myself. "Are you planning to leave Valerie?"

"No. Of course not." Yet he touches his face, a sign he's untruthful.

"Why not?"

"I'd lose half." Another lie. I know Valerie signed a prenup.

Time for honesty now. I lean forward in my chair and peer at him. "Is that the main reason?"

"That and our daughter."

"What about after she graduates?"

"I'd still stand to lose a lot."

I try not to groan. *What a saint you are, Atwater*, I muse. "What about Sandy?"

"What about her?" He shifts his gaze to the open doorway, making sure Sandy is out of earshot.

"How is she with this *arrangement*? Does she want your daughter gone?"

He sputters at the question. "Allegra doesn't know about

our plans to divorce, and Sandy is just happy with the time we spend together."

Bingo. I knew he'd walk himself into that trap. Valerie told me he asked for a divorce. Now Darren's acting like it's out of the question for him and Valerie to split.

"You sure of that? Teens are more perceptive than we give them credit for."

"I've never paraded Sandy around Allegra. My daughter sees her if she stops here, of course, but that's it." He flashes his expensive watch at me, checking the time. "I don't mix business and pleasure."

"Is that so?" I can't help but add, "Isn't that how you met Valerie?"

His eyes narrow into slits. "Watch it, Delaney. I golf with your superiors."

"And the DA," he adds smugly.

I ignore his self-righteous attitude and continue, "Doesn't Sandy want more from you?"

He shrugs, "Sandy knew what she was getting into."

"But people change, and so do their minds."

"Of course, and so their opinions. And in my opinion, Delaney, you have a suspect in mind and are trying to make it work in your favor. I'm the cheating spouse, so I must be involved in my only daughter's disappearance. Don't forget, I had a wife when I met Valerie. She can try and rewrite the past as it suits her, but it's not reality."

"You had another daughter, right?"

His face goes ashen, "Are you implying I murdered her, too?"

"Whoa!" I hold up a hand. "No one said anything about killing." I shake my head back and forth, "Now if there's something you want to tell me..."

He takes a deep breath, "I lost my first child when she

was a few years old. Now I have a teenager who is the pride and joy of my life. She's missing. Find her, that's all I ask. I'd do anything for her."

"What about your business associates?"

"What about them?"

"Anyone have a reason to harm your family?"

"Absolutely, people want what I have." Darren touches his ring finger, twisting where his wedding band would be if he were wearing it. "Listen, Delaney, don't think you're pulling the wool over my eyes. I know Valerie paints me as this overbearing, controlling monster."

"That might be so," I tap my chin. "But if you want your daughter back, why then haven't you paid the ransom?"

Mouth behind his hand, his voice comes out muffled. "What ransom?"

"The ransom note the kidnappers sent to you directly."

"No one sent anything."

He doesn't know I haven't seen it. I call his bluff. "It was sent here."

"How do you know?"

"Because I talked to the kidnappers this morning." Now it's my turn to fib. "They sent a copy to Valerie when they didn't hear from you."

"Really? Then why didn't you mention this last night?"

"She opened the mail this morning." The lie falls easily off my lips. "It was intercepted by yours truly. I took it to the station after I left your house."

A look of disdain crosses his face.

"From where I'm sitting, it sounds like you want your daughter to die. I hope they don't make her suffer." I'm trying for a reaction, hoping for a confession, and worried he'll pummel me in the process. His beet-red face warns me he's about to flip his lid. I sit back in my chair and wait him out.

He slams his fist on the desk. "Enough!"

"You can explain to the authorities and the district attorney why you didn't communicate a ransom letter you received from the alleged kidnappers," I say quietly,

"But I'm not going to."

"Why would you keep this from the police unless you have something to hide?" I raise an eyebrow, "I can't wait to arrest you, Mr. Atwater."

"I am not going to get into a pissing contest with some stranger," Darren yells. "Just because he claims he has my daughter."

"Even if said stranger is holding your daughter hostage, and you just got her murdered?"

"How dare you?" he roars. "Coming in here with a bag of tricks you learned at some academy. It doesn't give you the right to parade your antics in my office."

I ignore his comment. "Not to mention, we got a report about a drug mule in your prized organization." I throw that in there for good measure. "So, what now, Mr. Atwater?"

"Now," he points at the door. "You get the hell out of my office."

"Great." I'm done with his charades. "I'll be in touch. Probably with cuffs and an arrest warrant."

"Like hell you will."

And just like a typical Atwater, he has to get in the last word.

33

VALERIE

Unable to stay at the house and calm myself after Brian heads to work, I scream at the walls and pound my fists in frustration. The nagging feeling that Darren has put our daughter in jeopardy grows. Anger and remorse are at the forefront of my mind as I drive to the trailer that houses his makeshift office.

I walk in as Delaney brushes past me. I'm tempted to follow him outside, but his set jaw and demeanor tell me to let him cool down.

Forced to confront both Sandy and Darren, my hands shake at my sides. Her eyes widen when I enter the office. She abruptly stands and comes around the desk, her mouth in a frown, as she keeps a couple feet of distance between us.

I say nothing, fixing her with an icy stare.

"He's in a meeting." She acts as if this will stop me.

"Really?" I say sarcastically. "Because his appointment just walked by me."

She doesn't have a response.

"I'm going to speak to my husband." I slam Darren's office door in her face, clicking the lock behind me.

Darren's not any less frazzled than Delaney. Staring out the window, his fingers snap the blinds angrily. "I'm calling the Chief of Police, dammit!" he snaps. "That fucking detective needs to be thrown out on his ass."

Coldly, I ask. "How could you?" I'm not strong enough to lift his desk and throw it at him, but at this moment, I feel like I could. "That's our daughter. What if something happens because the ransom didn't get paid? How could you be so *cheap* with her life?"

"They really called you?"

I nod. "This morning."

"We don't have the money," Darren sinks into his chair with a sigh.

"What do you mean?"

"Liquid assets. I don't have that kind of cash."

"You're lying," I glare at him. "Is this some kind of divorce tactic, so you don't have to pony up anything?"

"Christ, Val, listen to yourself. We are far from poor. But the kind of money they asked for, we don't have it."

"Then what do we do?"

He motions for me to sit in the chair Delaney vacated. "We need to talk."

I sit, but I don't dare move, my eyes misty with emotion.

Darren threads his arms behind his head. "You and I didn't think this through. We never should've involved the police to begin with."

I tilt my head, "It's not like the authorities wouldn't find out if we paid someone off in secret."

"And another thing." He slams his fist on the desk. "Why didn't you tell me you had a past relationship with Devon Delaney?"

"I was a teenager."

"Valerie, your ex-lover is tearing apart our assets, digging in deeper and deeper. You and I both know that's not going reflect favorably on either of us. I have to stop it."

"Why did you send Brian to the border?"

"I beg your pardon?"

"What did you have him take?" I stand up and lean my elbows on his desk. "Are you transporting drugs across the border?"

He sits deathly still.

"Did you set him up because you thought I was having an affair with him?"

His gaze is locked on mine.

"Are you? Answer me, dammit!"

"I don't owe you an explanation," He leans forward so I can see every pore and whisker on his face. "You can never leave anything the hell alone, and look where it's gotten us. Now get out of my office."

34

DETECTIVE DELANEY

I'm sitting on my back patio, feet perched up on the chair across from me, drinking a vodka tonic. My gentle giant is in his usual spot to my left, and I watch as his ears perk up at the sound of an engine motor.

He lets out a shrill bark, so I hold my drink in hand, pausing for a moment.

It sounds like the slam of a car door.

Falkor immediately rises and takes off down the steps, heading towards the front of my one-story house. I assume it must be okay since I don't hear another yelp, either from him or an intruder. Plus, my gun is never far from reach.

A voice hollers in the shadows, "It's just me," as the dark figure moves towards the patio.

Chief Bratton.

"Sir," I say in greeting.

"You didn't answer the bell, so I figured you'd be out here." He climbs up the wooden steps with Falkor on his heels. "You always did like to be outside when the rest of your world was imploding."

"You know me well," I agree.

"I know this is a tough case for you." He points to the empty chair to my right. "Mind if I sit down for a minute?" He never asks, usually forces his way into every situation and every crevice of my life. This can't be good.

"What is it?"

He ignores the question, "Got any beer?

"Inside," I say. "Help yourself."

"Be right back." He turns before he gets to the screen door, "Need anything?" I shake my head and watch as Falkor settles back down underneath the table as the door slams after him. I peer into the dark woods, wondering what he's going to come at me with.

A break in the case? A body found?

The rest of my vodka tonic dumps down my throat in one gulp.

He reappears with a can of Coors Light and a bag of peanuts he found in the pantry.

"How's Valerie Atwater?"

"Don't," I growl.

He sits down and rests his legs on the other empty chair. "I didn't come here to talk about that." He rips open the plastic. "I want to talk about the case."

"It's all the same, and maybe I don't."

He whistles through his teeth. "Not the way to talk to your superior."

"What's wrong?" I ask. "You don't like what's unraveling?"

"I don't think you do." He stares hard at me for a moment. "I think there's a lot more to this puzzle than what meets the eye."

"There certainly is."

"You're looking in the wrong places." His voice is gentle yet firm. "You have your sights set on Darren Atwater."

"I disagree. I do not think he's the only suspect."

"Right. It's either him or him and his mistress, Sandy," he frowns. "This is an Atwater, Devon. I'm getting so much shit from the state to get this handled." He runs a hand through his balding hair. "Not to mention, I'm being accused of nepotism, and his attorneys are pressuring me like I'm the one in the hot seat. Maybe you forgot what a small town this was."

"So, it's about politics, then?" I add, "And perception?"

"I can't end my career on this note," he grunts. "Accused of tunnel vision and mishandling this case. When you are running the damn department, you can sit in your ivory tower. Right now, you need to consider the broader picture."

He takes a swig of his beer, and I watch his throat constrict as he washes it down. "I want you to stop breathing down Darren Atwater's neck and poking your nose in his business dealings."

I correct him, "*Shady* business dealings." Falkor raises his massive head from underneath the table with concern as I slam my foot against the metal leg of the chair.

"I think you need to stop ignoring what's in front of you." He sits back a minute, chomping on a peanut before he spits it into his empty can. "Just because you and Valerie go way back doesn't mean life hasn't changed her, or the money, or her marriage to that pompous asshole."

"Well, we agree on one thing. He's *such* an asshole."

"I'm taking you off the case."

"Are you fucking serious?" I pound my fist on the table. "So much for pivoting."

"I changed my mind," he sighs. "I need Darren Atwater off my back. Off his friend, the DA's back, who is now on mine."

We sit in uncomfortable silence as I twist my glass in

hand, afraid I'm about to break it from squeezing it hard. "I'm going to have Segal and Kantz on the case from now on."

"It takes two men to do my job?" I whistle. "Suit yourself."

"What can I say, son. You're impressive."

I attempt a joke. "I'm just glad I'm adopted, so I'm not bald, just prematurely gray."

"You're not that young," he reminds me, "Didn't you turn forty-five this year?"

Falkor must agree because he gives a loud snort and then rests his furry face on my thigh. I rest my hand on his cold nose and give his ears a good rub.

Chief Bratton, my father, stands and stretches. With an awkward pat on my shoulder, he says, "You're my son, and I love you, Devon." I ignore the wetness that forms in the crease of my eyelid, and I don't know if it's because he never tells me this or if he's trying to ease his earlier news. In the next moment, he becomes gruff again. "And now I'll put my chief's cap on." He turns to me. "Tomorrow, you'll report to your office at eight am. Segal and Kantz will be waiting for you to brief them on the case."

"Fine," is all I can muster.

"Good." He gives my shoulder a final squeeze and addresses Falkor, who follows him down the deck stairs to the driveway. He's such a gentleman, I think, walking my father to his waiting car.

Frustrated, I rest my head in my hands. If Darren Atwater isn't guilty of involvement in his own daughter's disappearance, then who is?

An idea starts to formulate, and I wonder if I can pull it off.

35

CERULEAN

Just as my name changed to Cerulean in the confines of these walls, so did my focus on survival. I have to reestablish my identity, which meant Allegra had to die. The name sounds foreign to me in this house of sister-wives. It used to match my bubbly personality, a distinct difference from the girl I had to become in here.

As much as I miss her, I'm not that girl anymore. To survive, I had to become Cerulean. I'd hate to say I acclimated to the household, but I've had to adjust in some aspects. After a few weeks of crying myself to sleep, the sobs lessen, and I wake up resigned to the fact that this is temporary, or at least that's what I tell myself.

It works, until reality sets in and I meet John, the business partner. It's then I realize that even in a house like this, girls are still females, and jealousy rears its ugly head.

One afternoon, a man bursts into the house with no warning, not utilizing the three knocks Muscleman pounds before entering. It's my week for kitchen clean-up, and I'm on my hands and knees, scrubbing the floor in an oversized t-shirt and sweatpants. Everything is baggy on me, my weight loss food and stress-induced.

The slam of the door is followed by a hoot. This forces me to a standing position, sponge in hand. "You must be Cerulean." The man strides straight to me, his hands leeching onto my face as he tilts my cheek, then moves my chin side-to-side. The dirty sponge drips water droplets as I hold it in my grasp. I'm tempted to shove it in his mouth.

"Lovely, just lovely." He steps back and throws his arms in the air. "I have so much work for you, and well, this will be a valuable business endeavor."

I don't respond verbally, but my stomach twists into knots.

Up until this point, I hadn't had to go to 'work.' It's not that I thought I would be excused, but it was my luck that I had my period, which is an automatic dismissal, and then Muscleman said I wasn't allowed to. We haven't even had the dreaded ceremony. Ruby and the girls have kept me in the dark on when it's supposed to happen, either because they don't know, or are trying to keep me from worrying.

Ruby hears us and comes running into the kitchen. "John," she bites her lip with distaste, "I didn't hear you."

"You do now, sweetheart," John says. "I've just met the newbie."

"Yes. The girls have taken quite a liking to her." Ruby's voice is ice-cold. "You can go to your room now, Cerulean."

"I still have the laundry to do."

She raises her voice, "Did you not hear me?"

"Okay," I dump the sponge back in the pail and leave the room. I don't go far, deciding I'll eavesdrop from behind the corner of the wall.

"What're you doing here today?" Ruby seems disgruntled by his appearance.

Undeterred, John responds, "I didn't know I needed an appointment."

"I told you we needed to talk, and you ignored me."

"Maybe I'm not here for you," John slides into the corner booth. "I was asked to pick up the girl."

"What?" Ruby seems perturbed, "What for?"

"To work." He leans back against the seat. "She needs to start earning her keep."

"She hasn't even been initiated. I thought he wanted her for himself."

"He does. But he's a man, and he wants to make money."

"So, I need to get her ready?"

"He asked me to take care of it."

"That's not the process, John."

From my spot, he must be giving her a death glare because she lowers her gaze to her hands. "Are you arguing with me, Ruby?"

"Of course not."

"I don't like the tone of your voice."

"I don't like you taking advantage of..." Like a coiled rattlesnake that's about to strike, his hands lean forward to grip her throat. "What're you saying?" They lock eyes, and he must be squeezing harder because she gasps, then chokes.

"What I do with her is *none* of your business, do you understand?" She can't move with her neck in his viselike grip, so she slowly nods. "Good," he drops his hand to his lap. "I'm glad we had that talk."

"I need to speak to you about something."

Dismissive, he stands, "I don't have time."

"When can..."

"Jesus, Ruby, I've had it with you." With a blow from his fist, she goes flying across the damp floor, which is still drying from the soap and water I used to clean it.

"Stay down." He kicks her in the face, then the stomach. "If it's what I think it is, don't bother telling me."

Unable to stop myself, I lurch out from behind the shadows and pummel him, jumping between his foot and her abdomen.

"Stop it," I scream, "stop hurting her!"

I don't know who is more shocked to see me, him or her. John's mouth hangs open while Ruby quickly backs up and out of his reach. He doesn't stop, and I continue to suffer his wrath until he exhales and steps backward.

To make matters worse, I learn what the 'pantry' is really used for.

Punishment.

He forces Ruby to lock me in the pantry, watching as she does, and then instead of leaving, he disappears down the hall with her.

The walk-in pantry is about the size of a hall closet. You can't stand, shelves prevent you from doing that, you can only sit. There's nothing to do but close your eyes and keep your imagination from running wild.

The pungency is enough to knock me out, reminding me of the sheets on the bed when I first came. It doesn't smell like a pantry should, where nonperishable items are stored, and supplies are kept. It's worse than moldy bread rotting or meat left out too long. It reeks of something dead, and I wonder if a rat or mouse is above me on a shelf, stuck in a trap.

Sitting in the small, confined darkness, I hold a hand up to my nose and come away with the stickiness of blood. I rub it on my leg and shudder, a chill running down my spine.

I reach my hand out to touch the wall. Something's

etched in the paint like a pencil was dug in and left a permanent mark.

Later on, when I'm let out and told to finish scrubbing the kitchen, I use a flashlight hidden in a junk drawer and examine what's written.

I read what's permanently ingrained in the wall. My body responds by throwing up bile since I rarely get to eat.

I'm Olive now, but I'm Cynthia Watts, and I died here, followed by the date.

Olive died in this closet. That's the stench.

And with that, I resolve to not let that happen to me, no matter what.

36

CERULEAN

To make matters worse, now Ruby is mad at me.

Not only did I get a black eye and a nosebleed, I got the pantry and her silent treatment. When John comes back to collect me, he screams at Ruby to cover up the bruising underneath my eye. He waits in the kitchen, impatient, as she drags me into her bedroom to get ready.

"Why're you mad?" I whisper.

She ignores my question and pushes me into a chair facing the mirror. "It's hard to get the purple covered underneath your eye, but I'll use heavy concealer." Expertly she applies makeup, too much in my opinion, and finishes with a deep red lip liner and a matching lipstick.

I don't look like myself, I look like a whore. I didn't allow my mind to drift to nudity or what I would be dressed in. I guess I thought a silk nightgown of some sort. Instead, I feel like Julia Roberts in Pretty Woman on the corner in even less clothing.

I'm shocked at the amount of weight I've lost that was unnecessary in the first place. My gaunt cheekbones stare back at me as I stare at my too-skinny frame in the full-length mirror. If that's not bad enough, I have constant hunger pangs.

Ruby expects me to praise her work, but I can only stare at myself with apprehension, reminding myself this is *Cerulean*, not Allegra Atwater.

And that's the only way I'm able to exit her room and greet John, who stands and drops his lousy mood like a coat.

Giddy, he practically drags me out the door, Ruby a forgotten afterthought. I don't bother to turn and catch the murderous glances she sends my way when we depart.

He escorts me into a luxury vehicle, too new and classy for him and this side of town. My eyes gaze at the unknown scenery as we drive through an unfamiliar landscape. I try and memorize my surroundings, searching for points of reference.

When we pull up to a five-star hotel, John hisses at me. "You will listen to me and not talk to anyone, got it?"

Before the valet arrives, he hands me a coat. "Here, put this on," he murmurs. It's a long, black trench coat from the backseat. I don't dare ask whom it belongs to. Was it Olive's? Or does anything have an owner besides the men with these girls?

Thankful to cover my bare skin, I button the trench before the valet guy opens my door. It's weird to be outside in the evening, even for a minute. I stare at the sky, losing my balance when my heel meets the curb. I suck in a breath of air and look up at the stars, my lower lip trembling as I think of my mom and our talk when I was a child.

I love you, Mom, please don't give up on me, I'm out here, I whisper to myself.

The man gives me his hand as I stumble. His eyes exude concern. "Careful, young lady, those shoes look lethal." I give him a forced laugh and almost gasp when he remarks, "You act like you've been in prison and need to get as much air in your lungs as you can."

You have no idea, I want to shout. I'm about to make a comment when John replaces the valet's light grip with his rough one. If I thought I could run for help, I would, but John's touch is already back on my arm, his fingers twisted around my elbow. He acts like we're a couple, his hand lingering on my back like you would your significant other.

Hotel key in hand, he leads me to the elevator.

"Did you enjoy the drive?"

"Yes."

He issues a stern warning, "Sir. Yes, sir."

"I thought that was only for him," I murmur.

"No. We are both your masters." He reaches forward to push a strand of hair off my face. "You look good with curls."

"Thanks," I utter miserably. "Thank you, sir."

He stares at me intently, "If tonight was your last night on earth, what would your last meal be?" My face scrunches up in horror, and I try to wrap the coat tighter around my waist, shivering behind the thin cloth. Is this John foreshadowing what's going to happen this evening?

He ignores my pensive stare. "What would it be? Any combination of food or restaurants, including dessert."

I pretend to think, tilting my chin.

He offers, "If it were me, I'd want Wagyu steak, truffle mashed potatoes, my grandma's sweet potato casserole, and an entire peanut butter chocolate cheesecake."

"That sounds delicious." My stomach sounds an alarm, the only meal I've had today hardly counts as one. I was given oatmeal that was more water than the actual substance. John's still waiting for a response as the elevator halts on the top floor. It opens, but he makes no move to exit, his gaze locked on mine.

"Steak. And potatoes," I finally say. "And rhubarb pie."

"What about to drink?"

"A Coke."

"Not vodka?"

I muster the confidence to respond with, "I'm not old enough to vote, let alone drink." His earlier smile twists into a frown. "Well, don't go around advertising that tonight." His eyes light up as he thinks of something. "Actually, they'd probably love to know that."

I shrug noncommittally.

"Steak it is, if you do well tonight. I will take you to dinner."

"Do what well?"

He squints at me like I'm an exotic animal. "Are you serious?"

My eyes drift down to the expensive but highly uncomfortable heels I'm wearing. I'm tall already, and these make me tower over everyone.

"They want models," John had insisted when Ruby was picking out my wardrobe.

"Just do what they ask." He shakes his head in annoyance, and the elevator beeps at us again, signaling it will close if we don't act.

He leads me to a room, inserts the key, and I'm shocked to see it's the size of most of my friend's houses. It's not a regular-sized hotel room, it's a penthouse suite. I hear a loud racket as the sound of glass being smashed echoes to the foyer, and a wave of terror envelopes me.

John notices and whispers. "It's just a poker game."

When we enter a spacious room, sure enough, four men sit at a card table, all of their eyes concentrating on the cards in hand. Their expressions try to remain neutral, hence the term 'poker face.'

They're all different ethnicities. One is Hispanic, one is black, one is mixed, one is white, and all are dressed in various levels of suited attire. One has a tie loosened around his neck and a jacket hanging over his chair, another is wearing a navy three-piece, the third has his pants unbuttoned and his collared shirt untucked, the last guy wears a gray suit that brings out the salt and pepper in his hair. All look around my father's age, give or take a few years.

I try not to gag, forcing that comparison out of my head.

They don't pay attention to John and I at first. One is staring at the broken glass he just presumably threw at the wall, judging by the distance it is from him. Cards are laid out on the table along with a white powder and beer bottles. One is smoking a vape pen, another is strangling a cigar between his lips.

The jacket keeps me covered, but I still feel naked when their eyes focus on me, or more precisely, my body. It takes them a while to meet my eyes as if it's inappropriate to stare at me head-on. Or maybe deep down, they're ashamed of having to pay for this.

Involuntarily I shiver, goosebumps rising on my skin.

John motions to me, "Gentlemen, I have your evening's entertainment."

"As if poker wasn't enough," the navy three-piece suit says.

The unkempt one smirks, "I like what I see."

The third one claps his hand, and the fourth one, now named Gray, remains silent.

John elbows me in the ribs, my cue to speak.

The red lipstick on my mouth opens. "Hi gentlemen, I'm Cerulean." I practice a small curtsy, "At your service."

All four give me their definition of a smile.

"Sa-real-a-what?"

"Can we just call you sexy?"

"Take it off already."

Gray stoically sits in his chair, his hands folded in front of him.

"Okay, doll, take it off," John sneers, backing away from me, "And try and look seductive." I give each man a small smile, my eyes drifting from face to face as I beg them to see the uneasiness.

I remove the belt of the trench coat, then the jacket, unsure how to be provocative and sensual. Because my lip trembles and signals an onslaught of fresh tears, I spin around as if it's rehearsed and let the coat tumble off my shoulders.

There's a mirror in front of me, and I refuse to meet my eyes in it.

Instead, I look over my shoulder but over their heads.

When I turn and place a hand on my hip, the lacy black bustier and fishnet stockings seem to further amplify my sexuality. A part of me I do not want to share.

The men leer at my breasts, pushing over the tight material. Even John licks his lips. My face flames in embarrassment, and I'm grateful the room is dimly lit.

"Drinks?" The man in gray stands as if repulsed by my show.

For a minute, the men refocus on alcohol consumption. "Everyone but Randy," the three-piece suit jokes, referring to the sloppy one. "That glass is a reminder he can't hold his liquor."

"Yeah, he's still like a frat boy," another one prompts, "I think we should cut him off."

"Then, I get a turn with the girl first." He settles back in his chair as if he won a contest.

"I've set up private quarters across the hall." John points behind us across the foyer.

"What if we want to watch?"

"Better yet," the fully-suited man says, "what if we all want to join in?"

"I'm not gay," one protests.

"It's not gay if a chick's involved."

"How old are you, sugar?"

"Old enough." I scowl.

Gray takes notice and hands me a drink. "That'll help take the edge off."

I don't know whether to pummel him or be grateful, so I nod my thanks.

John pinches my arm and hisses. "You better behave, or you'll end up like Olive." I assume he expects Ruby to use it as a scare tactic with us.

I gulp, letting my lips twist into a smile. "I'm old enough to know better but young enough not to care."

"That's better," Relieved, John gives me a wink. "Okay, gentlemen, if you need me, I'll be over here." He sinks into a couch across the palatial room, and the men ignore him, going back to their poker game for a moment.

"So, we can do anything with you?" The drunken one raises an eyebrow.

"Uh, I have limits," I say.

"What?" Navy three-piece complains. "He said nothing was out of bounds."

"Randy," the drunken frat boy in a man's body, reaches forward to rub my ass appreciatively. "I'd like a turn."

Choking on my own fear, I have to slink away to the bar to fight the tears that are starting to threaten my expertly-applied makeup. "Okay, who's first?"

The silent one, Gray, raises his hand. "Can I have a turn?"

"Why does the best-looking one get to go first?" Fully-suited throws down his hand.

"Save the best for last," someone else retorts.

"You'll all get a turn," John yells from across the room. "Cerulean, they aren't paying for you to stand around. Get to work."

And with that, Gray takes the lead by grabbing my sweaty palm, pulling me down the foyer to the bedroom.

37

CERULEAN

Gray shuts the door behind us, locking it.

A moment later, there's a tug on the handle. "Unlock the door, you know the rules," John yells. "Hurry, or you'll lose your turn."

He abides. "Sorry, John, my mistake."

"Uh-huh." He smirks. "You know I have to keep an eye on her."

"She's feisty, I get it." Gray shrugs. He reaches into his suit pocket. "I got you some good stuff. The best." He hands John a baggie, but I don't know what it is-pills or powder. Appeased by this, he steps back while Gray closes the door again.

I'm frozen to the beige carpeting, watching their exchange when Gray turns to me, a scowl on his face. "What's wrong?" He questions. "You mad I didn't share?"

"What do you want me to do?" I whisper. "Just tell me so we can get this over with."

"I usually like to savor these kinds of moments."

"I can't...I can't do this." I moan.

"Aren't you supposed to like this kind of thing?" He attempts to make eye contact, but I twist around to consider my surroundings. The side table sits empty, where a telephone should be.

On the other end, a vase of flowers and a bowl of foil-wrapped candy rests. As I focus on the dish, I realize it's not for your sweet tooth, it's the shiny packaging of condoms. Frantic, I run to the window, staring out at the city lights. There's no sliding glass door, no balcony. I'm stuck.

"Help me, please," I say out loud. "Please!"

His reflection behind me in the glass shows a tilted head and narrowed eyes. He takes a step toward me. Anticipating his touch, I cringe. He's not a bad-looking man, but he's old. And this forced closeness is not what I want. I want to go home.

"Huh?" He stands behind me but doesn't press up against my back. I catch a whiff of what smells like aftershave, the expensive kind like my father wears. Pressing my eyes closed, I push the memory of my father away.

"What's going on?"

"My family has money, lots of money," I offer.

"Let me guess," he chuckles, "this was the opportunity of a lifetime to show them you could make it on your own?"

Disgusted, his gold wedding ring catches my eye when he hooks his arms around my waist. "There are cameras in here." He loosens his grip but doesn't let go. Giving me a second to catch my breath, he whispers in my ear. "Please nod your head to tell me you understand."

I shake my head in response.

"John mentioned you were the virgin special. Is this your first time?" My mind races. In this type of situation, *yes*, I want to scream. I didn't set out to be kidnapped and sold for male pleasure. But I'm Cerulean now.

"Uh-huh," I swallow.

"Good," he swivels me to face him. "You have to play the game. Act like we're having fun, that this is enjoyable."

"Okay," I sigh.

"Lean in and pretend to lick my neck."

I follow his instructions, breathing heavily near his throat.

"Good, that's right," he moans. "Why did you mention your family?"

"Because I need help getting out of here."

"You're not here by choice?"

I rest my hands awkwardly on his broad shoulders. "No."

Keeping his face close to mine, he says. "How old are you?"

"Seventeen."

I watch his throat constrict. His face burns red.

"Do you have any kids?"

"Don't you fucking dare," he seethes through clenched teeth.

"Please," I beg. "I can make sure you're set up for life. They would pay you a lot of money. More than you could ever spend."

He's silent.

"Maybe," he thumbs his chest. "But these guys would kill me."

I shudder at the thought. Not that I devalue my life, but why would the bad guys care if they have one less girl?

"Let me think." He yanks me toward the bed. "We need to go through the motions at least."

Shakily, I lean down to remove my heels. "Can you buy me for the night and take me home?" I plead, "Back to my parents?"

"I don't know what to do," he says helplessly, pulling me

down beside him. "I can try, but I've never been allowed to do that before. Are most of you girls underage?"

I shrug.

"I don't want to get in trouble." He instructs me to remove his suit jacket. "I'd go to jail for soliciting, not to mention you're underage. I'd lose everything."

"There's gotta be a hotline or some way to stay under the radar."

He points to the pristine white comforter. "I want you to undress," his eyes hold mine, "but underneath the covers. I don't wanna touch you since you're a minor."

I gulp.

"Just keep yourself wrapped up in the sheet, so it at least looks like you're naked."

My terrified expression gives me away. Immobile, he gently tugs me toward his body. "If you're covered, it looks like we're doing something. If you don't, you're going to have bigger problems with your pimp."

Pimp? I never thought of a word to describe what John or Muscleman does. But it's the truth, they pimp girls out. It seems foreign on my tongue, and I hate the sound of it.

Trembling, I remove what little fabric I'm wearing, which now seems like a lot compared to my nakedness. The thin sheet and comforter are not enough to keep me warm when I'm internally frozen.

After I lose the minimal clothing I have on, Gray joins me underneath the covers, pulling the comforter over our heads. "We have to put on a show. I'm going to pretend to take my clothes off, and then we have to make noises."

He unbuckles his belt and tosses it on the floor. Then his shirt. Fortunately, he leaves his pants on.

"Like moaning and other noises?"

"Yes." He reaches his hand out for a condom by the bed

and unwraps it. He holds the latex in his fingers. "I have to pretend to, you know..."

"What about your friends?" I whisper to Gray as he caresses a spot on the bed beside me. "Please don't let them come in here."

"I'll do my best." He seems preoccupied as he stares at the wall, his eyes avoiding mine. I keep talking. "My real name is Allegra Atwater, look me up."

I don't think he hears me until he mumbles, "Sure."

"Do you do this a lot?"

"Don't judge me, I thought you girls were prostitutes," he says defensively.

Gray asks me a few questions as he messes up my hair, and I do my best to dishevel the sheets. We make sounds, and I feel like I'm shooting a movie which, if we're being filmed, I technically am.

John busts through the door to check on us. He says it's to make sure Gray is satisfied, but I know it's to make sure I'm not causing problems. "Time for another." John motions for him to get lost. When he exits the room, I take the opportunity to beg one last time.

"Please," I try to remain calm, "I need you to get your phone."

"They take our phones when we arrive." Gray gently touches my cheek as tears start to roll down my face. "I can't help you," he winces, "I'm sorry."

After he dresses himself and steps out, I wipe my eyes and say a silent prayer that I got through one alleged liaison. Not all will be as understanding as him, I remind myself.

Keeping the sheet pressed to my naked body, I hear Gray asking John if he can rent me for a house party, along with a couple of my friends.

Waiting for John's answer, I settle back against the pillows.

It's not a positive one.

He flings the door open and jumps on the bed to grab the nape of my neck. "What the fuck, Cerulean!"

I stammer. "Uh, I'm sorry."

Shit, did John hear what I said to Gray?

"You know better than to tell clients you're allowed to do outside jobs." John shakes me as Gray stands behind him, his eyes nervously darting around the room before they land on the floor.

"I...uh, I'm sorry." I apologize, "I'm sorry, sir. I didn't know..."

With a final slam, John shoves my face down into the pillow. He snaps his fingers at Gray, screeching, "It's time for your friends to have a turn."

He leaves me gasping for air on the bed as he yanks Gray out of the room. When he returns, it's with another man. This one, three-piece navy suit, is in a mood to get rough. When I'm alone with him, his clammy hands claw at my skin. After I huddle underneath the covers and scream, John flies into the room like there was a fire and I sounded the alarm.

Navy suit guy complains I'm not following instructions, and before I know it, John reaches into his pocket and pulls out something tiny. Before I can respond, I'm stabbed in the vein with a sharp needle.

Thrashing, both John and the man both hold me until I settle down. With a hand still on my chest, the man shakes his head. "This girl is trouble."

My vision blurs, and John slaps my cheeks with his hand to coerce me to stand, but it's useless. Dizzy, I close my eyes as the room becomes a blurry mass of shapes and muted colors. When I wake up, I'm in a foreign bed, not the one in either the penthouse suite or room number four at the sister-wives' house.

38

CERULEAN

"What the fuck happened?" I hear screams. The house is so tiny it sounds like the fight is beside me. It takes me a moment to realize who the voices belong to.

Muscleman howls. "How dare you? I fucking bought her. She wasn't yours to take."

"Calm down, man." John's voice is shaky, the earlier confidence gone.

"I'm not going to *calm* down." Muscleman's voice raises another octave. "Why would *you* tell me to relax?" I hear a thud, and I'm pretty sure he pushed John by the sound.

"It was fine, the night went well. I made, I mean, *we* made a lot of coin."

"That's not the point. I didn't want Cerulean taken out of the house."

"Why not?" John protests.

"This girl isn't our usual. I know her family on a pretty intimate level."

"Whaddaya mean?"

"Her mom and I, we have a thing." He lowers his voice to

a reasonable level. "Lots of people are looking for her. "Authorities. Private investigators. Her parents. Everybody you don't want. I didn't want Cerulean spotted in public. Did anyone seem suspicious?"

My blood runs cold. He knows my mom? What kind of a 'thing' could they possibly have going? I know my parents have a fucked-up marriage, but my mom's seemed so focused on my own happiness.

"No," John sounds contrite. "I'm sorry. We only went to one hotel, and it was a penthouse suite."

"Her family is loaded, like major wealthy. She's not a throwaway or a runaway or some teen down on her luck." Muscleman snaps. "Her rich daddy better come through with the money soon."

"I need to know the gentlemen that were there," Muscleman demands, "I need their names. Are they the regulars?"

I hear John go through a list. I wonder which one was Gray.

"You better go," Muscleman says. "She'll probably wake up, and you drugged the shit out of her."

"She was making a scene," John argues. "I had no choice."

I can imagine him gritting his teeth as he says, "Get out and let me handle this."

"Okay." I hear the door slam after him, and a lock clicks into place. Then the toilet flushes and the sink drips before I feel Muscleman's hot breath on my face. I want to push him out of the way, but instead, I groggily open my eyes. I need to know about his ties to my family.

"What happened to me?" I yelp.

"You had a rough night."

"What...did they?" I can't finish my sentence. The reality is unspeakable.

"Go to sleep."

"How do you know my mom? And how do you know my family?"

He sighs, but says nothing.

"My mom?" I moan. "What is she to you?"

He gives me a small shove. "Stop talking." Muscleman isn't in an explaining mood. "The drugs will wear off soon, and you'll feel well-rested."

I can tell he's troubled by the evening, but for a different reason than I am.

"Tomorrow, we'll have a talk about your future here." He lays down next to me, but for once doesn't hover. "Just sleep." I try to fight the fogginess, but like a light switch being turned off, I close my eyes and am transported to another time and place. A happy place. My childhood. Allegra's.

I think of one of my favorite memories when my parents took me to Disneyland. They were glowing with pride, holding hands, and they acted like big kids, riding every ride along with me. My father begrudgingly wore the Mickey Mouse ears I begged him to.

They were happy together.

We were a family.

And nothing else mattered.

When I wake up, I'm not in a hotel, and I'm not in bed. Muscleman is nowhere to be found. My head lolls back when I realize I'm in the basement, restrained again.

I vaguely remember waking up, thrashing around until Muscleman reappeared by my side. I started to question him about my family, and specifically, my mom.

He did not like the inquisition.

Refusing to answer my questions, he dragged me by the nape of my neck outside. I figured he would tie me to a tree or something sinister, but his intentions were equally sadistic.

He brought me to the backyard to show me something in the garden. I freaked out when he showed me a shallow spot in the dirt. With the toe of his boot, he uncovered what had to be plastic.

It had to be a Halloween prop. It just happened to be shaped like a bone. And it was buried in the dirt. Muscleman claimed this would be my new resting place if I didn't stop upsetting him.

My recollection is blank after that, except for the throbbing headache at the base of my head. I don't know how much more of this I can take.

A guttural sound I think is mine, escapes my lips. Until I realize there's another *me* down here, a girl I've never seen before.

PART III

PRESENT DAY

39

MADELINE

When I wake up, I'm in a small room, a bare room. Concrete on all sides. Zero windows. It's empty, and a sinking feeling twists my stomach into knots.

At least I thought I was alone until I hear a whine.

Startled, I see the fragments of another girl. I say *fragments* because of her gaunt appearance like she's about to blow away. Her long hair's blonde and greasy, and her pale skin is dull and colorless.

Sickly is what Brian would say.

When I raise my arms to motion at her, they only raise halfway, since I'm forced to stop at my elbows, I'm latched onto something in the wall, a type of restraint.

Defeated, I stare at my knees and pick at a scab. "Where am I?" I whisper.

No response.

"Where are we?" I ask louder.

"Hell," the girl remarks.

"Please," I tremble. "Can you help me?"

"Probably not, since I'm chained to this wall." It should sound harsh, but it's full of pity.

"My boyfriend, he was shot," I shriek. "They just left him."

"Who did?"

I explain what happened. She tells me she has a boyfriend in California.

"What's your name?"

"Cerulean," she answers automatically. I watch as her mouth twists into a grimace. "I mean, Allegra."

"I'm Maddy," I say.

We stare at each other. I don't know about this girl, but I'm memorizing her face. I bite my lip, afraid to ask her any questions in case someone's listening.

After another moment of silence, I can't stand it. "How long have you been here?"

Her voice quivers. "Long enough to know I don't want to be here."

"So, you didn't just get here?"

"No. I'm in here for punishment. Usually, it's solitary confinement. I asked questions I shouldn't have."

"What?"

"Never mind." She sounds hollow. "You'll find out about Olive some enough." To herself, she mutters, "She's buried in the garden."

"Who are they?" I scratch at the rope cutting off the circulation to my wrists. "And who's Olive?"

She shakes her head at me. "I just told you not to ask."

"Then don't tell me." I tap my knee in annoyance. "But you shouldn't mention something unless you plan on telling the whole story."

"Whatever," she scoffs.

I ask Cerulean, or Allegra, where she grew up, and when

she tells me, my pulse quickens. "You must be joking, that's where I'm from."

In hushed voices, we share our stories on how we were lured by strangers. I must be more scared since I'm new to this place, but having another girl ten feet away, one from my hometown, comforts me on some level.

It isn't long before a woman walks in, her lips swollen, and it's either from injections, all-natural, or swelling from a fist. She's barefoot and wearing a kimono, her hair loose.

"Ruby," Cerulean perks up. "Can I go now?"

"No. Sir sold you."

"What?"

"Someone wanted you bad and bought you." Ruby shrugs.

"But don't get a big head," she adds. "You won't see any benefits."

Cerulean stubs her toe angrily on the cement. "Who bought me?"

"A man offered an exorbitant amount of money for you. He has a clientele that I could only dream of. You'll get California, *and* you'll get to be on camera." I'm not naïve enough to think her new gig is strictly acting on film. At least not in the traditional sense of Hollywood.

"I thought he didn't want to sell me?"

"Are you unhappy with the arrangement?" Ruby's eyes glint at her. "You should be thrilled, absolutely *thrilled* to move on."

"But what about you?" Allegra cries.

"I have to run this place. Keep the sister-wives in line. Speaking of," she turns to me. "It's time for you to meet your owner, John. But first, you two need to get cleaned up."

Relieved to be separated from the restraints and this room, I rub my sore wrists and follow Ruby and Cerulean.

When we exit, I realize we are in a damp basement that smells of rust and sulfur.

Upstairs, Ruby points to an ugly bathroom. I sneeze as I examine the pink bathtub and the dusty fake flowers. We aren't allowed to take separate showers, so Cerulean and I both take turns standing under the nozzle.

I drink the water as the low pressure spits out a crappy stream. She takes pity on me and lathers my hair, turning over my wrists to examine a jagged line of rope burns and sores from the metal. She traces the scar on my right shoulder but says nothing.

To make me laugh, Cerulean acts like an elephant, lifting her trunk, or in her case, an arm, and I cup my hand to keep the giggles from escaping.

Ruby barges in through the open door to rip the shower curtain from my grasp. "No more talking. Shut up. I want silence." Her lower lip trembles, and I think she might cry, but I don't know what's causing her reaction.

Apologetic, Cerulean nods, and I chew my lip.

When it's her turn, I help wash her back, trying not to show my outward horror at the bruises. The imprints describe a cruelty that's worse than even the abuse I endure at the hands of Brian. She was struck by something sharp, certain parts have a deeper indent that will surely scar. Her ribs show underneath the translucent skin, and her hip bones jut out. With a swallow, I wonder if this is foreshadowing of how I'll look, my skin reminiscent of a boxer after a match.

Ruby stands impatiently as we towel off, a makeup palette in hand. "Come with me," she instructs.

We follow her to another door, and when we enter, I assume it's Ruby's room by the bed and the minimal personal effects. Clothes are laid out on her bed for us to try on.

Ruby explains I will call John "sir," and overwhelms me with the house rules, most of which I forget because I'm filled with trepidation at what's to come.

After we are made-up, Ruby tells us to have a seat in the living room. As we sink into the couch, I notice it's empty of modern technology. Weird. We used running water, and there's electricity, so they must not be some bizarre cult that lives off the land.

With Ruby out of earshot, Cerulean moans, "I was supposed to get a Jeep and finally have some freedom, and instead, I've lost every part of myself. Here I thought I had it bad when I didn't have a vehicle. I didn't know it could get worse. What a stupid thing to worry about, right?"

"I don't have a car, either." I sigh. "Brian's a mechanic and owns a garage, and I *still* don't have one."

"What garage?" she questions, "and is Brian, like, your boyfriend?"

"No, my dad," I tell her the name of the garage, and her mouth drops in surprise. "You call him Brian?"

I wrinkle my nose. "Yes."

"That garage sounds familiar."

Cerulean opens her mouth, and I'm positive she'll ask why I call my dad by his first name. A rumble from the back of the house interrupts us, and we exchange nervous glances. Someone is here, and loud footsteps thump before the man emerges from the hallway.

This must be John.

His hair is slicked back with too much gel and a few too many spritzes of cologne. Shifting his gaze between us, he smirks. "Looks like you two have been talking."

I wait for a cue from Cerulean. She stares down at her hands.

"Cerulean," he thumbs at her. "Let's go."

She slowly rises, and I observe her face. Her expression matches how I must seem - alone and frightened. Her eyes dart around the room as if too scared to focus on one thing. Her fingers clamp onto the hem of her skirt as she tries to tug it down, make it longer.

"Bye," I whisper. "*Allegra.*"

Her eyes light up for a brief second, and she stands tall. She doesn't speak. She only nods in return as she manages a small wave. Then her slumped shoulders retreat to the kitchen, and I sit, hands in my lap, awaiting my own fate.

40

CERULEAN

When I follow John outside to his vehicle, a different one from the other night but still a high-end brand, I slide in, my bare thighs cold against the wind.

"You ready?"

I take a deep breath, so I don't snap. "Yes, sir."

"This change will be good for you."

"Why didn't he come? I thought he owned me."

I wait for him to yell or berate me, but he doesn't. "Because you have a new owner now."

"He's mad at me?"

"Nah," John doesn't waver from the road. "He's over it."

"Anything I should know about this man, sir?" I ask. "Anything he likes or dislikes?"

"You've met him, actually."

My face swivels to look at John's side profile and the big mole on his cheek that I never paid attention to before. "We've met?"

"Yes, at the penthouse suite."

I feel my palms start to sweat. I wonder which one? What if it's drunken Randy?

We drive in silence, the only sound the hunger pang that rumbles in my chest. Funny, the steak dinner John promised me that night at the hotel never happened.

It takes about twenty minutes, and I switch between counting down the minutes and staring at the world that seems to go on blissfully unaware of my existence around me. It feels unfair that people can go on with their day, a disregard for the fact I'm missing.

And what about the other girls? Doesn't anyone care about us?

A sense of self-pity starts to take root, and I push it away. I don't want to go down a negative path right now.

Instead, I tell myself I will now have a bedroom the size of my old one with my own private bathroom. The towels will be fluffy European cotton instead of threadbare.

We arrive at another five-star hotel, and instead of pulling into valet parking, we head towards the employee parking lot. Did someone who works here approach John about me? I can't stomach the word "bought" since humans are not meant to be owned.

John parks in the very last row and at an angle. I assume it must be a signal to the man we're here. His phone trills and he rests it against his shoulder as he rolls his window down. "Yeah, the black one."

I watch in the side mirror as a burgundy Lexus slowly pulls into the lot and moves toward us. The car seems to halt in hesitation before moving into a space three spots away from us.

"Stay here," John instructs, pointing to the gun in his waistband. He shuts the engine off, locking me in the vehicle as he walks away. Strolling to the passenger side of the other vehicle, he lowers his head to peer in the window. John exchanges words with someone, but I still can't see who it is because John's silhouette blocks his profile.

When he saunters back, it's to the passenger side. He ushers me out as a bead of perspiration rolls down my back and into the waistband of my pleather miniskirt. Holding my hand tightly in his, he silently wills me to try to break his hold on me.

We stop by the Lexus, and all I can make out are the dark sunglasses the man's wearing behind the tinted windows. John poses me in front of the driver's side, his fingers digging forcefully into my back, along with the gun in his waistband.

The window slides down to reveal the man's face.

"You remember Cerulean?" John pushes me toward the open gap. When he lowers his shades, he reveals himself.

Hazel eyes burn into mine.

With a sharp intake of breath, I start to speak, then stop. I didn't know his name then, but I called him 'Gray' because of his suit and matching silver hair. He looks the same except for a different outfit. Today he's wearing a blue suit and tie.

"Yes, Cerulean, I do remember you." Gray breaks the lull. "I promise you are in good hands. I think you'll find my network of friends to be accommodating to your desires."

I shudder as John drags me backward so Gray can exit the vehicle. He reaches for my hand, kissing it lightly. "Let me open your door for you." Gray walks me around to the passenger side, guiding me to a seated position as my knees wobble.

Is he taking me to meet his friends, the ones from the poker game? I try not to cry out as the door shuts and locks behind my tearful gaze.

Another lock, another key, another prison.

John and him are deep in conversation, and before Gray returns to his car, he hands John a package. Is it more drugs, I wonder?

When he slides into his seat, he turns to me, lowering his shades. "Hi, Cerulean."

"Hi," I say shyly.

"Are you ready to see your daddy?"

I swallow. The thought of some old geezer putting his hands on me is more than I can handle.

Retching, I hold my stomach in pain.

Frantically, Gray reaches around in the backseat for something he can hand me, so I don't throw up on his beige leather interior. John is waiting for us to exit the lot, his car still idling.

Gray backs up and says, "Probably bad timing, but are you hungry?"

"I was," I whisper. "Why did you want to buy me?"

"I didn't," his eyes dart to his mirrors. "Your father is waiting for us, Allegra. Sorry if it was a poor choice of words by calling him 'daddy.'"

I turn to him, not trusting myself to speak. *Allegra*. I can be Allegra again.

"I'm serious."

"Don't lie to me," I whisper, the tears falling fast down my cheeks, ruining my makeup. If Ruby were here, she'd smack me across the face for messing up her effort.

"I can assure you, I'm not." He keeps his eyes trained on the traffic light in front of us. "Do me a favor, reach underneath your seat. You'll find my badge."

Carefully, I clasp a small pocket-sized leather wallet type thing in my hand. I let out a little whoop. "Detective Delaney?"

"At your service."

I'm still skeptical. "When did the police start driving high-end cars?"

"It's borrowed."

I start to sob, and he pats my arm. "Don't worry, you're safe now."

"What about the other girls?" I cry. "There are other ones at the house. A new girl just got there."

"They're going to be saved real soon." He glances at the dashboard clock. "In approximately twenty-two minutes."

Resting my head back against the seat, my shoulders start to shake. I bury my face in my hands. "What about my mom?"

"Valerie?"

My eyes shine. "Yeah, my mom. Is she with my father? I mean, I know they hate each other."

"They do?" He tries to keep his mouth from curling up at the corners. "I wouldn't have guessed. Let's get you some food, and we can talk. Afterward, we'll go to the hospital." He explains doctors will want to examine me.

"Can I call my boyfriend and tell him I'm alive?"

"Soon," he promises. "Not yet."

My face falls. "He's got to be so worried about me. I bet he thinks I'm dead. Everyone forgot about me."

I start to bawl, and Delaney sits patiently while I sob. He finds a box of tissues and presses some into my hand. "I promise everyone has been looking for you. You saw me before this, didn't you?"

"Yeah," I shake my head.

"You were not forgotten." He tilts my chin up. "You have a family that loves you dearly. Not everyone has that."

I nod, wiping the last of my tears off my face. "The other girls, known as the sister-wives, they need help."

I tell him about what I saw, the dead girl, Olive, and what I remember. Detective Delaney takes me to a small diner where I scarf down a bowl of soup and some crackers, not wanting to upset my stomach. It's nice using real silverware and not having to ask permission for the cabinets or refrigerator to be unlocked.

When we arrive at the hospital, it's dark. My tentative steps follow the detective through the emergency room doors. It seems surreal as a doctor and nurse greet us, both wearing big smiles and overjoyed expressions. The nurse reaches forward to embrace me in her arms. Detective Delaney waits outside the room while they ask a million questions, and I feel numb, my answers stilted and monotone. After my examination, I hear hushed voices outside the room while they converse.

A few minutes later, Delaney reappears with an overnight bag. *My* overnight bag. Inside are my own clothes, and I weep at the smell of the familiar laundry detergent and fabric softener. "Let's get you home," Delaney says, his eyes misty as he gently leads me back to his unmarked vehicle, his grip light on my elbow.

After we're settled in the vehicle, I force out the question I'm not sure I want to know the answer to. "Did my father not want to come to the hospital?"

"I thought it was best we meet him in private." Detective Delaney brushes a strand of hair off my face. "I'll take you to him now." I struggle to hold back my emotions. I want to scream one minute and then sob the next. I'm grateful he saved me, but homesick for my parents and Coye.

"Why don't you shut your eyes?" he suggests. "We won't be back to the city for a couple hours." I'd rather stare out the window, but my lids are heavy, and it doesn't take long before I'm out.

It isn't until I'm awakened by a hand grabbing my shoulder that instinctively, I scream, "Don't touch me!" My eyes are wild as they meet Delaney's calm, hazel ones.

He jerks his hands back immediately. His voice is soft. "Sorry, that was my mistake. I should've alerted you first."

Blinking, it takes a minute for me to recognize I'm not in the company of Muscleman or John or other men. We are parked in a secluded lot, and the only light comes from the bright headlamps.

"Where are we?" I murmur.

"Your father is going to meet us here."

"Why can't we go to my house?"

"Because it's not safe yet."

My blood curdles at this. "I'm not safe? They can still hurt me?"

"No, Allegra," His tone is firm. "They're being apprehended, but I didn't want to run the risk of taking you there too soon. It's a network that has multiple layers to it, and people."

Hopeful, I ask. "Can I use my phone now to contact my boyfriend, Coye?"

"Very shortly."

My eyes start to fill with tears.

"Hang in there," he says. "We have more to discuss, and then you can. I promise."

41

DETECTIVE DELANEY

I watch as the Silver Jag pulls into the lot. Allegra's face immediately lights up, and the dullness lessens just a bit. I clench my fists, not wanting to think about how long it will take her to get back to a semblance of normalcy, if ever. She'll need the best therapists in town, the best support system around. And she'll need parents that care.

Speaking of parental figures, the Chief wasn't pleased to hear I had gone undercover. Obstruction of justice, he spat at me.

In fact, father or not, he was going to hand me my walking papers. It wasn't sanctioned by the department. Since I was removed from the case, I was supposed to stay the fuck out of the way. But I couldn't do that. I didn't want to let Valerie down again. Something inside of me told me to keep at it...

It's not until I told the Chief I located Allegra that he went absolutely still, a rarity for him. His jaw went slack. If it were any other occasion, I'd have laughed.

But this was serious. This was an Atwater.

I step out of the vehicle as Allegra jumps, practically

tumbling to the ground as she closes the gap to her father. "Daddy," she cries, "Daddy!"

Darren's almost unrecognizable in athletic pants and a hooded sweatshirt. His smile matches Allegra's, and tears run down his face as he wraps his arms tightly around her waist and presses her to his chest.

"I'm sorry, Daddy," she wails.

"You didn't do anything wrong, Sugar." His voice breaks. "Nothing at all." I wish I could say the same for Darren Atwater. Allegra doesn't need to know the father she loves will be arrested after this. I did him a solid by letting him think we believe in his innocence and reuniting him with Allegra.

My phone buzzes in my pocket. It's time. I'm given a five-minute warning before the police will break up this reunion with sirens and handcuffs. And as much as I love taking this man down a peg, I don't want Allegra to see him arrested. She's been through enough.

Striding up to them, I say, "I hate to do this, but I need to get Allegra down to the station."

She turns from her father, puzzled. "I wanna be with my father," she pleads. "Can't it wait until tomorrow?"

Darren's temper flares. "There's no need to send her to the station after her ordeal. What she needs is some sleep."

"I agree." I say, "but we have to finish some paperwork."

"Not without my lawyer, you don't."

"Mr. Atwater, this isn't the time or place to discuss this. Allegra and I need to have a chat about her mother."

His eyes narrow. "What about Valerie?"

"She has a right to know her daughter's safe."

Darren can't argue this. Slumping his shoulders, he leans against his car. "Can she at least ride to the station with me?"

"I'm afraid not." I run a hand through my hair. "It's police protocol until a parent signs off that she be escorted by an officer."

"Why can't I sign the necessary papers?"

"Because we aren't at the station."

"You're a dipshit." His brow furrows. "Then why couldn't we have met there instead of in the middle of an abandoned lot?"

Sneering, he asks, "Is this payback because you got *removed* from the case?"

I shoot a warning look at him. "Let's go, Allegra."

"I don't want to," her voice quivers. "I appreciate everything you've done, Gray... I mean Detective Delaney, but I want to stay with my father."

I'm struggling to keep control of the situation and my patience. I need her in the car to avoid the impending arrest. "Allegra, in the Lexus, now."

My tone has the desired effect. Now she has to decide who's in charge between Darren and me. Is it her father or the police? He must feel the pressure because he starts to argue with me.

This, in turn, causes his daughter to pause. At my wit's end, I pull out my trump card. "We don't want to hurt your mother's feelings."

"Is she at the station?" Without waiting for a response, Allegra gives Darren another hug and hurries to the vehicle.

When I'm certain she's inside with the door shut, I turn to him. "Hey Darren," I smirk, "I'm the reason Allegra is home, you ungrateful prick. Enjoy prison."

Confused, his face contorts into a grimace.

I hurry into the Lexus, the sirens starting to blare.

We drive out of the lot and are back on surface streets when the flashing lights approach and then pass us.

Even though I know what they mean, I say nothing out loud, my mind drifting to Valerie. At a stoplight, I shoot her a quick text.

"You didn't see that," I tell Allegra.

"What?"

"Exactly."

At the station, Allegra pressures me to let her call Coye.

I hand her my phone. "Five minutes," I say.

"That's..."

I interrupt, "Not enough time. I know."

She pouts.

"Trust me, you can call him back later. Your mom will be here soon."

I shut the door. My palms perspire as I pace the hall, watching for her. I'm nervous about seeing Valerie, and I don't know why.

42

VALERIE

I'm aimlessly pacing the halls of the empty house. I've spent the evening chain-smoking cigarettes and wandering like I'm lost in my own residence.

In a way, I am.

Being alone in this massive estate makes me realize how isolated I really am. Darren hasn't bothered to come home again tonight, the papers served to me yesterday by his attorney. He's not backing down from our imminent divorce.

My phone beeps.

It's from Devon. Detective Delaney.

Allegra is in my office.

It's one sentence, but the meaning of his words is priceless.

I struggle to breathe. It must be a jumbled text. There's no way.

Allegra??? I text back.

She's here. Come now.

I don't bother locking the doors or shoving shoes on my feet. My purse isn't even on my arm when I get into my G-

Wagen. I have to run back in the house to throw flip-flops on and bring my wallet.

Speeding down the hill, I dial Darren. It goes straight to voicemail. Annoyed, I try again. Shaking my head and cursing, I don't bother leaving a message. If he wants to start over with Sandy and cease all communication with me, even with Allegra missing, I can't force him to participate in the journey.

Squealing into a parking space at the station, I realize it's reserved for the Officer of the Month. Indifferent about being towed, I grab my purse and head inside. In my mind, I keep waiting for Delaney to tell me he's pranking me, that Allegra's not really here.

Hands in his pocket, he's leaning against the station desk when I walk in. He's wearing blue dress pants and a collared shirt with the sleeves rolled up. If I went into his office, I'm sure I'd find his suit jacket ditched in a heap. Never one for restrictive clothing, he always preferred loose garments.

"Devon," I scream. "Where is she?"

"I found her." His eyes burn a hole in my heart. "Valerie, we need to talk a minute."

"You found her?" I start to sink down to the floor, my knees buckling. "I need to see her now." Tears flood my eyes. "I need to know my baby's safe."

"She is. But I need to fill you in on some developments." He guides me gently by the elbow down the hall.

Stopping abruptly, he swivels to face me. "Darren was arrested tonight."

My mouth drops.

"He did see Allegra. I made sure of that."

I have so many questions, but I can tell he's exhausted. Purple circles rim his eyes. "Allegra was being held by human traffickers. She's okay physically in some respects, but she's going to need a lot of assistance. She went through some traumatic shit." He clenches my wrists. "Valerie, she's going to need you now more than ever."

"Devon," I swallow. "She's going to need *us* more than ever."

"I will do what I can to help."

"Who are they?"

"We can talk about it after you're reunited with your daughter." Delaney knocks before entering his office. Hunched over, Allegra's body shakes like a leaf. Poor girl.

Muffled, she tells who I presume is Coye on the other end she has to go. Allegra hands Devon the phone but has a hard time letting it out of her grasp, her fingers wrapped tight around the screen. That is, until she spots me standing behind Devon.

Shrieking, she throws herself into my arms. I hold her close, her shrunken body significantly different from the one I parted with that day at the mall. "Allegra, I am so, *so* sorry you had to go through this." Our tears run together, the top of her head wet from my cheeks.

"Why don't you sit down?" Devon moves his swivel chair next to the one Allegra just vacated.

"Is my father coming here to meet us?" Allegra asks. "Are we going to go home together now? Like a family?'

Sinking into the chair, I hold her on my lap like she was a child and not an adolescent. Wrapping my arms tightly around her, I nod at Delaney. "Why don't you sit next to us? I'd like to say something." A curious look passes over his face.

I nuzzle Allegra's neck and whisper her favorite lullaby in her ear. She's drowsy and headed for sleep. We sit in blissful silence for a few minutes, both focused on the rise and fall of Allegra's chest.

"Devon, I owe you an explanation, and this is the absolute worst time, and I'm sorry." I take a deep breath. "I hope you can forgive me for my silence somewhere down the line. I didn't intend to hurt you...or her."

He appears to be holding his breath as he waits. I'm worried he's going to pass out if I don't break the news. "Delaney, in the hall, you mentioned Allegra would need the full capabilities of her parents."

"Yes, I did." He lowers his voice. "Is there some kind of problem with that statement?"

"You don't understand." I shake my head. "Devon, she's *ours*."

Allegra's body purrs on my lap as he intones. "What are you saying?"

"Allegra is your daughter."

His face goes ashen. Even his hazel eyes seem devoid of color. "What're you talking about? Is this your idea of some sick game?"

"I didn't lose our baby, Delaney. I married Darren when I was a few months pregnant and told him the baby was his."

"No. You couldn't have." He brushes a hand over his face. "No. Darren wouldn't have believed you."

"You and Allegra both have such similarities," I whisper. "It scares me at times."

"You're lying, Valerie. You said you lost the baby. I believed you."

"I couldn't raise a baby without you, Devon. You were gone. Emotionally and physically."

"Valerie..." He watches Allegra's face in shock. "I don't think this is the right time to discuss this."

"I agree, but we can do a paternity test if you don't believe me."

"Valerie..."

"I'm not lying to you. I swear."

"Darren never questioned it?"

"No."

Allegra stirs, wiping a hand across her face. He swallows. "And she doesn't know?"

"Not an inkling."

"She's going to have a lot of questions."

"And I have the answers."

"I don't think you should tell her yet." He leans forward to touch Allegra's translucent skin. "She's been through one hell of a rough time."

"I know." I reach for his hand, and he gives it willingly. Squeezing his fingers, I murmur. "We can tell her when we're ready."

A knock at the door startles all three of us. Delaney and I break contact as Allegra groggily swipes at a piece of hair on her cheek.

I recognize the man instantly. It's been a long time since we've been in the same room, but even with age on his face, his mannerisms remain unchanged. The Chief of Police. Chief Bratton. Devon's father.

"Hi, Mrs. Atwater."

I start to rise, but he motions for me to say seated. "Hold your daughter, Mrs. Atwater, she needs you."

Tears spring to my eyes, and it takes a moment to speak. "Thank you for all your help, both of you. And the entire department. I can speak for both my husband and I when I tell you how much we appreciate your diligence in getting her back."

Chief Bratton nods. "The public will be thrilled to know Allegra's home. I'm relieved this little lady is safe."

"Detective," his tone is professional. "Would you mind

coming with me for a minute? We have a couple loose ends to tie up."

They step outside of the room. I hear the Chief mention Darren's name, but their voices are muffled as the tap of their footsteps echo down the hallway.

Then it's just silent. And peaceful. Allegra and I are together. I'm finally getting everything I want. My family is slowly, but surely, coming back together.

43

BRIAN

I catch Delaney by accident as I enter the police station. When I call his name, he turns to acknowledge me before realizing who the voice belongs to.

Disgust is written all over his face. He puts his hands on his hips. "Now's not a good time," he admonishes.

"This can't wait," I say. I don't bother to add that I finally know what hell must feel like. It's laughable, considering I thought I wanted my daughter gone, out of the picture.

It's clear Delaney's frazzled, his movements jarred. "If it's about Madeline, I don't have an update," he grits his teeth. "You need to leave."

"Why is Valerie's SUV parked outside?" I ask. "Did something happen?"

"I can't tell you that. Now, if you'll excuse me," he tries to brush past me, but I grab his elbow.

This displeases him, and he throws his hands up. "Unless you came to confess, I don't have time for your shit, Brian.

"I know you hate me. You've expressed this, I get it. But this isn't about me. This is about your earlier question."

I swear I see a vein pop out of Delaney's temple. This is my final warning, so I make it fast. "You asked if anyone has it out for me."

He snaps, "When I say I'm busy, what am I not clear about?"

"This is about the case," I take a deep breath. "I have a confession to make."

"You came to admit you killed Madeline?"

"Not exactly."

"Leave," he points to the door.

"Not before I see Val."

"She's occupied." Something crosses his face, maybe sadness? "Now's not a good time."

"I told her what I found," I jut my chin out. "You can ask her."

Delaney looks bored. "Unless she witnessed it, it's hearsay and doesn't matter. She can't corroborate anything you confided in her."

Turning on his heel, he walks away. I take two aggravated steps before sputtering, "Dammit, Delaney, this is about a *body* I found."

As soon as Delaney hears the word 'body,' he swivels.

"What did you say?"

"I found a young woman."

"And you bring this to me now?" His nostrils flare. "In the middle of the night?"

"It might be connected to the disappearance of Maddy. Maybe even Allegra."

Delaney sneers. "I thought Maddy ran away from a bad situation?"

I don't react to this. I shrug my shoulders. "I did a delivery for Darren Atwater last week. I think he has it out for me."

The mention of Darren captures his attention. "My office is being used right now. Let's go to Chief Bratton's office."

When we enter, the Chief motions me to have a seat. Delaney shuts the door and leans against it. I expect Detective Delaney to be a younger version of the Chief of Police since Valerie clued me in that this was Delaney's father. Staring into the brown eyes of Chief Bratton, I can't find a shared feature between the two. The Chief is balding and of average height, with a bulbous nose. Delaney has a masculine face, gray hair, and hazel eyes.

Hmm...interesting.

"Is there a problem?" The Chief peers over his glasses at me.

I shake my head.

"This is Brian Pruitt, Madeline Pruitt's father," Delaney says by way of introduction. "The other girl who disappeared recently, Maddy, is his seventeen-year-old daughter."

"And you are Valerie's boyfriend?" The Chief squints his eyes at me.

"God, no. Her brother," I shrug. "Or if you want to be specific, half-brother."

"I knew Val growing up. Didn't see you around. Are you the Hewitt's' kid, the one that went into the military?"

"No. Valerie and I didn't meet until about eight months ago. Our mother abandoned us as children, and we went our separate ways."

Delaney mutters behind me. "You'd think you'd be a better father,"

It's painful, but I ignore his comment. So does the Chief. I'm uncertain if he heard it from his location behind the desk.

"Sorry to hear. Always a shame when that happens." He

motions at Delaney. "His parents did the same. He was in and out of the system until he was eight."

"Oh, you aren't his biological child?" The lack of commonalities between the two now make sense.

"Chief," Delaney whistles. "Can we stick to the matter at hand?"

"Sorry," the Chief seems embarrassed. "I shouldn't air out our laundry. I guess I wanted to make a point, it's great when foster kids can be reunited with their siblings. Did your fosters adopt you?"

"No. I bounced around." Now it's my turn to step around the topic. Delaney senses my discomfort and saves me for once. Cutting to the chase, he tells the Chief I found a body doing a run for Darren Atwater. He stretches the name out smugly, clearly making a point to the Chief. They confirm I'm willing to be audio recorded, and I explain how I came to meet Darren and his men. Both listen attentively as I tell them about my drive to the border of Nuevo Laredo.

Delaney listens to my story with interest. "The body you found was left at the ranch then, with the load you dropped off?"

I stammer, "Not exactly."

With a sheepish glance, I stare at the floor.

The Chief murmurs, "Go on. Out with it."

"I dumped the body."

"You dumped the body?" Delaney and the Chief both say in unison.

"Yeah. At a rest stop in Texas. Near Laredo, Texas, to be exact. It's close to Nuevo Laredo, which was the drop-off point."

I don't dare shift my gaze to Delaney, whose breathing pattern has changed. Out of my peripheral vision, I keep him in my line of sight, worried he's going to pummel me.

"Did I miss something?" The Chief looks down at his notepad. ""Why would you do that?"

Delaney smirks. "If you were innocent, why not call the police when you found the body?"

"If I didn't drop the steel drum off at the ranch, I guarantee I would've gone missing along with the dead girl." I rush to add, "And it's not like I could just phone the authorities. Darren's main guy, Mickey, the one who set this up, tracked every movement I made on that trip. I couldn't risk being arrested or drawing attention to myself. Especially if his gang is hooked up with a cartel or doing illegal shit."

"You know, *besides* murder," Delaney says curtly. "I'm starting to wonder if Darren's crew had you transport drugs since it was so close to the border."

"I wondered that," I sigh. "I couldn't dig into those boxes because I couldn't reseal them."

The Chief puckers his lips. "Weren't you worried about what would happen if they discovered the girl was no longer in the fifty-five-gallon steel drum?"

"Yeah," I admit. "But I hoped whoever was involved would assume the female was still sealed in whatever liquid they kept her in. If they didn't know about her to begin with, then it would just be an empty drum to them."

The two exchange quick glances. "I'm going to need some information from you. A written statement and a description of the woman," Delaney doesn't miss a beat. "Then I'll reach out to the great state of Texas and see if anyone reported missing is a match. Could be that someone found her in the dumpster or at the landfill."

He runs a hand through his salt and pepper hair. "This is going to be one hell of a cluster fuck."

Uneasy, I wait for my next instruction.

Chief Bratton dismisses me. "Thanks for coming forward. That couldn't have been easy."

A tinge of sadness laces my voice. "Now if only we could find Maddy."

44

DELANEY

This day has gone off the rails in so many directions. I'm looking at shrapnel in both my personal and professional life.

When I finish with Brian, it's after two in the morning.

I don't bother to tell him I think I've located his daughter. He mentioned the name of one of Darren's crew members, and I want to delve deeper into the men working for him before this case becomes public knowledge.

She was found in the house, where the sister-wives live, with Allegra AKA Cerulean.

Threading my arms above my head, I settle into the pillow. The girl I thought I rescued, Valerie's daughter, is mine. She might've disappeared for a while, but I've lost seventeen years with her. And Brian gets to be a shitty dad while I was robbed of the opportunity to be a stellar one.

But I know it's not that simple. Val is right about my emotional and physical presence back then. I was a train wreck, and now I'm in pain. I shut off my emotions, but when it comes to Val, they are raw and deep-rooted in our shared history.

I avoided seeing Valerie and Allegra off. If I stopped back in my office to say good-bye before they left, there's no way I could stare at both of them and not lose my composure. Sure, I could feign happiness at Allegra's safe return, but the agony in my eyes would be an easy read.

My mind drifts to the hotel room, and I'm suddenly disgusted.

Just thinking about being in the penthouse suite with Allegra makes me feel dirty. How the men leered at her in the hotel room, the one that had his way with her. Tears prick my eyes. I didn't protect her from the big, bad, ugly world.

I could've grabbed Allegra and ran, but I wanted to save more girls than just her. Does that make me a hero or a villain? It's an ethical question I don't have an answer to. One I'll wrestle with internally long after this case ends. If I had tried to remove Allegra the first time we met, the likelihood of either of us being alive is slim to none.

45

BRIAN

In the morning, a knock at my door startles me but doesn't wake me. It's not like I went to bed. The television was on mute as I sat fully-clothed.

Waiting. I knew it wouldn't be long until I was summoned.

Beer washes down my pain pills. Between the insomnia and sedative, my head's in a fog. I'm unable to think clearly, but it's a welcome distraction right now.

My steps are unhurried toward the front, as if I'm walking toward a death row executioner.

I peer out the curtains, dumbfounded to see Valerie on my stoop. Pushing past me when I open the door, she eyeballs the dirty apartment. Her bewildered eyes flicker at the mess. "Are you okay, Brian?"

"No," I rub a hand over my eyes.

"What's going on?"

"Maddy's missing," I tap my fingers on the table. "And so is my vehicle."

The blood drains from her face. "This is all my fault," she wails, "I got you mixed up with Darren."

"No! It's mine," I wipe a hand across my mouth. "I haven't been a good dad."

We settle on the couch and wordlessly, I hand her a pack of cigarettes we can share.

A few minutes later, the voice of Detective Delaney filters in through the half-opened door that one of us hadn't fully closed.

He solemnly asks, "May I enter?"

"Sure," I say, inhaling the smoke.

Speaking Valerie's name as a hello, he turns to address me with a curt nod. "Brian."

The detective looks terrible. His eyes are half-swollen with dark circles underneath.

"Do you need me to leave?" Valerie's voice sounds hollow.

"No. I'm glad I caught you both at the same time." He sounds like he's choking as he asks how Allegra is.

"Sleeping soundly. I left her with our housekeeper, so I could sneak out for a few minutes." Shameful, she peers at Delaney. "I'm going to go back to her in a couple minutes. I just wanted to check on Brian."

"Wait. Allegra's home?" I run a hand through my hair. "Since when?"

"Last night," Valerie says.

I tilt my head. "Is that what all the commotion was?"

"Yeah," she sighs. "They suspect Darren was involved in her disappearance. He was arrested."

"Why didn't you call me?" I suck longer than usual on the cigarette. "I was at the station. Delaney wasn't letting me near you."

"Why not?" She looks first at me, then at Delaney.

Delaney snaps. "The night went down a rabbit hole. A lot of unexpected explosions caused by reckless people and their selfish actions." Valerie sinks back against the couch as if the words slapped her across her cheek. Puzzled by her reaction, it's like she's suddenly ashamed.

As I try and figure out that riddle, I'm interrupted by a clinking sound. Dismayed at the sight of Delaney unfolding handcuffs from his pocket, I groan in protest.

He stares in earnest at both of us.

Even though I knew this was coming, I'm still shocked to hear Delaney's authoritative tone. "Brian Randall Pruitt, you're under arrest for the kidnapping of Allegra Atwater and Madeline Pruitt."

He reads me my Miranda Rights.

Valerie watches in awe. "I knew it." She shakily stands. "I knew you had something to do with it after you told me about the body you found. You're involved with Darren's gang, aren't you?"

"Just because CPS has been called in the past doesn't make me guilty now," I argue.

"True," Delaney concedes.

A long hush lingers between the three of us as if we're paused, no one daring to breathe or change positions. Valerie leans against a wall, I choke on one last puff, and Delaney has the cuffs in his outstretched hand.

Finally, I toss my burned-out cigarette in an empty beer can. "I'm ready," I hold my wrists out so he can shackle them.

Instead, Delaney pivots and connects the metal with Valerie's tiny ones. "Valerie Maureen Atwater, you are under arrest for the kidnapping of both Allegra Atwater and Madeline Pruitt. You have the right to remain silent..."

Her jaw drops. "You can't be serious?"

"Oh, but I am."

"You found both girls," she says quietly. "Alive."

"Hardly. Allegra is malnourished and looks like the size of a twelve-year-old. Do you know *what* they did to her?" His eyes are wild. I've seen him angry, but this is different. This is primal. He's like a rabid animal, ready to tear apart his prey. In this case, Valerie Atwater. "Do you know what they did to *our* daughter?"

My soggy mind is playing ping-pong with the information spewing from their mouths. What motive would Valerie have for kidnapping my daughter? When Valerie and I reconnected, I had high hopes our daughters would meet.

But not like this.

And he made it seem like he has a daughter with Val. That Allegra is his.

"Wait! You also found Maddy?" I'm ignored as the tension mounts between the two of them. Their eyes are locked on each other in hatred.

Valerie whispers. "It wasn't supposed to be like this."

"What do you mean?" We say in unison.

"Do you really think I'd let men sell my daughter?" Valerie fumes, "*Sell* my daughter?"

"Wait! Back up," I'm on a rollercoaster, having been practically arrested and then informed my half-sisters now involved in Maddy's disappearance. "Delaney, what the hell's going on?"

He shoots Valerie a death stare. "Do you want to tell him, or should I?"

"How do you even know what Maddy looks like?" I'm stunned. "You've never met her."

She slides down the wall, Delaney making no move to stop her. Now seated, she sniffs. "You have her picture at your shop. You always complained she was ruining your life.

You wanted to start over with your girlfriend. I was only trying to help."

"Help *how*?" I'm struggling to breathe. About to hyperventilate, Delaney takes a step forward to put a hand on my shoulder.

I shrug him off me. "What happened to the girls?"

He doesn't mince words. "After I was removed from the case, I did my own surveillance and went undercover. I did it without the Chief or the department's blessing, so I had no back-up. I hate to say *luckily,* but lucky for me, I met Allegra at a penthouse suite. She had been sold to a human trafficking ring."

"Where's Maddy?" I rise too fast, dizziness washing over me. "Was she with her?" Lightheaded, I sit back down.

"Allegra was alone that night. To my detriment, I couldn't save her then because I had to find out where she was being held." As if Delaney's trying to reassure not only us but himself, he adds, "I knew I'd find other girls in the same predicament."

Valerie cries. "You had a chance to save her *then*, and you didn't?"

He fixes her with a steely glare. "I needed her physical location. Where she was living. Plus, I needed to know who was behind this particular ring." Delaney scoffs. "Turns out, Valerie Atwater is the mastermind behind this group."

She snorts. "I would've give me that much credit."

Delaney turns to me. "The contraband you moved was *illegal*, but not in the way you thought. It was counterfeit goods, think fake luxury brands like Gucci or Chanel. Knock-off purses and accessories. That's the load you hauled to Nuevo Laredo. Not drugs."

I rest my hands on my knees. "Okay, but the body…"

He rubs a hand over his face. "Darren wasn't aware of the dead body."

"So he says," Valerie snipes.

Delaney ignores her. "But Valerie was. She knew ahead of time you were asked to be the driver."

"How did you know before I told you?" I stare at her. "You hired me to follow your husband, and uh, help investigate him."

Delaney responds to my question. "Valerie suggested your name to Mickey, who in turn mentioned you to Darren. Darren would've never taken Valerie's input, so she put the idea in Mickey's head. Darren stopped by your shop because he was looking for more than a tire, he was looking for a new guy to drive for him. Val said you were hard up for cash and were savvy."

She cuts in. "I kept out the part about you being an alcoholic without a license."

"After Darren came to your shop, he investigated you. He was worried you and Val might've had your own thing going on, but Mickey knew better. He knew you and Valerie weren't sleeping together, that you were in fact related, because he was having an affair with her."

This is too much. I light up another cigarette.

Delaney has more to say. "Valerie had agreed to help Mickey out with his side business, and an issue came up with a girl. She was killed and tossed in that steel drum you delivered. She'd been dead for a little while, but you'd never know because she was stored in fluids that kept her from developing rigor mortis or going through the actual decomposition process..."

"...so, they could control when the time clock starts on death," I finish.

"Exactly," Delaney sighs. "Mickey's crew hid the fifty-five-gallon steel drum behind the shipment. Valerie didn't think you would peek inside, either, I'm guessing."

"It was an empty container when I got to Vincent's..." I say.

"...and they unloaded it without question. In fact, Vincent asked Darren why an empty steel drum was part of the load, and he had no idea."

Delaney continues, "Mickey has been running this ring with a couple other men. Unfortunately, Mickey promised Valerie the world and a new life while trying to access money he thought she had. He wasn't aware of the prenup."

"Allegra was never supposed to be in harm's way," Valerie interjects. "Arrangements were made so Allegra and I could leave Darren and start over in California. You have to believe me, I would never, *ever* hurt my daughter. Allegra's boyfriend, Coye, lives there, and I thought it would be a nice change for her and me."

Delaney seethes. "You knew about Mickey and his 'side project,' and you became an accomplice. You have a fucking child, and you still helped them kidnap and drug young girls for unspeakable acts."

"No," the color drains from her face. "I agreed to dispose of a body for them," she says miserably, her eyes bloodshot. "It was in exchange for transporting Allegra to California. She was supposed to be escorted by an acquaintance named Pierce. Pierce was instructed to call me, except he never did. *He never did.*"

"Instead, he called Mickey," Delaney clenches his fists. "And she became part of a ransom game. He had his own ulterior motives."

"But where is Maddy?"

Again, I'm discounted.

"In what universe would Allegra not be scared out of

her mind?" Delaney plays with the collar of his shirt. "Did she have any prior knowledge about this?"

"No," Valerie's crestfallen.

I can't sit any longer. I spy a thin gold chain in the carpeting and reach down to pick it up. It's a bracelet that belongs to Maddy.

Keeping my hands busy, I focus on unraveling a knot so I don't wallop my half-sister.

She stiffens her shoulders, "It was only supposed to be for a short time."

"And just like that, happily ever after?" I snap. "Do you hear yourself?"

"She was supposed to be brought to..."

Delaney interrupts, "You mean *kidnapped*."

"No! Never," She bites her lip. "Mickey let Allegra and I stay at the house in California in June. He told me he owned it. I found out differently later on."

"So, that's why you flew to Cali that day?" I ask.

"Yes. But when I got there, I saw it was a ruse," Her shoulders slump in pain. "Mickey didn't own the house. It belonged to a couple that rents the one out next door on a vacation site. They had never heard of him. I found out from Walt, the owner, there was a company hired to fix some plumbing issues. I guess Mickey was friends with a guy in the crew. He made a copy of the key. The property we stayed at isn't used for rentals, so they didn't have a paper trail or realize he stayed there that weekend."

"And Mickey thought if he took Allegra himself and used her as collateral, he could bleed money from Darren and Valerie," Delaney adds.

"Where is Maddy?" I pump my fist at her.

"She's at the hospital," Delaney yanks Valerie and her cuffs up.

"When can I see her?"

"Right now." Delaney leads Valerie down the stairs. Katrina's curtains move, and I know this is the height of entertainment for her.

I follow Delaney to the squad car he has waiting to reunite me with my daughter.

46

DETECTIVE DELANEY

After speaking with the officer that picks up Brian, I turn to Valerie. "Time to get you booked," I say.

Her face is haggard, and even since last night, she's aged.

"Devon," she wails, grabbing at my arm.

I twist out of it. "What?"

"Why did you arrest Darren?"

"Because he was still selling counterfeit goods." I help guide her into the backseat of my borrowed Lexus. "Plus, this way, the other suspects, including *you*, thought they were off the hook."

I meet her eyes in the rearview mirror. "Looks like it worked."

"I can't sit up front?"

"No."

"Devon?"

"Uh-huh?"

"Will you take care of Allegra?"

"I don't even know what that's supposed to mean," I retort. "You kept her from knowing me all these years."

"Tell her when you're ready about us. Anything you want. But I don't want her to feel alone. She's losing both Darren and I in some aspects."

Is Valerie that delusional?

She'll be heading to prison. One day, Allegra will learn the truth about her mother's actions.

"I have one last question," she says. "What made you suspect Mickey?"

"When I went to pay Darren's warehouse a visit, I met Mickey. There was a paper receipt in his office from Caval's Department Store shoved under the desk calendar. After we executed a search warrant, we found the actual shopping bag and Allegra's purchases hidden in a closet. When I tracked his movements, it led me to the house where the girls were. Had you ever been there?"

"No, of course not," she yells. "I didn't know Mickey was going to take her to a house. Allegra was supposed to be driven to California, not kept for his own sadistic purposes."

Head down, I hear her crying, but her tears don't garner sympathy from me. Valerie goes berserk when they lead her away in handcuffs, and I quickly exit, not wanting a scene. Her screams drown out any words that are said.

It's going to be a long day, an even longer road ahead for those of us involved.

At the hospital, I visit Madeline and Brian. Madeline has been keeping watch on Dane Burns, her boyfriend. She's been glued to his side since she was released from police custody after her physical exam. Dane's starting to improve and his vitals are stable. He also has his own road to recovery. He was shot by Mickey and had no prior involvement with Darren's crew, even though they tried to allude to it when they kidnapped Madeline to throw her off.

I'm relieved that Madeline and Brian are seated next to each other, holding hands.

I watch as tears run down their cheeks, a mixture of sorrow, and I hope, forgiveness. I hear him ask Madeline about a concert. "As soon as Dane gets better, I'm taking all of us," he promises.

I watch them for a few minutes before I interrupt. After introducing myself to Madeline, I ask her how she is doing. A SWAT team rescued the girls shortly after I picked up Allegra from John and the parking lot.

Allegra, who is my daughter, I think to myself.

"How is Cerulean, I mean, Allegra?" Madeline shudders as Brian rubs her arm. We both know Allegra was wasting away, and Madeline saw her at the end of her stay with the sister-wives.

"I'm going to go see her after this," I say. "I'll let you know."

"That could've been me," she whimpers.

"But it wasn't," Brian says softly. "It wasn't. You're safe now. Even from me. I'm going to quit drinking. I want us to be a family." His voice cracks. "I love you, Maddy. I've made lots of mistakes, but you have to know, you're not one of them."

Before I leave the two of them, I ask to speak to Brian in private. "I heard from one of my guys. The girl in the drum was nineteen-year-old, Cynthia Watts, known as Olive to the others. Another girl in the house provided us with her information. We haven't located the body you dumped, but we know her identity, and that's a start."

"Were there other girls in the house?"

"A woman named Ruby ran the household. She had befriended a man that turned into her boyfriend, then her pimp. John Lazario. She disappeared from a bus stop in

Ohio years ago. With a history of drug abuse, no one expected her to resurface. The assumption was she was dead."

"Another girl, Violet, was a transient, and Ivory is a recent runaway. Her parents are both dead, she turned eighteen and was picked up during a routine shopping trip to the grocery store. A woman pretended she needed assistance with her bags. Suffice to say, Ivory was caught off guard when a man pretended to rob the woman and took Ivory in the process."

I exhale. "There's another woman, the one your daughter and Dane encountered. Her name's Sapphire. She doesn't live at the house, just acts as the traffickers' intermediary, using a variety of tactics to snare young women. She lured both Dane and Madeline by selling concert tickets online."

"I can't believe Dane was with her, and it still happened."

"They get creative, trust me," I pat his shoulder. "Go be with your daughter. You have another chance at this. Take it. Don't fuck it up. If I get another call from CPS, you and I will meet in a dark alley."

"Understood," he says gravely.

"Delaney," I hear him call out after me.

I turn to face him. "Yeah?"

"What did Valerie mean about Allegra?"

My mouth tightens. "I beg your pardon?"

"What she said earlier." He stumbles over his words. "Val referred to her as 'our' daughter."

"Stay in your lane, Brian," I shake my head at him. "If you do better at being a dad, maybe I'll tell you someday when our kids get together."

Over my shoulder, I murmur, "Parent to parent."

EPILOGUE: ALLEGRA

I'm at home when I hear the intercom beep twice.

Rose, one of our housekeepers, is helping me bathe. After being naked most of the time, I've lost any shyness I had. It feels like heaven to take a simple bath in a clean tub. With my own soap. And unlimited water. Hot water.

"I'll go check who that is," she offers. "Your mom should be back shortly."

"I don't understand why she had to go into town," I sigh. "I need her."

"She had to stop at the police station, I think."

Leaning against the edge of the tub, I wonder why my father isn't home. Tears burn my eyes. I won't say this out loud, but it hurts, this shield my parents have put between us. It's like they don't even care I'm home, their priorities elsewhere.

When Rose appears at my doorway, her face is haunted. "Get dressed, Allegra. You have a visitor."

My energy sorely lags. It takes me longer than usual to throw on some sweatpants and a t-shirt. They hang off me like when I was a child playing dress-up in my mother's clothes.

Before I go downstairs, I inhale the scent of my bedroom, the smell that comforts me the most.

Is Coye here, I wonder?

He has to be getting close. He left California early this morning. With no phone to check, I trust he'll call the house phone when he needs directions to the compound. He's never been here before, and the thought of him around my father makes me nervous.

My mother insisted it would be fine, but my stomach knots at the idea of my father meeting my boyfriend, who, until recently, was a secret.

I swallow my unease. I can worry about that later.

At the bottom of the landing, I spot the visitor.

To me, he's Gray.

To others, Detective Devon Delaney.

"Hi," I run a hand through my tangled wet hair.

"Hey," he shifts his eyes, suddenly nervous. "Mind if we sit down and talk?"

"Uh, no. My parents aren't here, though." My lip starts to quiver. I turn my face away from him. "I'm not really sure where either of them are, to be honest."

"It's okay. I came to check on you."

Rose stands protectively behind an interior door. She nods her head at us. "Go have a seat in the sitting room. Coffee, detective?"

"Sure. Thank you."

Gray follows me, but in a way that tells me he's been inside the house before. There's no hesitation in his steps.

As soon as we're seated, his confidence nosedives again. He keeps pulling at his collar before he abruptly stands. Anxiously, he paces the room.

Epilogue: Allegra

Wringing my hands in my lap, I notice the stubble on his face and his wrinkled shirt.

He looks like how I feel. Battered and exhausted. Suddenly, I feel sorry for him. He was probably up all night, and his job to find me couldn't have been easy.

"I appreciate what you did for me," I say with sincerity. "And for the others."

He nods. "You're welcome. I couldn't just leave you there..." He rests a hand on the mantle. "I'm sorry. This is probably driving you nuts."

I say nothing for a second. Tucking my feet up underneath me, he asks. "Are you cold? Do you need a blanket?"

"No," I lie. I just want Gray to tell me what's causing him this much pain or insecurity. "What do you want to talk to me about?"

"Your mom and I go way back," Gray offers. "In fact, we used to date."

"You guys dated?" I make a face. "You mean, before my father and Mom got married?"

"Yep. A long time ago."

"Must've been like a hundred years ago."

He shrugs. "It feels like it."

"Are you married now?"

"No."

I snort. "What happened to the wedding ring you were wearing at the hotel?"

"Good eye," he stares down at his bare ring finger. "I was undercover and playing a part."

"And you had to be married for it to work?"

"Sometimes, I have to disguise my own reality."

I don't know what he wants me to say next. Either does he. We both sit in silence for a moment. The only noise is the chiming of a grandfather clock in the house.

Luckily, Rose appears with his coffee. He gratefully takes the mug from her hands.

"We need to get you fed," She smiles kindly at me. "Soup for lunch?"

"Yes, please." It'll be a while before I can eat full meals without feeling sick. My body needs to readjust to solid foods outside of watery oatmeal.

Gray sits down on the opposite end of the couch. Holding his mug, he leans forward. "I don't know how to tell you this, so I'm going to just say it. Your mom and I got pregnant when I was in the military. I didn't...I wasn't the best candidate to be a father, and I was deployed."

My eyes widen. "But how?" I gasp. "What are you talking about? Darren is my father. Wouldn't he have said something? They would've told me."

"Yes, he's raised you like his own," he says. "But I'm your birth father."

I chew my lip. "Why weren't you around, then? Did you not live here?"

"I only moved back a few years ago."

"And you just left me all this time?" I glare at him. I'm already emotional and wounded by my parents' seeming rejection, but this puts me over the edge.

Anger laces my voice. "And you chose *now* to drop this on me?"

"Why now?" I whisper. "Why would you tell me this right now?"

He takes a swig of coffee, his hazel eyes never leaving my face.

"I want my father. Will you call him to come get me?"

The truth follows. One I'm not ready for. "Your father was arrested last night."

Epilogue: Allegra

Accusingly, I say. "How is that even possible? We were just with him."

"I wanted to give you the courtesy to see him."

"The courtesy? Are you serious?" I jump up from my seat. "You planned this all along, didn't you? You're punishing him for my mom's fuck-up."

I put my hands on my hips. "She had an affair, didn't she? With the man that took me, the big, tattooed guy." Now it's my turn to pace the floor. He says nothing, and even though his face remains impassive, I can tell I'm right.

"Allegra, I'm just as overwhelmed as you." Gray's eyes are warily watching me, but he keeps his distance.

"I just get home, and now you're telling me my father's in jail, and not only that, he isn't even my real father." I stop to slap my hand against the wet bar. Twisting my lips into a scowl, "How could my mother do this to me? I thought we didn't keep secrets."

He pats the seat next to him.

"No way," I cross my arms in front of my chest.

"Allegra, let's talk."

"We did."

"No. I'm not done." He curses. "This isn't fair."

"What?"

"That I'm..., that we're in this position. This sucks."

"Did something else happen?"

"Allegra, *wow*," he mutters. "I don't want to have to tell you this."

I stare at him.

"I'm not telling you until you sit down."

"I'll sit over here."

Again, he taps the spot next to him. "Right here."

I'm already tired from standing, but I don't tell him that.

"Please."

"Fine." I brush a strand of hair off my face.

"Your mom," he starts, unsure how to proceed, his voice cracks. "She told me last night that you were my daughter. And now she's in trouble."

I feel like I'm being squeezed, my lungs about to burst. Leaning forward, I grab my knees and rock back and forth. I cry, "What kind of trouble?"

"With the law. She did a terrible thing."

"What?" I shriek. "What could she have done?"

"She's going to jail for a long time."

"Because of the man? She helped him, didn't she?"

I don't realize I'm the one sobbing hysterically until Gray puts a hand on my arm. "I'm here." We sit like that for a long time. He gently touches my elbow as I bury my head into my knees.

"Why were you there that night?" I whisper. "In the suite?"

"To find you."

"But you didn't know then I was your daughter?"

"No. But I knew your parents were worried, and I knew you needed help."

"That night, at the hotel," I take a deep breath. "What did you give the man named John?"

"Drugs," his voice is flat. "Cocaine."

"Did you know those men?"

"Only for the intent and purpose of arresting them. I supplied drugs so I wasn't ratted out."

I start to tremble. "Who are they?"

"Bad men."

"But why me? Does my father do business with them?"

"It's complicated, Allegra." He rubs a hand over his face. "We can talk about it, but let me do my detective work first."

The tears stream down my face. "There was a man

Epilogue: Allegra

named Pierce and his driver Freddy. Then a couple named Jeff and Eva, all before I ended up at the house with the other men and girls."

"There are a lot of people involved, and they're part of a criminal trafficking ring. Law enforcement is putting the pieces together." He leans his head back against the couch. "And as far as being your father, I don't know what we're going to do, but you got me. Better late than never, I think."

"What about my parents? Will I see them again? Do I have to leave my home? I'll see them soon, right?"

"Yes. Absolutely." He thumbs a tear off my cheek. "You have a lot of healing to do, young lady. I don't have the answers to everything. One day at a time, deal?"

I nod.

"I can promise you one thing. I'm not leaving you again."

"I don't know you."

"I know." He gives me a stiff smile. "But you will. Do you like dogs?"

"Sure, but my parents won't let me have one."

"I have one. A big furry Great Pyrenees." He whips out his phone to show me a picture. "Falkor. I'll introduce you."

"Okay," I agree.

"And here, I know you probably want to call Coye."

"He should be here any minute."

"I'm glad. After you guys are reunited, I want a couple words with him." His phone rings, and he steps out of the room to take it. I hear hushed voices, but I can't make out the words. When he returns, he has a stunned look on his face, like he heard something he didn't anticipate.

"Is everything okay?" I murmur.

"Yes," he sighs. "We found, well, let's say we had a truck driver come forward that listened to the news bulletin about a missing woman. Cynthia Watts is being returned."

"Olive?"

"Yes, Olive."

"I thought she was...dead." I clench my hands in my lap. "I found her bones outside in the garden at the house."

"She is," he shoves his phone in his pocket. "Those bones at the house belong to a cat or type of animal. They were inconsistent with human remains. From what we know, Olive was disposed of at a truck stop. A truck driver that passed through Texas claims she's buried on his property. I don't have all the details, but it will help with our case."

I struggle to maintain my composure as I break down again.

Gray reaches his hand out, and I take it. Sitting in silence, neither of us speak. I let the tears flow, and he encourages me to squeeze his fingers when I need to.

Rose comes in a few minutes later to announce the arrival of Coye.

Gray gives my hand a final tug before we stand.

"Just remember, Cerulean gave you strength, but you're Allegra, inside and out."

His words ring true.

I'm a little bit of both. But more than that, I'm a fighter, and no one is going to take that power away from me.

NOTE FROM THE AUTHOR

STOP HUMAN TRAFFICKING!

The National Human Trafficking Hotline connects victims and survivors of sex and labor trafficking with services and supports to get help and stay safe. The National Hotline also receives tips about potential situations of sex and labor trafficking and facilitates reporting that information to the appropriate authorities in certain cases.

Per their website, https://humantraffickinghotline.org, the toll-free phone and SMS text lines and live online chat function are available 24 hours a day, 7 days a week, 365 days a year. Help is available in English or Spanish, or in more than 200 additional languages through an on-call interpreter.

<u>**Call 1-888-373-7888 (TTY: 711)**</u>|

Text 233733

ABOUT THE AUTHOR

Marin Montgomery is the author of Because You're Mine, The Girl That Got Away, The Ruined Wife, All The Pretty Lies, Into the Night, The Perfect Stranger, and The House Without A Key.

Her first novel for Thomas & Mercer, What We Forgot to Bury, is now available for preorder on Amazon. It will be available in May 2020.

Proud to be an Iowa native, she now calls Arizona home.

Marin is represented by Jill Marshal of the Marshal Lyon Literary Agency.

Connect with Marin at authormarin@gmail.com or follow her on Instagram @marinmont18.

ALSO BY MARIN MONTGOMERY

Into the Night

When Blair and Bristol Bellamy's overprotective parents agreed to let their daughters spend spring break in Oahu, they never anticipated that only one of them would return. What should have been a week of soaking up the Hawaiian sun next to pristine blue waters takes an unexpected turn when Blair wakes up on the beach one morning with no purse, no shoes, and no memory of what happened the night before.

And worse?

No sister. Bristol had vanished into the night. Gone without a trace.

All the Pretty Lies

What does the tragic death of a twenty-seven-year-old Portland beauty have to do with a suburban mother in Houston?

Everything.

Only Meghan Bishop doesn't know it yet.

When the married mother stumbles upon evidence suggesting someone close to her may have ties to the heinous crime the nation can't stop talking about, she's forced to dive headfirst into an ocean of secrets she never knew existed.

Unraveling her life one startling piece at a time, Meghan realizes she believed all the pretty lies she'd been told.

And the truth? It's uglier than she ever could have imagined.

The Ruined Wife

Alastair has found the perfect partner in husband Steven. Together they've built a successful life, had a beautiful child, and still behave like newlyweds long since the day he carried her over the threshold.

But all of that changes in an instant thanks to a thoughtless deed that has lifelong repercussions.

With secrets bubbling to the surface, the pair find their American dream life suddenly in jeopardy, and neither one of them are willing to let go at any cost.

Made in the USA
Coppell, TX
07 April 2020